Murder at Glen Athol

Murder at Glen Athol

Norman Lippincott

Coachwhip Publications
Greenville, Ohio

Murder at Glen Athol, by Norman Lippincott

First published 1935
Norman R. Lippincott, c.1873-1963
CoachwhipBooks.com

ISBN 1-61646-508-5
ISBN-13 978-1-61646-508-7

1

"It is Mr. Marshall, the old gentleman from next door, sir."

I looked up from my writing to find Jeffries at my elbow.

"Show him in, Jeff," said I; and, with ill grace, I laid down my pen.

Damnation! Would the middle of the Sahara afford seclusion!

A moment later I rose to receive my ruddy-faced caller. Very spic-and-span he was, in a black-and-white Harris tweed suit, entering the library jauntily, advancing upon me with outstretched hand. His wide smile disclosed teeth too good to be true.

It was not my first glimpse of the fellow. Already I had identified him as Reuben Marshall, brother of Mrs. Randel, my next-door neighbor. Each morning since my arrival at the bungalow, two weeks before, I had noticed him in company with a younger man—one of the Randel boys, I surmised—in the middle distance of the widespread lawn, practicing swings with a golf club. Twice, looking beyond the hedge which separated me from my neighbors, I had seen them joined by an attractive woman, of slim, athletic figure and dark bobbed hair, whose youthful appearance made it hard for me to realize that she was Mrs. Randel, the mother of two grown sons. On another occasion a smaller and younger woman, very chic in her smart sport clothes, had made one of the party. Probably Harry Randel's wife, about whom some odd stories were whispered. Nice-looking people, I thought.

However, it was not for social amenities that I had come to Glen Athol, and I had determined that as long as the dwellers in the valley left me to myself I would do the same by them. And now here they were, breaking into my coveted privacy.

I took my visitor's hand.

"Very good of you to call," I said, with assumed cordiality.

"I fear you must think us laggard in hospitality, Mr. Holt," he replied; and his voice was like his appearance, easy and pleasant. "As a matter of fact," he went on quickly, "ever since Judge Hammond told us that you were to occupy the bungalow while they wintered at Miami, all of us have been anxious to make your acquaintance."

He paused, smiling, his blue eyes alight with good-fellowship.

"Very nice to have you feel that way," I thanked him; and we seated ourselves before the open hearth, where a beech log smoldered—though the weather was warm for nearly the first of November.

"I should have been over before this," Marshall proceeded, sinking back in his chair, "but I know how it is. When a man has done things that are important and interesting, people are always running after him, boring him to death."

"On the contrary," I smiled, "I have never done anything very startling."

His derisive snort refuted my denial; and he ran on: "I told our crowd, 'Now don't let us go bothering Mr. Holt the first thing. Give the man a chance to settle down.' But now Muriel, Harry's wife—she was divorced from

Campbell Snowden, and she's a handful—Muriel wants to have you over for dinner and some contract. She has been after Ann—my sister, Mrs. Randel, you know—for the last week, deviling her to invite you. . . . By the way, you do play contract—and golf, I hope?"

"No bridge; but as a golfer I usually get back the same day I start out," I admitted.

"Well, that's something, at any rate; Tom will be glad to hear that—Tom Randel, my nephew," he explained, off on a new angle. "He is home on a visit; has lived in Paris for the last three years. A fine boy! Did the judge tell you? Tom was an aviation pilot during the war. Started, a kid of nineteen, in the Lafayette Escadrille. When he heard that you had been in the Secret Service he was mightily interested. . . . Smoke?"

He extended a handsome Russia-leather cigar case.

"No, thanks; I'm a pipe smoker," I declined; and reached for my briar.

He was holding a match to the end of his cigar, igniting the Corona with slow, gentle puffs.

"And none of you must get the idea that I have done anything very important," I told him.

"According to the judge, you have," he smiled. "He and Mrs. Hammond had dinner with us the night before they started south—they and Dr. McClennen and Jane Maxwell. By the way, you haven't met the doctor, have you? A fine chap, though he does like to run things. He and Ann and I have been great pals since they were youngsters—I'm their senior by ten years. . . . And that reminds me," he broke off, regarding me critically: "You look very young. I expected to meet an older man." His reproachful tone made me smile.

"I shall never see forty again," I admitted.

"Is that so?"

"Forty last month," I confessed.

"Well, you don't look it. . . . Getting back to what the judge told us the night of the dinner—all about your being in the Secret Service during the war, and the time you had with Oppermann in Africa later on—I told the judge you should have him for your publicity agent."

I glanced at the manuscript on the desk, work interrupted by this caller. For the past two weeks I had been engaged in writing my recollections of those African adventures.

"Once I had the pleasure of serving the judge. Since then he has overrated me," I explained.

The old chap's face brightened. "Yes, he told us about that. You solved the mystery of his cousin's death, didn't you?"

"It wasn't much of a mystery," I assured him.

He proceeded to put me through an interminable cross-examination.

"And you got a bullet through your shoulder, I understand," he said at length, still harping on the subject. Plainly, the judge had omitted no detail.

"It didn't amount to much. I was out in a week," I said, devoutly wishing the fellow would take his leave. But no, he was still curious.

"By the way," he droned on, "the judge told us that you have his cousin's man with you. Is he the chap who let me in?"

"Yes," I told him. "That is Jeffries. I inherited him from George Bennett; and a very fine fellow he is."

My caller nodded appreciatively.

"A fine fellow, indeed. Humph! Yes; a husky individual; all of six feet two, I should say."

"A good guess; and tips the scales at a hundred and ninety, stripped," I replied, smiling at his enthusiasm.

"Humph! A tough customer in a fights, eh?"

"Tough enough," I admitted, thinking of our numerous friendly set-tos in which, Jeff lacking experience, I could hold my own, despite his advantage of four inches in height and some twenty pounds of good honest muscle.

"Well," declared Marshall, surveying me appraisingly, "the two of you look as though you could hold the castle. No other servants, eh?"

"Just the two of us; and we get along famously," I assured him.

Somehow the mention of our housekeeping suggested hospitality. I rang for Jeff and had him bring a bottle of rye whisky and some Apollinaris.

"Is this Colleti's?" Marshall asked, pouring a drink with an ungrudging hand.

"Colleti's?" I repeated.

"Possibly you haven't yet had the pleasure of meeting Mr. Augustus Colleti, local purveyor of liquid refreshment."

"A bootlegger?"

"The admirable Crichton of the breed. Well, here's happy days. . . . The very prince of all bootleggers," he resumed, setting down his empty glass. "That is how some people consider him." His face darkened. "I think he is a bad egg; and that's putting it mildly."

His voice had taken on a serious tone.

"It is disgusting—the way he is tolerated. You know," he ran on, the judge's hundred-proof Overholt beginning to get to him, "Muriel and Harry were as thick as thieves with the fellow. Why, before we had to send Harry to the sanitarium—"

He came to a sudden stop and shot me a quick glance. "There!" he exclaimed, looking scared. "I shouldn't have said that! You mustn't give me away—you won't, will you?"

"Certainly not," I assured him.

He tossed the end of his cigar into the fire and reached for the whisky bottle.

"Shall we have another little drink?" he proposed.

After we had followed his suggestion, he lit another of his big black cigars, and there the two of us sat. At length, to make conversation, I spoke of his unfortunate relative.

"Harry is your married nephew, isn't he?"

He turned on me fiercely. "Married! Yes! That infernal wife of his is the cause of all his trouble. Ruined him—that is what she has done!"

Unprepared for this outburst, I sat noncommittally with my pipe.

"Before he married her I told them how it would be," Marshall went on, half to himself, staring into the fire and wagging his head. "I said to Ann, 'What do you suppose the ex-wife of Campbell Snowden will turn out to be?' But no! Ann wouldn't hear a word against her—and she won't today."

For a time, lost in thought, he seemed to forget my presence.

"Damnable fascination!" he muttered, gazing vacantly at the smoldering logs. Suddenly he looked up and caught my eye.

"You see, it was this way," he went on, instantly returning to his former manner. "Before Harry took up with Muriel, he was practically engaged to Jane Maxwell—a fine girl, Mr. Holt! Before he lost his money and blew out his brains, her father was one of the wealthy men of the valley. Then Jane had to work for a living. She was Harry's secretary for a while. But Ann would not have it. In spite of me, she nagged at the boy till he broke with Jane. I told Ann, 'It isn't that you care particularly what becomes of Harry—Tom's the mother's darling; it is just your damn family pride!'"

Once more he lapsed into cogitative silence. As a conversational stopgap I asked what had become of the lost lady love.

"Who? Jane?" he said, half musingly. "Oh, Jane, poor girl, was pretty well out of it for a time. Now she is right back in the old crowd. Even Ann is nice to her—since she has made a name for herself. You should see her place—the most exclusive style shop in the valley."

Jeff's entrance with a log for the fire stopped him for the moment. I hoped that he had completed his saga of the Glen Atholians, but when we were alone once more he was at it again:

"Harry is supposed to be out on the coast. He is a junior member of the law firm of Jennings, Wilberforce & Grant. They are in sympathy with us and allow it to be thought that Harry is away on legal business."

He paused, with a lugubrious shake of his head.

Notwithstanding the mournful expression on his ruddy face, I foresaw his account running to an interminable length. Hoping that it might serve a double purpose, once more I tendered liquid hospitality. However, I had reckoned without my guest, for, after he had replaced the empty glass upon the tray, he settled back in his chair, his visage not a whit less doleful.

"It was this way," he resumed, anxious now, it seemed, to tell me the family history. "Harry's troubles came to a head shortly after Tom returned home—that was in August. For some time we had noticed that the boy was acting queerly. Then one night he and Muriel and Tom had an awful scene."

He broke off to relight his cigar, and suddenly I realized that the old gossip was thoroughly enjoying himself.

"Well, sir," he added, "we sent for McClennen, and he had them come and take Harry away."

Again he paused, thoughtfully puffing on the black Corona; then, inclining his face a little forward, he said in a low voice: "I wonder whether you have noticed, about halfway up to the city, the very large, red-brick house that sits back on the hillside?"

I shook my head.

"Ever hear of Piermont?"

"No," said I. "A hospital?"

His voice sank to a whisper.

"An insane asylum, Mr. Holt! That is where Muriel Randel's husband is—in an insane asylum!"

"A sad affair," was my guarded comment.

"Yes; it is," sighed Marshall. "Bitterly sad. Well—"

Thank the Lord! At last he was rising to leave.

"And here I have been doing a lot of talking," he smiled, with one of his sudden changes of manner, "and haven't yet delivered my message."

He was buttoning his well-cut tweed coat, patting it and smoothing it down.

"As a matter of fact," he went on in his former jovial style, "I am commissioned by my sister to ask you over for dinner—on Friday night, the twenty-third. We are to have a week-end party for a house guest. . . . And that reminds me," interrupting himself in his odd way: "Have you an ear for music?"

"I like music, certainly," I told him, smiling at his earnestness.

"Prepare for a treat!" he exclaimed, greatly pleased. "Our expected guest—she lands in New York in a day or so—is returning from a year's study of singing, in Paris. Lea was born and raised down here in the valley—the Donnays live out in the East End now. She is *some* girl! Sings like a bird! Now say you'll come!"

I didn't want to go. On the other hand, I didn't want to appear crabbed. I told him that I should be glad to accept the invitation. Later I had cause to regret my weakness.

He looked pleased. "That's fine! You will meet the persons I have been talking about—Campbell Snowden included."

"Campbell Snowden?" I repeated. "Still in the picture, eh?"

"Very much so." He paused, a sardonic smile showing his white teeth. "You don't cherish old-fashioned ideals, do you? Why, man, we are living in a modern age—not bad, just modern."

"Today there is more opportunity," I grinned. "People are just as moral as they ever were."

"Exactly!" he agreed. "It is the times that have changed, not human nature. Well—at any rate, you'll see Campbell Snowden tagging after Muriel, much the same as formerly."

Out on the veranda I bade good-bye to the loquacious old chap. Watching the spruce figure stepping along the path to the opening in the hedge, I found myself liking him, notwithstanding his boresome garrulity.

"But, Lord!" I thought. "If his family could have listened-in to his broadcast, wouldn't he get a warm reception!"

2

A few mornings later when I sat down to breakfast I found several letters beside my plate. There was a note, I discovered, from my young niece in Boston, a special favorite of mine. She was, she wrote me, soon to make her debut, and she was full of excited anticipation of the great event. She ended by reproaching me for my failure to answer her last letter. Regretting my negligence, I determined to make the usual amends. Clearly a present was indicated. I decided that she should have the nicest thing obtainable in evening frocks sent to her that very day.

After breakfast I had Jeff get the car, and we proceeded up the lane to the state highway. Some three miles to the north the road developed into the main street of the village of Glen Athol, lined on either side for several hundred yards by the stores of the business quarter. Halfway down the street we stopped at a shop bearing a brass sign on which appeared the name, "Jane Maxwell," and the words: "Gowns—Lingerie—Tea Gowns."

It was a two-story building, its red-brick facade broken by a wide display window and a white Colonial doorway. Mauve velvet hangings made a background for the contents of the window. These consisted merely of a single garment that seemed, I thought, a superior kind of nightie, diaphanous of texture and pinkish in color, draped over a chair of ornate design by the side of a table on which was a bowl of roses.

Somewhat intimidated by the exhibition, I entered the shop and found myself on the heavy pile of a one-tone carpet that matched in color the drapery of the window and the velvet portières that hung at the rear of the room. There were some easy chairs, upholstered in rose silk damask; a low, round-topped table bearing a bowl of yellow roses; and some Edward prints, splashes of color against the creamy background of the plastered walls. However, I had come to buy a dress, and of such a thing I saw no sign.

I faced the velvet portières and coughed shyly.

At once the curtains parted to admit a tall, dark girl, dressed in an orange-colored knitted-silk sport suit which frankly revealed the firm and rounded contours of her perfect figure.

"Miss Maxwell—" I began; and suddenly it occurred to me that I was jumping to conclusions. "You *are* Miss Maxwell, aren't you?" I asked.

She nodded, smilingly appraising me. Her eyes were hazel in color and merry of expression; her mouth was large, though shapely.

"Well, Miss Maxwell," I went on, "I want to buy—a present for an eighteen-year-old niece—the nicest evening frock you have in your shop."

Instantly she was all business. "What does she look like?"

I gave the information.

"Can do," she declared brightly; and disappeared between the portières.

Almost immediately she was back, holding up for my inspection a creation beyond the description of a mere man.

"Isn't it chic?" she proudly demanded.

"It has to be," I told her. "It is for the dearest little *poulette* in the world"; and I gave her the shipping directions.

Then, checkbook in hand, I asked the price of the poem in chiffon. She told me and I whistled.

"What do you handle them with? Jewelers' tongs?" I asked, writing.

"'The quality lingers long after the price is forgotten,'" she grinned at me; and as she took the proffered check I noticed her hand, large, white, and beautifully formed, the wrist round and muscular. A remarkably strong-looking hand, I thought.

"Are you a golfer?" I asked irrelevantly.

"Scratch!" she informed me, proudly; then, looking up from the check: "Oho! *Now* I know who you are. 'Francis Holt,' she said, reading the signature. "Well, Mr. Holt, I've heard stories about you. I should have spotted you more quickly, but when you spoke, I said to myself, 'He's English.'"

"It was the Bostonese that fooled you," I explained. "Remarkable how the brogue persists after all these years. The accent lingers long after the place is forgotten," I added, mimicking her.

"You're living at Judge Hammond's place, aren't you?" she said, ignoring my persiflage.

"Yes, I am," I replied. "Right next door to your friends the Randels."

Her face suddenly became serious.

"My friends the Randels," she repeated. Her voice held a touch of irony, I thought; and I said: "Well, they are your friends, aren't they? Mr. Marshall called on me the other day, and he had all kinds of nice things to say about you."

She gave me a quick look. "He does talk, doesn't he? Oh, yes," she went on, "we're very good friends. He's a nice old soul; and Ann is a darling. You see, it was at their house I first heard of you—from Judge Hammond."

"And that reminds me," I said; and I told her of the invitation I had received. "Will you be there?" I asked.

Yes, she would, she said; and added: "I'm to be a week-end guest. Of course Mr. Marshall told you of Lea Donnay?"

"She was offered as a chief attraction," I replied. "Marshall describes her as something very much out of the ordinary."

She was all of that, Miss Maxwell affirmed. "You see," she proceeded, "I practically grew up with her. She is a beautiful girl, talented and charming—as long as she gets what she wants. Otherwise—well, she can be a Tartar on occasion."

"Temperamental, eh?" I asked, and at her nod: "That will make two of them, won't it? I understand that young Mrs. Randel is rather of the emotional order."

She gave me another quick look, and her face hardened.

"Oh, Muriel is of quite another type," was her brief reply.

"No love lost between you, I'll wager," was the thought that went through my mind.

At that moment there drew up in front of the shop the cream-colored Isotta sport job that I had often seen on the drive before the Randel house. Its single occupant, a girl—and my first glimpse identified her—got out, with a generous display of legs, and slammed the door.

I caught Jane Maxwell's low-voiced exclamation: "'Speak of an angel . . .'"

I glanced at her. Her white forehead was puckered in a frown, and she smothered her quotation as the door opened and the girl came into the shop.

"Hello, darling," she saluted Jane Maxwell, and her quick glance, cool and appraising, scanned me.

"Don't let me butt in; no hurry at all," she went on, turning her eyes away from me. "I just wanted to see if I could pick up a golf jacket; a knitted Jaeger sweater, for choice."

Her voice was husky, deep and full as the voice of a man; a remarkable voice, coming from that flat-chested little figure.

Jane Maxwell turned to me with the merest suspicion of a shrug. As she presented me to young Mrs. Randel, her manner was coolly formal.

If the intruder sensed the hesitation—I might almost say dislike—that was to me perfectly evident in Miss Maxwell's reception of her, she showed no sign of the knowledge. She gave me a slow smile and, pulling off her loose buckskin driving glove, thrust out her hand in a gesture that was masculine in its bonhomie.

"Hello," she greeted me.

I took her hand, which was soft and cool, and I experienced an odd sensation—not unpleasant at the first touch—that I find it hard to put into words. There was, in the contact of her clinging flesh, an indefinable suggestion of something insidious and sinister. Suddenly, unaccountably repelled, I withdrew my hand and caught a fleeting mockery in the eyes turned up to mine. Remarkable eyes they were, odd as her voice was odd. Yellow around the pupils, deepening gradually to a dark jade green, they held for the instant a look of evil wisdom and experience. I had the feeling that I had glimpsed behind a curtain that now was drawn. The episode was a matter of seconds, my sensation brief and undefined. I found myself studying the girl with no little curiosity.

She was a small bit of a thing, two or three inches over the five-foot mark, and the heather-brown pullover that she wore disclosed with uncompromising exactness the straight lines of a figure which might have been that of a boy of twelve. The hair that showed below the fillet of the green scarf that was bound around her head was the color and texture of oakum and was cut to a bob which formed a cloudy background for the small oval face. She wore no make-up, and her wide, thin lips— whether by art or nature—were vividly red against the pallor of her flawless skin.

She gave me another amused glance and said: "Don't run away. I want to see you when I get through here." She turned to Jane Maxwell, who had, I felt, been regarding us with interest.

"How about it, darling? Do you have what I want?" she asked brusquely.

The next quarter-hour was spent in trying on sweaters and was accompanied by a running fire of talk between the two of them. Among other things, I learned that Tom Randel and his mother were in New York and would return the following day, bringing Miss Donnay for the house party. At this stage young Mrs. Randel turned to me.

"Don't forget that you're slated for the blowout Friday night," she reminded me. "Not that you'll enjoy it. Bore you stiff, probably. You'll practically cut your throat."

A remark that in the light of after events was to assume a horrid significance.

Finally she got what appeared to satisfy her. She settled herself into her jacket and smiled up over her shoulder at me.

"Now come on," she said, ignoring Jane Maxwell. "I'm going to take you for a ride. We'll go places and see things." She moved towards the door. "So long, darling," she called to Jane.

Jane Maxwell's face brightened, and she held out her hand. "Good-bye, Mr. Holt. Thanks a lot for the order."

"Friday night," I reminded her and went out to where the little figure stood by the long bonnet of the Isotta.

"The carburetor needs seeing to. Open her up," I was commanded.

I undid the catches and lifted the hood. The girl pushed me away and bent inside over the big engine. Jeff, looking back from our car, saw something was wrong and came to offer his services. Mrs. Randel's head and shoulders returned into view. Erect once more and drawing on her gloves, she sized up Jeff in quick scrutiny.

"It's O.K. now," she smiled at him—and I laughed to myself to see the way Jeff stiffened. "The damn thing was flooding," she explained; and swung herself in behind the wheel. I told Jeff to take our car home and got in beside her.

Following the thoroughfare, we passed the remaining business places. At once the street narrowed into the state highway, running north by west along the river. On our left was the broad and muddy Ohio; on our right the hills came down to the side of the road, with now and then a valley and a view of rolling country to the east, and a glimpse of an occasional house, imposing and remote, back on the highlands.

My companion drove with the skill of a professional. I said something complimentary about the car, adding: "And you certainly can handle it, Mrs. Randel."

"Oh, cut out that 'Mrs. Randel.' Muriel is the name." She asked abruptly, never taking her eyes off the road: "What's your first name?"

"Francis," I told her.

"That's a hell of a name," she assured me. "It doesn't suit you, darling; it doesn't suit you at all. You, with your cold gray eyes, and your funny hooked nose, and that bristly toothbrush on your lip. Why, it's a girl's name." She flashed me a quick glance.

"Well," I laughed, "I'm not responsible for it. And you might call me Frank, you know. That's what my friends call me."

She shook her head. "No, darling; that wouldn't do. That wouldn't do for a minute. Then I'd think of the other and be liable to be sick."

I asked her what she thought we should do about it.

"I don't know," she admitted. "Anyhow, you've got a perfectly lousy name."

We were silent for a time. The splendid car ticked along at fifty, quiet as a watch. At length the girl came out of her brown study.

"Old-timer," she muttered, thinking aloud; then, glancing up at me: "That's what I'm going to call you. Old-timer. It sounds safe and dependable, and it suits you."

"It can't be possible that someone is trying to flatter me," I grinned.

I was advised not to kid myself. "Honestly, I wouldn't flatter you," the young woman assured me. "When I first saw you at close quarters—back there with Truck Number Six in her style shop—I thought: 'Here's a guy that can help you a lot, if he will.'"

"What's your trouble?" I asked; and I added: "By the way, when you mention Miss Maxwell to me, just call her that, will you? She's a friend of mine."

"Oh. Like 'em big, do you?"

"Never mind what I like," I told her. "Let's hear how I can help."

A mile or so had slipped by before she spoke again:

"Listen, darling—old-timer, I mean—if I tell it to you, mum's the word, you know."

"Mum's the word," I promised.

"Then, not to deceive you, I'm in a hell of a bad jam!"

For the last half-mile we had been running through the ragged fringe of the outskirts of a town, a grimy hinterland with a succession of jerry-built cottages, each with its quota of dirty-faced children in the dooryard. Hugging the banks of the river, a multitude of long and narrow buildings, horned with smokestacks, sent out a clamor of activity. In the foreground the darkened letters of a great electric sign formed the words "Cambria Bridge Company."

Suddenly my companion stopped the car with a jerk.

"Oh, good Lord!" she exclaimed. "I meant to take you to the country club! We passed *that* road ten miles back. I must be going nuts!"

She started the car and drove slowly past the gim-crack houses with the dirty-faced youngsters. As we proceeded, our surroundings improved, and before we had gone much farther I was surprised to see what a thriving, up-to-date place the town was. There were some good-looking stores, a couple of imposing banks, and the people on the street appeared busy and prosperous. Finally we stopped before a hotel; "Cambridge Arms," its sign read. It would have been a credit to a good-sized city.

Mrs. Randel glanced up at me. There was a look on her face that all at once made me feel sorry for her. Somehow I got the impression that the girl was scared to death about something. I found myself sympathetic and wanting to help her.

"You interrupted yourself back there. You wanted to tell me something," I suggested.

She shook her head. "No, old-timer; I've changed my mind. Not now, anyhow." She reached forward and cut off the ignition. "Come on, let's go in and eat."

Inside the hotel, I found that my companion knew her way about.

"We'll eat down in the grill," I was told; and she guided me to a stairway to the left of the lobby.

We descended, walked down a corridor, passed a subterranean barber shop and a beauty parlor—both surprisingly grand in metal, marble, and plate glass—and came to a long, low-ceiled dining room, which—it being past the lunch hour—was almost empty. A dark, thickset fellow in a tuxedo was chatting with thc blonde cashier. At sight of us he came forward, a smile on his face, his eyes upon Mrs. Randel.

"Hello," he greeted her.

He gave me an inquiring glance, then his eyes—brown and humid, like a seal's—went back to my companion. She seemed to take his familiarity as a matter of course.

"Hello, Tony," she said. Her husky voice was friendly. She called to the cashier: "Hello there, Kitty"; and the blonde smiled back at her: "Hello, Muriel."

"By George!" thought I. "Certainly we have landed among friends."

3

We followed Tony halfway along the length of the room to where a number of booths, screened by six-foot partitions, afforded semi-privacy. Into one of these clandestine retreats he smilingly bowed us. Muriel slipped in between the leather seat and the table, and I took my place on the opposite side.

Immediately it transpired that young Mrs. Randel suffered from thirst rather than from hunger.

"My tongue's hanging out," she admitted; and looked up at Tony who, menu card in hand, awaited instructions.

"Get me some gin. Have you any of the Old Tom left? . . . You have? Well, I want some of that; and I want a tall glass, and a couple of limes, and some White Rock. Rush it, Tony," she told him.

"Right away," he promised and turned to me. What would I have? The same? No, I said, no gin. Well, he could let me have some very good whisky; Scotch or rye.

"If the Scotch is that filthy Johnny Walker that you gave me the last time I was here, it's a crime," Muriel put in. "You had better lay off the Scotch," she advised me. "It's all cut to hell and gone. No kick to a gallon of it."

I told Tony that I would chance the rye, and he left us. Somewhere in the room a Victrola was touched off into the strains of a popular song. Muriel, her elbows upon the table, her chin resting on interlocked fingers, regarded me quizzically.

"What do you think of this dump, old-timer?" she wanted to know.

Everything seemed very friendly, was my somewhat sarcastic response.

She wrinkled her nose at me.

"Don't be snooty. As for its being friendly here, why, 'you ain't seen nothin' yet'. . . . Fast work, Tony," she said, addressing the fellow, who now appeared with a loaded tray.

Muriel squeezed a lime into a tall glass of gin and White Rock. She kept her eyes downcast. The man leaned over the table, changed by an inch the position of a bottle, and smoothed the cloth, bringing his face close to hers.

I heard his low-voiced aside: "Gus is out front."

Muriel had her glass to her lips, and she finished it before setting it down. Then, unheeding the man's byplay, she reached for the square bottle and poured a good four fingers of gin, leisurely adding some mineral water.

"Play fair, old-timer. I'm one down on you," she said, lifting her glass to me.

The girl had drunk the larger part of a half-pint of gin, and whatever her capacity might be—considering that the alcohol had gone into an empty stomach—it was time that she had some food. Besides, I was hungry myself.

"Let me have that bill of fare," I said to Tony, who, apparently unwilling to leave us, still hovered at the entrance of the booth.

I handed the card to Muriel.

"I don't see anything that looks good to me," she protested, after a quick scrutiny.

"May I offer a suggestion?" asked a pleasant baritone voice.

It startled all three of us. Tony did a quick side step, and I looked up to see his place taken by a medium-sized young fellow, remarkably alert-looking in a well-cut double-breasted suit of brown serge. There he stood—enjoying our surprise, I suppose—his dark eyes fixed upon Muriel, an expression of ironic satisfaction on his swarthy face. He got little enough for his pains.

Muriel gave a raucous chortle.

"As I live! It's my old friend, General Humidity," said she. "And with more suggestions," she added meaningly, eyeing him in no friendly way.

He inclined his sleek black head towards her, and his smile widened.

"And you will find some of my suggestions very good ones," he assured her.

Muriel ignored that. She turned to me.

"Old-timer, this is Mr. Augustus Colleti, Gus for short. In these parts, not to know Mr. Colleti is to argue oneself unknown." She grinned impudently at him. "Gus, this is Mr. Holt, a very good friend of mine. Gentlemen, be seated." She raised her glass to us. "Mr. Tony Basconne will now give his celebrated imitation of a man serving lunch!"

"And none too soon," thought I, reseating myself.

Colleti remained standing.

"No, no," he laughed. "That brings us back to my suggestion. Let me give you lunch up in my rooms. We'll get Kitty up for some music—have a little party, eh?"

I glanced at Muriel. She was eyeing Colleti. Her face wore a look of scornful amusement as she hummed a line of old-time doggerel: "'Will you walk into my parlor?' said a spider to a fly. . . ."

She broke off with one of her hoarse chuckles and said to me:

"What do you say, old-timer? Shall we 'walk'?"

Not waiting for my reply, she rose and edged her way out of the booth to Colleti's side.

"Come on," she said. "Let's go."

"Fine!" he said; and as I signaled to Tony for our check: "No, no; please. You are my guests." Bowing, he turned and led the way out of the dining room.

At the cashier's desk Colleti stopped for a word with the blonde Kitty. Muriel and I proceeded towards the stairs to the lobby.

"I don't know what I may be letting you in for, old-timer," she said to me hurriedly; and then shot this bolt from the blue:

"I don't suppose you have a gun on you?"

Nonplussed, I told her I hadn't.

"Well," she said, "here's hoping that you don't wish you had."

Before I could ask what she meant, we were joined by Colleti. We ascended the stairs and crossed the lobby to the elevator. At the top of the house he led us down a long hall, at the end of which he unlocked a door and, stepping back, invited us to enter.

It was a spacious room. Two very large Chinese rugs covered most of the floor; a concert-size grand piano, its lid raised, occupied the central space; there was a variety of chairs, upholstered in Spanish leather; a number of low tables followed the line of a wide sofa—leather-covered, like the chairs—which extended round three sides of the room. Against the fourth wall was a handsome mahogany bar—complete in all its details, even to the brass footrail—the back bar, with its profusion of bottles and glasses, paneled in green mirrors.

Naturally, I didn't get all this as I followed Muriel over to the piano and helped her out of her jacket. She sat down on the bench and began to play "Chop Sticks." Colleti stood grinning at her.

"Wonderful! Your technique is superb!" he laughed.

"I can sing, too," she informed us, and with a one-fingered accompaniment sang a version of "Frankie and Johnnie" that was a masterpiece of ribaldry.

Colleti roared with laughter.

"You little tramp! You ought to be spanked," I told her.

"Francis of the High Hat," she jeered at me and sprang to her feet. "Go ahead, Gus," she said, turning to Colleti. "Let this guy from Boston hear a real number."

Colleti shrugged and smiled. He seated himself at the piano, and his fingers spread over the keys. He looked up at Muriel; a whimsical smile lighted his dark face, and at once, softly and exquisitely played, the strains of "A Venetian Love Song" stole through the room.

I looked at Muriel; there were tears in her eyes. She caught my glance.

"He always makes me cry when he plays that," she said.

From Nevin, Colleti turned to Greig; and seldom have I heard the *Peer Gynt* suite played as he played it. The fellow was a wonder. Then lunch and the blonde cashier arrived at the same moment. I was presented to Kitty—a good-looker, but for her slightly prominent teeth. The two waiters carried in a table loaded with a variety of food and equipment; and when they had arranged things a bit and had plugged in the electric connections of a coffee machine and a chafing dish, one of them spoke in Italian to Colleti. After a survey of the ensemble he nodded in curt approval.

"O.K.," he told the man. "We'll not be needing you. Scram."

The girls, both apparently quite at home amid their surroundings, had taken their stand at the bar.

"A little service, please," cried Muriel, rapping loudly for attention.

Colleti looked at me and shrugged.

"A great couple of twists—one barbed wire, the other a pushover; and both of them with their legs bored out. Come on; you'll see," he chuckled. "At your commands, ladies," he told them, going behind the bar. "What shall it be?" He smiled at us over the mahogany.

Later, when we gathered round the lunch table, we found further proof of our host's discrimination.

Bedded in ice was a large bowl of caviar—and very good caviar it was. There was a chafing dish that contained lobster Newburg; there were sandwiches of chicken, and sandwiches of ham, and sandwiches of pate de foie gras; and that Colleti had not departed from the traditions of the land of his fathers was evidenced by the presence of a couple of forbidding-looking Bologna sausages, dishes of sardines, of anchovies, of tiny artichokes in olive oil—the immemorial antipasto.

Kitty and I did justice to the spread. Colleti, it transpired, had breakfasted shortly before our encounter. Muriel's fancy ran to alcoholic refreshment. So far, Colleti's opinion of her capacity seemed justified. However, visioning our drive home, with her at the wheel, I foresaw disaster.

To make matters worse, Colleti was doing his best to encourage the girl to drink; also, he showed a desire to get her off to himself, leaving me with Kitty. I soon decided that the blonde had been introduced into the party to that end. I recalled Muriel's hint of impending trouble. "Well," I said to myself, thinking of her behavior since we had come upstairs, "she deserves all she gets."

Kitty had reached the stage that induced chatter.

"He's goofy about her,"—she nodded toward Colleti, who lolled beside Muriel on the sofa at the opposite side of the room. The two were in deep conversation, low-voiced and earnest. Somehow, the sight angered me.

"He would be," I shrugged.

Kitty raised her mascaraed eyelashes at me.

"I expect you've been hearing funny stories about her. Well, don't believe all you hear, dearie"—she looked at me over the rim of her glass. "Of course, there's Campbell Snowden—he's sixty, if he's a day. And old Rube Marshall." She sipped her wine reflectively. "But I always say, 'Only believe half of what you see, and nothing you hear.'"

"Marshall?" I repeated. "You don't mean her uncle?"

"Sure! He's only her uncle by marriage."

"You're crazy," I told her.

"I am *not* crazy," was her indignant retort. "Why, dearie, people don't know that old guy. You'd be surprised."

"Well," said I, "you're all wrong about his attitude towards Muriel. He thoroughly disapproves of her. He told me so himself."

She laughed heartily.

"You bet he does—now. He hates her internal organs since she trimmed him for three grand—and then took a run-out powder on him."

She paused and gave me a reproachful look.

"My glass is empty, dearie."

I corrected the condition and she went on:

"That was at the time Tom Randel got here. Once she met him—good-night nurse! She fell for him like a load of lead. Just now he's the white-haired boy."

"You seem to know a lot," I told her, fed up on her gossip; and I looked at my watch. It was later than I had thought. Wishing myself at home, I turned in my chair to see what was going on at the other side of the room. Muriel and Colleti had disappeared.

4

"We seem to have lost our company," I said, turning to Kitty.

She remained silent, ogling me slyly, her eyes humid and drowsy from the alcohol she had absorbed.

"Where did they disappear to?" I asked her sharply.

She laughed. "Don't get hot and bothered about them, dearie. They ankled out on us a while ago."

Again I thought of Muriel's hint to me.

"Hell!" I exclaimed and got to my feet.

My action, and the look I gave her, put the blonde in a bad temper. There was acid in her voice when she demanded:

"You're not going to do a kibitzer, are you? Why, Mr. Holt, I thought you were more of a gentleman!"

Puzzled, I looked about the room. The table at which I had been seated was near the entrance from the hall. They hadn't gone out that way. I could see no other exit. Perplexed, I glanced at Kitty and got my cue. She was looking down the room towards the bar. I picked up an empty wine bottle and started in that direction.

I'd get myself killed, the blonde called after me. "You go trying to spoil his game. He'll shoot you in two," she warned.

I stepped round the corner of the bar. There was a closed door, screened by a portière. The door was unlocked, and immediately I was in a combination dressing room and bath. It was dark, save for a narrow streak of light at the edge of a door, slightly ajar, a dozen feet beyond me. From the other side of it came the voice of Colleti:

"And don't think your Airedale out there is going to get you off the spot."

"I tell you I haven't got it," I heard Muriel's reply and the man's response: "Then what was your crack about showing it to Holt?"

"I *will* show it to him—right now, too, if you don't play fair," she shot back at him; and added something about my connection with the Secret Service. She had been misrepresenting things a bit, I could see that; using me as a club to threaten the fellow.

There was the sound of a hasty movement, and his snarl:

"By God, then you *do* have it!" and the girl's cry: "Let me alone! Don't you dare touch me!"

I kicked open the door.

The scene was a sybaritic bedroom, fantastic in its exotic appointments. Even in the stress of the moment I got that impression; also, I saw that already Colleti had made considerable progress in his search for whatever it was the girl had concealed on her person. She was fighting him like a tiger cat, half of her clothes torn off. Thus far she had been successful in retaining the one article of apparel the modern woman uses for a pocket. Though grievously threatened, her brassiere still served its appointed end.

At sight of me Colleti threw Muriel to the rear, and his hand darted inside the breast of his coat. I let fly the wine bottle at his head. He went down like a shot rabbit.

"Now," thought I, foreseeing annoying complication, "I hope I haven't killed the fellow."

A look showed that I hadn't. There was a lump on the side of his head, and for the moment he was dead to the world, but his breathing was satisfactory. He would be all right, barring a bad headache, in a couple of hours. I took an automatic pistol from a holster under his left arm and turned to Muriel.

Looking very much the naughty little girl she was, and appearing interested rather than frightened, she sat on the side of the bed against which Colleti had thrown her. Her hair, no longer confined by the green scarf, spread in a copper-hued nimbus, and her small oval face was white; however, she was smiling and apparently none the worse for her experience.

"Good work, old-timer!" she grinned at me.

I could have smacked her for getting me into such a mess and for her air of nonchalance.

"Get your clothes on and we'll get out of here," I told her.

"How's our friend?" she asked, glancing at Colleti as she fussed with the tattered remains of her blouse. I said he would soon be all right. She shrugged.

"And that will be just too bad—for both you and me," she assured me.

I told her to hurry, and presently—after another look had convinced me that Colleti was regaining consciousness—we made our way back to the outer room. It was deserted. The fair Kitty had flown from the scene of impending homicide. We stopped to get Muriel's jacket and my hat and Burberry. Then, without further happening, we descended to the street.

Our homeward drive was rather a silent one. My companion made no reference to Colleti's attack, nor did she allude to the matter under discussion at the time of our arrival. For the first few miles neither of us spoke; then suddenly Muriel said:

"I suppose you think I'm a bad egg, don't you?"

I was too much disgusted with her to dissemble.

"I think you need a damn good spanking," I told her.

"It's too late for that, old-timer," was her somewhat sad rejoinder. "That boat has sailed."

We were silent for another spell; then she said:

"My trouble was getting off to a bad start. If I hadn't been thrown to the wolves—a kid, like I was then—maybe I wouldn't have turned out to be so rotten."

I kept quiet. There was nothing for me to say. She was merely thinking aloud, anyway. At length she broke out:

"If I had met the right man earlier, I know I should have been different. And now that I have met him—it's too late!"

She thought this over for a while; then she cried out so that I was startled:

"Like hell it's too late! I'll show them all!"

And she gave the big car the gas, and we flew over the road at a mile-a-minute clip. But it wasn't for long. She slowed down to a respectable forty-five, glanced up at me and said:

"That's all Greek to you, isn't it?"

This time I did dissemble.

"I don't know what you're talking about."

"Didn't get the idea that you might be the man, did you? You might be, you know. I might change my habits for you."

We had entered the home borough, and at that moment we passed Jane Maxwell's establishment. Muriel indicated the place by a toss of her head.

"No, I guess you like them big; don't you?" she derided; and: "Truck Number Six!" she laughed maliciously.

Knowing that she expected me to resent her expression, I kept silent. My refusal to take umbrage seemed to madden her. She allowed the car to come to a stop and turned in her seat to confront me.

I gave her a pain in the neck, she informed me; and she went on:

"I don't know what kind of a canvass that number gave you this morning, but if you have the idea that she's any better than I am, you've got another guess coming. She's no white-robed saint, take it from me."

She paused in her tirade, and we resumed our way. In a minute she was at it again.

"It makes me sick to see how she's got everybody buffaloed, from Ann on down," she declared spitefully. "They can't see through her. But I can. I know her. And oh, boy, does she hate me! I took her sweetie away from her. She wanted him then, and she wants him now. If she could see me laid out with a lily in my hand, she'd be tickled pink."

"You shouldn't take yourself so seriously," I told her.

"Oh, nuts!" was her response. For the remainder of the way we maintained silence.

When we had descended the lane that led to the Randel place, Muriel drove in past the garage and stopped at the back of the house, just at the beginning of the path that ran through the hedge.

She cut off the ignition and leaned back in the seat.

"Well, here we are back home again. The end of a perfect day." There was a note of bitter irony in her husky voice.

"And you certainly kept your word," I laughed. "You promised that we should go places and see things. We surely did."

She reached over and laid a hand upon my knee.

"I hope you're not sore at me."

No, I told her. I wasn't sore at all. It had been quite an experience. "Only," I said, "I hope you haven't got yourself into a mess."

She laughed.

"Mess!" she said and laughed again. She surely was in a mess, she declared. "And the worst of it is that now—I'm afraid—I've got you into it, too," she added.

"Why not tell me all about it?" I asked.

She was tired and didn't want to talk, she said.

"Friday night I'll tell you. I'll shoot the whole works then, old-timer," she promised; and before I knew what she was doing she had slipped an arm round my neck and her lips were on mine. Again I experienced the repugnance I had felt when I had touched her hand that morning. Instantly I seemed to lose every iota of sympathy and forbearance. I think she knew it, for at once she drew away from me.

"I don't get to first base with you, do I?" she laughed spitefully. "Lucky you're so near home. You won't have far to walk."

She took the hand I extended, and I helped her alight.

"I *was* going to ask you in for a drink," she said. "Now, just for that, I won't."

In the gathering darkness she looked very small and forlorn, standing there by the side of the big car. There was a chill wind from the river, and she drew her jacket more closely about her.

"Better run into the house and get warm," I suggested. "Have some dinner and go to bed. You've been through a lot this afternoon."

"Not a bad idea at that," she said. "So long. See you Friday night."

Without further remark she turned and went slowly towards the house, leaving me to make my way along the path to the bungalow. And glad I was to get back to it.

5

Friday night brought regret for my lightly given word.

I didn't want to attend Mrs. Randel's dinner, and, arriving at her front door, I promised myself that I should be the first of the departing guests.

My ring was answered by a middle-aged, stocky little butler with a ruddy, cheerful face and an English accent.

"Good-evening, Mr. Holt; come in, sir," he greeted me.

Over his shoulder I saw Muriel at the farther end of the big hall. She was talking to a tall, well-set-up young man. When she saw me she came forward, the boy at her heels.

"How charming to see you again," she drawled. Evidently the little imp was on her good behavior.

In her evening dress she seemed infinitely more demure and feminine that I had conceived it possible for her to be. I visioned her as I had seen her seated at Colleti's piano, singing her risqué song; I recalled how she had looked when I had seen her half naked in the rococo bedroom. I could have laughed in her face. Perhaps she read my thoughts. She widened her eyes at me and turned to the young fellow at her side.

"This is Tom Randel," she said; and added, speaking to the boy: "Mr. Holt was with me on a tour of adventure the other day. We went places and saw things—didn't we, Mr. Holt?"

It had been both interesting and instructive, I affirmed.

"I am sure it was," declared Tom Randel, laughing. "I've been a fellow voyager with this little lady on one or two of her excursions."

He was about thirty years of age, with a tanned face and honest brown eyes. Not the type, I thought, to be the "white-haired boy" of Kitty's description.

"Now you must meet the others," Muriel said.

She led us into a spacious room, lighted by two crystal-festooned chandeliers that descended from a high ceiling frescoed and painted in the old style. At the farther end was a great stone fireplace, before which, seated on a long davenport, Jane Maxwell and Reuben Marshall conversed with a man who stood, his back to the fire, looking down at them.

There were a number of persons in the room. I was presented to Mrs. Randel. She was altogether charming, I decided. She seemed remarkably youthful, with her slender figure and smooth-skinned olive-tinted face from which looked out a pair of intensely blue eyes, peculiarly vivid in their concentrated gaze. Her voice, too, was delightful—softly modulated and free from the intonation peculiar to the speech of dwellers in that section. She said some nice things concerning the record of my doings as recounted to her by Judge Hammond, and proceeded to make me known to her other guests.

There was Miss Donnay, a tall girl, exotic in appearance in an amber-colored dress, her black bobbed hair, thick and curly, drawn down smoothly over her head and held by a narrow gold band just above her ears. She wore no jewelry, and her manner was cold and affected.

I met Dr. McClennen, burly, thickset, and fifty or so, whose Mephistophelian visage—Vandyke and all—was redeemed from hardness by a pair of twinkling gray eyes behind gold-rimmed spectacles. I liked his manner, with its polished professional air, and his deep-toned voice.

Then there were two sisters, the Misses Winans, youthful, sophisticated, and blasé, who considered me critically through wise young eyes. Also, there was a Mr. Cotton, a blond youth with marcelled hair and a manner of jocund gladness which merited a birching. A Mr. McKee might have been cast in the same mold but for the fact that he was dark of marcel and complexion.

Over by the fireplace Jane Maxwell beckoned to me, and I joined them. When he saw me, Marshall jumped up.

"My dear Holt, this is a pleasure indeed!" he greeted me effusively.

The man before the fire said:

"Ah, so this is Mr. Holt, eh?" He stepped forward. "I have heard of you, sir." He offered me his hand and added: "My name is Snowden."

"So," I said to myself, "you're Campbell Snowden, the ex-husband, are you?" and I studied him with curiosity.

Stoutish and pot-bellied and of middle height he was, with a bull neck and a fat face topped by a retreating forehead from which his thinning reddish hair was brushed straight back. His faded blue eyes, humid and protuberant, were widely spaced, giving him—with his fleshy little aquiline nose and receding chin—a striking resemblance to a Belgian hare.

In the talk which followed I speedily discovered that the man's personality was as objectionable as his appearance. Full of the importance of his position as the richest man in the valley, he took the opportunity to impress me with the fact. In the space of ten minutes, with a finesse that no doubt was the result of long practice, he managed to convey to me the information that his large estate back on the highlands included a Grecian swimming pool, a private golf course, an art gallery of distinction, and no fewer than three Rolls-Royce automobiles. How much further we should have progressed with the inventory of his possessions is uncertain, for the appearance of the butler with cocktails created a diversion and enabled me to get a word with Jane Maxwell.

At dinner I sat to the left of my hostess, with Muriel beside me. Opposite to me was Lea Donnay, with Tom Randel on her right. He was solemn and grim-faced. I could see that something was troubling the boy. Several times as the dinner progressed I noticed his low-voiced asides to Miss Donnay. She, with a manner that bordered upon actual rudeness, received his overtures with a frigid indifference. At length, when she ignored him completely and turned to speak to Mrs. Randel, I caught a delighted giggle from Muriel.

"Remember what I told you the other day?" she asked me.

"I remember there was something you *didn't* tell me," I replied. "Something that I was to hear tonight."

"Oh, I didn't mean *that,*" she said airily. The need for making me her confidant no longer existed, she declared.

"That's out now, old-timer; so you won't be bothered, after all."

She glanced quickly up at me. "He was here today."

Whom was she talking about? Colleti? I asked.

"Sure. He brought this wine you're drinking. Gus isn't such a bad fellow at that. I don't think he was at all sore about the other day."

"I should hope not!" I retorted indignantly, and asked what the fellow had to say for himself.

"I didn't see him," she replied. "Ann had called him up and placed the order. When he brought the wine she let him in. But I'm sure he wasn't sore."

Afterwards, when I remembered that I had unwittingly diverted her allusion to our talk of two days before, I wondered if things might have turned out differently if I had let her go on and tell me what she had to say. At any rate, the chance was gone. Before she could tell me more we were interrupted.

At the other end of the table Marshall and Campbell Snowden, greatly to the amusement of the younger guests, were vying with each other in their reminiscences of their early indiscretions. An argument had developed as to the more recent conditions in the scene of some of their activities. The Latin Quarter was the subject of the discussion.

"Ah, that's the place!" Marshall gushed. "The happiest days of my life I spent in the old Sorbonne district!"

"That's ancient history," Snowden broke in. "Things change over there the same as they do here. Nowadays it's Montparnasse where you find the lively times, Bohemia at its best. The old Quarter is a back number."

He paused and looked up across the table at us.

"Why, I'll leave it to Muriel," he went on, in execrable taste, I thought. "You remember, Muriel, when we were in Paris. The real thing was all the other side of the Luxembourg; isn't that right?"

I glanced over at Tom. His face was like a thundercloud as he leaned forward, glaring down the table at Snowden. Lea Donnay—the faintly mocking smile just visible at the corners of her carefully rouged lips made me want to shake her—let her eyes sweep over Muriel and rest, in malicious satisfaction, on young Randel. However, having pretty well appraised Muriel's reaction under fire, I thought if Miss Donnay happened to be looking for trouble it was extremely likely she would find it. At once I had proof of the soundness of my judgment.

Snowden was quite right, Muriel asserted; Montparnasse, by all means.

"The other place is like nothing human," she declared; and she proceeded: "Fancy your remembering that we were there together, Campbell; it's really touching."

She indulged in one of her husky chuckles and went on quickly, giving him no chance to reply:

"Speaking of Paris reminds me of a story that was told to me not long ago. It had to do with two Americans—a girl who lived in an apartment in one of those medieval fortresses on the Boulevard Raspail, and a man who was—well, let us say he was a friend. One night they went to the Ritz for dinner. They danced, and so on, till it got to be midnight. Then, when they got back to the Boulevard Raspail, it seems that the girl had lost, or forgotten, or mislaid her latchkey. Careless of her, wasn't it? And they just *couldn't* wake the concierge. You know how those Frogs are. Once they're in bed it takes a fire to make them get up. Well, anyhow, there they were. Midnight, and out in the cold world. Intriguing situation, don't you think?"

On the other side of the table the blasé Misses Winans, with Mr. Cotton of the blond marcel between them—and none of them the better for the wine they had drunk—loudly clamored for further details.

"You can't leave them out there in the cold," Cotton protested. "What's the rest of the story?"

"That's all there is; there isn't any more," Muriel chuckled delightedly. The absence of denouement added piquancy to the tale, she insisted.

"Quit kidding us, Muriel," Campbell Snowden demurred. "I'll bet a dollar you know what happened. Go ahead and tell us."

He must let his conscience be his guide, his ex-wife told him; and she added:

"Personally, Campbell, I like to think that the two spent the night strolling through the Gardens. Or perhaps they were like the Babes in the Wood. Maybe the Luxembourg nightingales provided the leaves."

There was no doubt in my mind as to the identity of the actors in the episode. There was no telling how far the little devil might go in her revelations. It was high time to stop her, I thought. I bestowed an admonitory nudge. She flicked me a quick glance from the corner of her eye, and there was a relentless look on her face as she smiled at the girl opposite to us.

"Oh, look at Lea!" she exclaimed.

Miss Donnay, her eyes closed and her face pale beneath its make-up, swayed forward. Tom Randel caught her as she slipped from her chair.

6

The situation was not without emotional appeal. Naturally, everyone was startled. It was Dr. McClennen who smoothed things over, making light of the incident as he did. At once he was round the end of the table, bending over the girl.

"Merely a fainting spell," he announced, after a quick scrutiny. "Come, Ann"—smiling reassuringly at Mrs. Randel—"we'll take her upstairs"; and he raised the girl in his arms, holding her—she was no lightweight—as though she were a child.

After the three were out of the room we resumed dinner. No one displayed much appetite. Campbell Snowden lit a cigar; Marshall did likewise, and there was a general lighting of cigarettes by the younger guests. I saw Tom Randel, looking very uncomfortable, offer his case to the Winans girl who sat next to him. Debarred from my pipe, I lit a cigarette and offered one to Muriel. It occurred to me that I hadn't seen her smoke. She shook her head.

"No, that's one bad habit I have never formed," she declared; and added; grinning up at me: "Got all the others, though."

"Including overweening arrogance," I reproved her. "I hope you're satisfied with the demonstration you have just given."

She scowled across the table at young Randel, the victim of Miss Winans's chatter.

"What did I do?" she demanded sulkily.

She hadn't added to her popularity as far as Miss Donnay was concerned, I told her.

"Oh, her!" she shrugged contemptuously; adding as she stared moodily at Tom Randel: "She's ditched; and she's beginning to realize the fact."

We men rose as Mrs. Randel, followed by McClennen, reentered the room. She gave me a rather wan smile as I held her chair. Miss Donnay, she assured us, was quite recovered. The doctor corroborated the statement.

"It was the odor of those flowers"—indicating the centerpiece by a nod—"and the heat," he laughed.

The room was too warm, Mrs. Randel agreed.

"Let us go into the living room for our coffee," she suggested.

As we left the table, Snowden hailed me:

"How about some roulette, Holt? Tom has a wheel in the billiard room."

Before I could reply, Mrs. Randel answered for me:

"No, Campbell; Mr. Holt and I are going to get acquainted. Take the others, if you like."

He turned to them. "How about it, gang?"

There was enthusiastic endorsement of the idea.

"Fine!" declared Muriel. "Will you back me as croupier, Campbell?"

"Surest thing you know," he responded heartily.

I wondered if any of the others saw the dark look Tom Randel gave him as they trooped out.

In the living room, before the great stone fireplace, I sat with my hostess. We talked of various things. She was charming. However, like many others, she had a mistaken belief in the romance and mystery of the Secret Service. That I had been an operative seemed to intrigue her immensely, and she was very keen to hear what she termed "the adventures." In vain I assured her that the work was largely a matter of prosaic detail, varied with episodes that one would rather forget. At length, disliking the topic, I switched the conversation.

"Really," I told her, "it is not nearly as interesting as some other branches of the service, aviation for example"; and I mentioned what Marshall had told me of Tom Randel's experience. At once her face lighted with a new interest.

"Oh, yes," she replied. "He was wonderful. I was terribly proud of him—a mere boy, you know, just starting college. Wait, I must show you."

She went to a desk at the farther side of the room and returned with an old-fashioned album of photographs.

"This is what Tom calls my 'rogues' gallery,'" she laughed, sitting down beside me, the big book on her knees.

It proved to be filled with photographs, every one of them, she assured me, Tom Randel at some stage of his development from his days of swaddling clothes up to young manhood. We viewed him as an infant in the arms of his nurse; as a curly-headed youngster of ten or so, proudly astride his Shetland pony; as "the schoolboy, with his satchel and shining morning face." Snapshots marked his passage through the years, until we saw him, a brave young airman, beside his plane in France. Then followed numerous views, all of them foreign and most of them taken after the war, each with its brief record of time and place—Cannes, Biarritz, Deauville, Paris. Several of the latter photographs showed Randel in company with a tall young woman whom I thought I recognized.

"Miss Donnay, isn't it?" I asked.

"Yes," Mrs. Randel said, "that is Lea"; and she added, an embarrassed smile on her attractive face: "She and Tom were the subject of Muriel's ill-timed pleasantries at dinner."

She raised her shoulders in a deprecatory little shrug. "Shocking taste; but the dear child is irrepressible—really, she is the best-hearted little thing."

"They make a handsome couple," said I, referring to the photographed young pair; and I added, laughingly: "You don't think much of your boy, do you Mrs. Randel?"

Instantly her face took on a look almost solemn in its intensity. Her blue eyes regarded me gravely.

"He is the dearest thing in the world to me," she said.

We were interrupted by Marshall, who came bustling into the room to ask Mrs. Randel if there was any Jamaica rum in the house.

No, she told him, she didn't think so. There was plenty of whisky, if that would answer. No, he declared, it must be Jamaica rum.

"You see," he went on, "Campbell Snowden has been telling us about the wonderful rum coffee he had the last time he was in New York. He got the formula from the chef. You put cinnamon in it, along with the rum—stick cinnamon, it has to be—and he says it's marvelous. We're going to have some."

Mrs. Randel smiled at me. "We may have the cinnamon, but I'm afraid you will have to dispense with the rum. Why not use brandy?"

Brandy might do, he admitted. "Come over; we'll ask Campbell," he said, making for the door.

In the room beyond the hall we found the party gathered round the billiard table, on which a portable roulette wheel with a single layout had been placed. At the end of the table Muriel, with Snowden beside her, was performing the office of croupier. We joined them.

"Come on in, the water's fine," the girl greeted me. She pointed to a stack of silver and bills. "I've taken these suckers for a hundred and seventy-eight dollars," she informed me.

"No, no," Snowden was saying. "Brandy won't do at all. Got to have Jamaica rum. Absolutely," He started to leave the room.

"Where are you going?" Marshall called after him.

"Going to call Colleti. He'll send us the Jamaica rum, all right," replied Snowden; and out he went.

I looked at Muriel. The mention of Colleti didn't seem to bother her.

"Now just look what boosters you've turned out to be!" she reproached us. "Taking the heavy-sugar man out of the game"—she scowled at Marshall—"you and your damn coffee!"

That idea, he protested, was entirely Snowden's.

At the other side of the table Dr. McClennen and Jane Maxwell were laughing at the squabble; Tom Randel was looking glum; and Cotton and McKee and the two Winans girls were clamoring for action.

"All right. *Faites vos jeux,"* Muriel warned them.

I dropped a bill on the double 0, and one of the Winans girls shrilled: "Go on, turn it, Muriel; everybody's down."

"O.K.; *rien ne va plus,"* she announced.

The ball fell, and she raked in the checks of the losers—my contribution was included—and paid the winners, all with a skill which might have secured a job for her at many a professional wheel.

Snowden returned, a smirk on his rabbit face.

"Who said I couldn't dig up some Jamaica rum?" he bragged.

It seemed that he had caught Colleti just as he was about to leave for the city. Passing through Glen Athol, he would stop and deliver the rum.

"He'll be along within the next half-hour. I know how that baby drives," Snowden added.

His prediction was verified. In a very short time the little English butler entered the room and approached

Snowden. Muriel saw him and said: "Is that Mr. Colleti, Simpson?" It was, the man replied. "Tell him to wait," she said; and turned to me: "Can you run the wheel, old-timer? You can? Then take my place for a minute, will you?" She slipped from her chair and hurried after Snowden.

I had made but a turn or two when suddenly I noticed that Miss Donnay had reappeared. She seemed none the worse for her recent indisposition. She watched the game for a bit, then came over to me and bought twenty dollars' worth of checks. Without hesitation she placed the maximum of ten dollars on the red. Everybody was down, and I made the turn.

It was an unlucky one for the bank. The ivory ball fell into the square labeled 24, a red number and the one on which the winsome Mr. Cotton had played the limit. Dr. McClennen had five dollars on pair, Jane Maxwell a like amount on the column.

With a squeal of joy, Cotton gathered in the eighteen dollars I pushed over to him. Miss Donnay smiled happily when she saw her four blue checks double. I paid McClennen and Jane Maxwell their winnings of fifteen dollars. Muriel returned just in time to see me pay the bets. She glowered at the reduced bankroll.

"As a mascot you're a total loss," she scowled, as she took my place. I was glad to relinquish it.

As it turned out, her luck was no better than mine. It seemed impossible for Miss Donnay to lose. She made no *en plein* wagers, leaving the numbers severely alone, but her *en carré* and *transversale* bets, paying eight for one and eleven for one respectively, were bad medicine for Muriel.

Campbell Snowden had returned, gleefully holding up a quart bottle which he assured us contained a superfine quality of Jamaica rum. With a grim smile he had watched his ex-wife's run of bad luck. Now, when she appealed to him, he turned a deaf ear.

"They have about cleaned me, Campbell. You'll have to stake me again," she told him.

"Take a little recess," he advised coldly; and turned to Mrs. Randel. "I took the liberty to tell Simpson to fetch some black coffee and the other fixings, Ann," he said.

Muriel spun the wheel violently and tossed down the ball.

"That will be about all," she announced; and proceeded to cash the checks of the players. She handed Lea Donnay what was due her.

"Go buy yourself a music lesson, darling," she said savagely.

Lea, a somber light in her big dark eyes, regarded the other steadily.

"A lesson may be dearly bought," was her somewhat cryptic response; and she turned to our hostess.

Muriel closed the check rack with a slam.

"Come on, Tom," she called, jumping to her feet.

Young Randel, wearing a hangdog air, came round the table and joined her. She spoke to him in a low voice, and the two, without further remark, quitted the room.

The butler and a maid appeared with a miscellaneous assortment of paraphernalia. We gathered round Snowden to see him perform the rites of his self-appointed office.

Into a chafing dish he poured the quart of rum, dropped in a handful of cinnamon sticks, a tablespoonful of cloves, and several lumps of sugar. When the rum boiled, he added a quart of very strong coffee. The verdict was that the excellence of the brew justified Snowden's enthusiasm. The butler, having served us, placed the big silver pot upon the table beside which Mrs. Randel was seated. She had been particularly complimentary in her endorsement of the result of Snowden's skill, and now she called to Muriel and Tom, returning from their excursion.

"Here, you two; try some of Campbell's rum coffee." She bent over the table and turned with a cup in each hand.

"Really it is very nice," she said, as Muriel took the cup and sniffed at it suspiciously.

Tom Randel waved away the concoction.

"I prefer my coffee and rum separate," he muttered glumly.

Muriel handed back the empty cup and announced that the combination was "all to the good."

"I always told Campbell that if ever he went broke he could make a success as a bartender," she laughed, wrinkling her nose at her ex-husband.

"What a wonderful partnership he and our friend Colleti would be," Tom Randel commented darkly.

"Now that just reminds me. I have a crow to pick with you, my lady." Snowden laid a proprietary hand upon Muriel's arm. "Suppose you and I step out on the porch and look at the moon."

"Lovely!" she assented, grinning at Tom.

They passed from the room, leaving the boy staring after them, an inscrutable expression on his handsome face and all unconscious of the equally enigmatic gaze directed upon him from his mother's blue eyes.

Out in the big hall somebody had started a Victrola. The younger guests were dancing. Dr. McClennen and Miss Donnay joined them. Tom and Jane Maxwell followed. I was about to ask my hostess to accept me for a partner, when one of the French windows giving upon the veranda opened and Snowden and Muriel came into the room. Immediately I sensed that their colloquy had not ended well. The man's face was flushed and wore a look of sullen anger comically out of place on that rabbitlike countenance. The girl was paler than I had yet seen her. With Snowden tagging on behind, she slowly crossed the room and sank into a chair beside Mrs. Randel.

"Ann," she said wearily, "I'm dead to the world; all in."

My hostess rose and bent over the girl.

"You're tired to death, dear; that's all." She turned to me. "Really she is not very strong, and she has been on the go all day." She laid a hand on the girl's shoulder. "Come, dear; let me take you upstairs to bed."

"Oh, don't run off like that!" Snowden protested. He glanced at his wrist watch. "Why, it's barely twelve o'clock."

Muriel rose unsteadily. She glanced at me and gave me a drowsy smile. I noticed her eyes—blank and darkened by widely dilated pupils.

"We'll finish our talk in the morning," she told Snowden, speaking with an effort; and to me: "Good-night, old-timer; I'll be seeing you."

Snowden seated himself in the chair vacated by Mrs. Randel.

"Of all the perverse pieces of femininity, that bit of fluff takes the palm," he irritably informed me.

"Probably she has overtaxed herself, as Mrs. Randel said," I reminded him.

"Humph!" he jeered. "You little know her! She's steel springs and dynamite. Out on the porch, just now, she was as full of hell as a nut is full of meat. Then, all of a sudden, she went sour and beat it in here." He took a cigar from his pocket and bit off the end. I heard him mutter something about "a damn good licking."

"'A plague on both your houses,'" I thought, pretty well bored by the lot of them—with the exception of Jane Maxwell.

"Suppose we watch them dancing," I suggested, hoping to make my escape.

Leaving the room, we were just in time to see Mrs. Randel, followed by Simpson, the butler, descend the wide stairway, which, rising opposite to the door of the billiard room, branched right and left from a mezzanine to the floor above. The record on the Victrola came to an end at that moment and the dancers ceased their gyrations and, seemingly actuated by a common impulse, followed Reuben Marshall into the dining room. Snowden—on the trail of liquid refreshment, probably—joined the crowd, so when I stepped forward to meet Mrs. Randel there was no one to witness my farewell—save the butler, who remained in the background.

"Not going already!" she protested, and she glanced at the tall clock that stood in a recess at the foot of the stairs. "Why, Mr. Holt, it is only ten minutes past twelve." I made appropriate excuses for my departure.

"To be truthful, I am ready for bed myself," the lady acknowledged, laughing; "I think Campbell's coffee must have a soporific quality. Poor, dear Muriel was asleep as soon as her head touched the pillow."

"The others seem wide-awake enough," I commented, as a burst of merriment came from the dining room; and I asked Simpson for my hat and coat.

Making my way back over the path to the bungalow, I congratulated myself that the evening was over. I decided that I didn't particularly care for the crowd, and, in woeful ignorance of what the future was to bring forth, I determined that from now on I would see little of my neighbors.

7

Though usually a ready sleeper, that night I lay awake a long time. At length from over at the Randel house came the sound of departing guests, laughter and shouted leave-takings. Some time after that I dozed off to sleep. I was roused to complete wakefulness by a sudden violent sound. Raising myself on an elbow, I saw the faint light of dawn showing through my windows and again a sharp, reverberating explosion broke the stillness. From the room above me came the screech of a raised window sash; then the patter of Jeff's bare feet crossing the floor. The next minute he was knocking at my door.

"What's the row?" I called to him.

"There is trouble over at the Randels'," he told me.

"Wait a minute," I said; and I got out of bed and pulled on some clothes.

As we made our hurried exit from the bungalow, one glance in the direction of the Randel place assured me that Jeff had not overstated matters. Several lighted windows, nebulous patches in the misty dawn, attested that the household was astir; through the open back door the glow from the hall blended with the illumination of the porch lamps to show moving figures on the driveway.

We went through the hedge and crossed the lawn to the scene of the disturbance.

Of the persons gathered round the supine figure on the fog-wet gravel, I first recognized Mrs. Randel, rigidly erect, a white negligee clutched tightly about her, her face ghastly in the light of the porch lamps. Seated at her feet, chastely indifferent to diaphanous night-gear, Jane Maxwell supported in her lap the head of a prostrate man, while Tom Randel was fussing with the fellow's upper clothing. There were also three females in nondescript dishabille—maids, I decided—and a very much frightened Negro.

Scarcely had I taken in the details of this picture, when from the lighted doorway there popped the stout little butler. Close upon his heels there emerged another figure, a woman bearing an armful of wraps. Her curly mop of red-gold hair, gorgeous in the lamplight, overtopped by half a foot the pudgy Simpson. He pushed his way through the circle of his fellow servants to fall upon his knees beside Tom Randel. The woman dropped a fur-trimmed coat over Jane Maxwell's bare shoulders, and with tender solicitude—so it seemed to me—enveloped Mrs. Randel in a similar garment.

Simpson spoke to Tom Randel: "I got through to the doctor, sir; he will be here at once." He covered his face with his hands, rocking back and forth distractedly.

I stepped forward and laid a hand on young Randel's shoulder.

"What has happened?" I asked.

He looked up at me, his face white and drawn in the growing light, and indicated the agonized Simpson by a jerk of his head.

"This damn fool has killed my brother," he replied dully.

"Oh, Harry! Harry!" moaned Jane Maxwell.

"Brother!" I echoed, nonplussed. I straightened up and, as though I should find there the answer to this riddle, my glance sought Mrs. Randel's face. The blue gaze of her remarkable eyes held the abstracted stare of a sleep walker.

"It is the judgment of God," she declared in a lifeless voice.

I had seen too many victims of gunplay to readily accept Tom Randel's statement that his brother was dead.

"Here," I said, "let me take a look."

There was considerable blood flowing, as nearly as I could determine, from a hole in the left shoulder, but his heart was going steadily enough.

Jane Maxwell was staring at me, her soul in her eyes, and Tom Randel sat back on his heels, his arms wrapped round his pajama-clad form. I glanced up and found Mrs. Randel bending over me, a look on her face that made me glad to be able to relieve her, temporarily at least.

"You will be happy to know that your son is alive," I told her, not caring to be too optimistic.

She continued to stare at me, unconvinced.

"You are sure?" she implored.

"No doubt of it," I assured her,

She drew a long breath and buried her face in her hands. From Jane Maxwell came a little sobbing laugh.

"Oh, thank God, thank God!" she cried.

Simpson jumped to his feet. "Here's the doctor now!" he exclaimed, pointing to a coupé coming down the lane. It was McClennen. Satchel in hand, he descended upon us, more bearlike than ever with his shaggy head, the hairy arch of his big chest showing through the open collar of the pajamas over which he had donned coat and trousers. Without a word he started to work. He had finished his rapid examination and had opened his bag to secure some needed article, when from the house there came the sound of a woman's scream—a sustained, piercing shriek of distracted terror.

Jeff was halfway to the door before I could rise. I entered the house only in time to see his vanishing legs at the turn of the back stairs. Following, I reached the second floor to find myself in a hall which, leading toward the front of the house and at a distance of some twenty feet, made a right angle with a broad dimly lit corridor. By the gray light from the window at the head of the stairs I was able to discern the two closed doors which, midway the length of the hall, faced each other across the passage. Jeff had disappeared.

I tried the door to my right. It was locked. My knock brought no response. The door opposite to me proved to be unfastened. I stepped into a bedroom which had recently been occupied, to judge by the appearance of the rumpled bed. A man's room, I told myself, noting the various articles of male attire lying about and sniffing the odor of cigar smoke.

Leaving the room, I ran into Jeff, in hasty retreat.

"Sure, sir, here is hell to pay," he announced, his brogue cropping out strongly in his excitement.

"It sounded like it," I agreed. "Who was doing the screaming?"

"Screaming, is it!" said Jeff, glancing fearfully over his shoulder. "And reason enough for screaming—with a couple of dead people lying in the room back there."

I waited for no more. "Come on," I said, stepping past Jeff.

Open to the roof, the rise of its walls broken midway by a mezzanine gallery that encircled it, the broad corridor, handsomely appointed and evidently used as a lounge, ran the entire width of the house. Looking to my left, I saw the great stained-glass window beyond the head of the staircase which led downward to the mezzanine that I had noted from the hall on the preceding evening. The other end of the corridor, some sixty feet to my right, showed an open door and a brightly lit room. We hastened toward it, past closed doors and, halfway of the distance, a stairway which ascended to the gallery.

I entered the room, Jeff at my heels. Just beyond the threshold I paused. It was a big, high-ceiled bedchamber. So far as I could see, it was in faultless order. Jeff laid a hand on my arm.

"There is the man, sir; lying there the other side of that settee." He pointed to an exquisite old Venetian chaise longue, in sage-green satin, that had its position beyond the silk-draped twin beds. "The woman is over there by the glass doors," he added, indicating the double French windows which opened upon a glass-enclosed balcony.

I moved forward and saw a foot, a man's foot in a blue silk slipper, the toe digging into the rug, the heel pointing upward, projecting beyond the edge of the chaise longue. Another step and I was bending over a figure swathed in a corn-colored silk dressing gown with a ridiculous great blue peacock embroidered on the back. The man lay outstretched, his head half turned, the left cheek pressing the carpet, the right side of his face concealed by his extended arm, the creases in the back of his fat neck—like parallel lines drawn in tallow—showing above the rich material of his costume.

I lifted the arm that hid the face, and looked at the ugly profile outlined against the rug. It was an unnecessary action, for already I had recognized the fellow— Snowden.

"Dead, is he?" Jeff asked in an awed whisper.

"No doubt of it," I replied, getting to my feet.

Extended on the floor in front of the French window, one curtained door of which stood open and partly hid the motionless form, I found the girl. A glance showed that I had been jumping to conclusions when I had assured myself that I knew who the other tenant of the room would prove to be. This woman would make two the size of the one I had expected to find. It was Miss Donnay, though I scarcely recognized the face that was turned up to me; the make-up scrubbed off, the tawny complexion most unattractive under a liberal application of facial cream; oddly shaped pieces of adhesive plastered at the corners of the mouth and between the brows. Suddenly the big dark eyes stared blankly up at me. A look of terror spread over the face.

"Don't be alarmed, Miss Donnay," I said.

She made an effort to sit up.

"Is he—is he dead?" she whispered.

"Don't you think you had better return to your room?" I asked. "Let me send Mrs. Randel to you."

"No, no," she exclaimed decidedly. "I mean," she hastened to add, "I am quite all right. I shall need no one." She extended her arm. "Help me up."

She clung to me for a moment, standing a bit unsteadily, her eyes averted from the body on the floor. When I asked if I should assist her to her room, she refused my help. It was only on the other side of the bathroom, she said, glancing at an open door at the farther side of the apartment. With that she turned away, and, giving the chaise longue a wide berth in her exit, crossed the room and passed through the door, closing it after her. I heard the sound of the shot bolt.

"Well, that's that," I said to Jeff; and I led the way back through the long corridor and down the stairs.

They had brought the victim of Simpson's marksmanship into the house and had laid him on a bed of pillows in the hall. The boyish face, showing above the plaid traveling rug with which they had covered him, was deathlike; the face of one long in ill health. Mrs. Randel, looking very shaken and wretched, sat by his side. The red-haired woman bent over her, and Jane Maxwell, a disconsolate figure, stood in the background. No one seemed to notice our return. However, just at that moment Tom Randel and Dr. McClennen, followed by Simpson and one of the maids, came in the back door, carrying a cot. McClennen's glance lighted upon me.

"What was the cause of that scream?" he asked.

"Merely a little demonstration of nerves by Miss Donnay," I replied.

"Humph!" he grunted and turned to Mrs. Randel. Had Muriel put in an appearance yet? No, he was told, she hadn't.

"Confound the girl! She must be one of the Seven Sleepers," he exclaimed angrily and went up the stairs, two at a time.

He was gone, I suppose, ten minutes; it seemed much longer. Tom Randel moved over to his mother and placed an affectionate arm about her shoulders; a quiet, loving gesture. She allowed her head to sink back against the support of his body. It comforted her; I could see that.

We stood awaiting the doctor's return. Outside it was quite light now. Through the open door occasionally came the sound of passing cars on the distant highway. Somewhere among the trees at the rear of the house, from time to time, a blue jay uttered his harsh cry. Behind a closed door to the right of the hall, a coffee grinder whirred; there was a faint clatter of pots and pans; a delicious odor of frying bacon stole through the cracks of the door.

"Evidently," I thought, "it is to be 'breakfast as usual.'"

Grimly amused, I visioned the fat body in the ridiculous peacock-bedecked robe awaiting attention in the room above. Should I tell the cook not to bother setting a place for Snowden?

McClennen came down the stairs, moving with a ponderous deliberation. He laid a gentle hand upon Mrs. Randel's shoulder.

"Ann," he said, his big organlike voice curiously subdued, "I find that Muriel is in no condition to be disturbed."

He paused, looking about him. "Where is my bag?" he asked, and when Jeff handed it to him, he took from it a bottle of white tablets, several of which he shook into a small envelope. "Jane," he said, turning to Miss Maxwell, "I want you and Olga to accompany Mrs. Randel to her room. Let her take two of these tablets at once."

The girl nodded. "Come, Ann," she said, extending her hand.

Mrs. Randel rose languidly. She stood with her sorrowful gaze bent upon her unconscious son. Mindful of the dead Snowden, I found myself saddened by the thought of the impending trouble which must immediately be added to the burden of those slender shoulders. Then Jane Maxwell slipped a sustaining arm round the older woman, and they turned and passed out of our sight.

8

We carried young Harry Randel upstairs and put him to bed in the room to the right of the short hall. His only visible hurt was the bullet wound in his left shoulder. Of course, there was the effect of his fall to be reckoned with, but I doubted that much importance was to be attached to that.

I was bending over the boy, straightening the bedclothes and easing the pillow under his head. I saw his eyelids tremble and his lips twitch apart. A faint groan escaped him, and he muttered a few unintelligible words.

"He's coming to," I said to McClennen.

The physician stepped to the side of the bed. He held a hypodermic syringe and a wet pad of absorbent cotton. As he bared the boy's arm and sterilized the patch of skin for the injection, Harry Randel's eyes opened. He winced at the sting of the needle as McClennen gave him the shot; his glance went from me to the doctor. Then:

"I settled that damn cur," he muttered.

With that his eyes closed and he seemed to relapse into unconsciousness. McClennen gave me a quick look, but made no comment. I wasn't sure that Tom Randel had understood. He said to McClennen:

"Shouldn't we get a nurse?"

"In the meantime, I want you to stay here," the doctor replied, returning the syringe to his bag. Then he turned to confront us, a look of determination on his dark face.

"Gentlemen," he said grimly, "I have a sad revelation to make."

He paused, and his glance traveled from the still form on the bed to the boy at my side.

"Tom . . . Mr. Holt," he said, regarding us in turn, the words coming with slow finality, "I regret to tell you that Muriel is dead."

For a moment there was silence; then: "Dead!" echoed Tom Randel in a hushed voice. I thought his tone expressive of surprise rather than grief. Suddenly, however, he threw himself into a chair and covered his face with his hands. I caught McClennen's eye. He shook his head, and the big shoulders hunched in a compassionate shrug.

"Brace up, Tom," the doctor admonished, laying a hand upon the boy's arm; and after a momentary hesitation: "That isn't all."

The young fellow threw off the sympathetic hand and sprang to his feet.

"I know it!" he cried, staring wildly at McClennen. He made a passionate gesture toward the unconscious boy in the bed. "He killed her—didn't he?"

McClennen lifted a warning hand. "Quiet!" he growled. A timid knock had sounded on the bedroom door.

I took it upon myself to answer the summons. I was confronted by Simpson, very ill at ease and apologetic.

"If you please, sir, it's the telephone," he excused himself, ignoring me and addressing Dr. McClennen over my shoulder.

"To hell with the telephone!" snapped the physician. "Don't you know better than to come bothering me?"

The man winced, but answered defensively: "The party is very insistent, sir. When I told them you couldn't be disturbed, and broke the connection, they rang up again." He paused, and after a furtive glance at me: "If I may say so, sir, I think it is Piermont."

"Tell them to hold the line," McClennen growled. "Come with me, Holt," he commanded, making for the door.

We descended the wide front stairway.

"Wait for me in there," McClennen said to me, with a flourish of his hand toward the door of the living room, and hurrying away to the telephone. He wouldn't, he added, be a minute.

Viewed by the somber light from the high curtained windows, the big untenanted room appeared lonesome enough. I located the switch controlling the lamps by the great stone mantel. I was seated before the fireless hearth when McClennen rejoined me. He deposited his weighty bulk beside me on the davenport with a grunt.

"It was Piermont, all right," he informed me.

They had just discovered Harry Randel's escape. They would have some explaining to do before long, McClennen declared,

"I called up the city police department," he added, moodily staring at the ashes in the wide fireplace. "A hellish business; but, of course, it had to be done."

There was a long silence. I experienced an odd reluctance to come out with the news of Snowden's death. At length McClennen got to his feet.

"There's a job waiting for me that I would give an arm to avoid," he frowned, buttoning his coat over the jacket of his pajamas. "Mrs. Randel must be told of Muriel's death. God knows what the result will be." He started for the door. "If you don't mind, please stop here till I come back. I'll have Simpson bring you some coffee."

"Wait a minute," I said. "There is something I have to tell you before you go."

He turned and looked back at me, his keen gray eyes filmed with suspicion.

"What now?" he demanded.

"Just this," I explained. "When Jefferies and I responded to that scream, we found Miss Donnay in a swoon on the floor of the room at the end of the corridor upstairs. What is more, she was not alone. The body of a man lay near her—the body of Muriel Randel's ex-husband."

For the moment McClennen continued to regard me; then the big shoulders raised in their characteristic shrug.

"Dead, I suppose." His tone was merely casual.

Somewhat nettled to see how easily he took the news, I made it plain that beyond a doubt Mr. Snowden had been gathered to his fathers. McClennen asked what had become of Miss Donnay.

"She went to her room," I told him; and I added that she had vetoed my suggestion that Mrs. Randel should go to her.

McClennen gave me an odd look, the suspicion of a grim smile showing at the corners of his lips.

"Humph!" he grunted. "Think of that now." And he turned to leave me. "The room at the end of the corridor, you said? Well, I'll have a look in there before the police get here."

After five minutes or so, Simpson entered with a silver tray bearing a coffee service, a welcome sight. He placed the tray upon a small table at my side and left the room without speaking. I had some of the coffee. Finding it comforting, I poured a second cup and was lighting my pipe, when a hand was laid upon my shoulder. I looked up to find Jane Maxwell at my elbow. She wore the knitted sport suit in which I had first seen her, and her face showed wan in contrast with the orange color of her apparel. A second glance convinced me that the girl was in a highly nervous state.

"Come," said I, extending my hand. "Let me give you some coffee."

She sat down beside me and accepted the cup I offered. Color returned to her cheeks, and her eyes lost the look of terror. However, when she spoke, it was apparent that she was laboring under tremendous excitement.

"Oh, Mr. Holt," she breathed. "It is a lie! He never did it. How can Dr. McClennen say such a thing!"

I took the cup from her trembling hand and placed it upon the table. There didn't seem anything for me to say, and I remained silent. The girl seized my arm.

"Say you don't believe him!" she demanded fiercely.

I knew none of the details, I told her; and I asked what McClennen had said.

"You know that Muriel and Campbell Snowden have been murdered, don't you?" she asked wildly, ignoring my question.

I nodded; and again I told her I was ignorant of the particulars. She released my arm and leaned back in her corner of the davenport, her handkerchief to her eyes. After a short silence she uncovered her face.

Again I asked what McClennen had said.

"Just now we were in Ann's room—Ann, Olga and I," she said. "We had given Ann the tablets, and she was on the bed; she wasn't asleep—just lying there in a kind of lethargy. Then Dr. McClennen came to us. He said that Muriel and Mr. Snowden were dead—murdered!"

"Did he say who had done it?" I interrupted.

"No; he didn't say it in so many words; but it was easy to see that he took it for granted that Harry killed them."

I asked how Mrs. Randel had reacted to the news. "Poor dear Ann was too crushed to say a word," she cried. "But I thought of you, and"—her voice became appealing—"I have come to beg you to find out who really killed Muriel and Mr. Snowden."

"But my dear young woman—"

"Oh, don't say it! Don't say it!" she broke in. "I have known Harry since we were children. Believe me, Mr. Holt, he is absolutely incapable of such an action." That was not the point, I said and proceeded to make it plain that I had neither the time nor the inclination to thus occupy myself. This outspoken avowal reduced her to tears, and I was filled with remorse.

"Stop crying and tell me just what you expect me to do," I growled.

But I reckoned without her intuition. She knew that I was won to her cause.

"Oh, you will!" she cried.

"You haven't told me yet what you expect me to do," I reminded her.

In a voice vibrant with feeling she replied:

"First, I want you to believe as I do—that Harry is absolutely innocent. They will rake up all kinds of things against him."

Once more she paused, her eyes downcast, her lips compressed.

"Poor boy," she sighed. "He has few friends—in this house or elsewhere."

"Granting all that, where do we go from there?" I asked.

She flashed her eyes at me.

"Then," she persisted, "I want you to use your brains and skill—all the resource that you have gained by your experience—to bring the guilty one to justice."

"You overrate my powers," I told her gruffly.

"Oh, no, I don't!" she insisted; and she went on to quote Judge Hammond on the subject. God deliver me from my friends!

At length, partly to silence the eulogy, I rose.

"All right, all right," I broke in; and I led her out into the hall and to the foot of the broad stairway. "Now you be a good girl. Go up to your room and get some sleep," I told her.

She gave me an anxious glance.

"And what are you going to do?" she wanted to know.

"Well," I replied, "if I'm to be of any help, there's some telephoning I've got to do."

This concession seemed to please her. She smiled at me gratefully as she turned to ascend the stairs.

I found my way to the back of the house, managed to unearth Simpson, and had him lead me to the telephone.

I put in a call for the city and leaned against the wall of the cubbyhole in which the telephone was located, waiting for my connection. Undoubtedly it was imagination which prompted the belief that I heard a voice, faint and husky; and the words were reminiscent:

"Like them big; don't you?"

And I seemed to catch a thread of cynical, elfin laughter.

9

I have a congenital distaste for the role of suppliant, and here I was telephoning to ask a favor.

It had so happened that, shortly after my arrival in that locality, I had, as a guest of Judge Hammond, attended a dinner in honor of a certain great man from Washington. This personage favors me with his friendship, and in his speech that evening he had brought me more or less into the limelight. Before the night was over I had not only renewed entente cordiale with my powerful friend but I had also met a number of men prominent in local politics. Among the latter was the district attorney, John Carlson. It was to him I proposed to appeal, asking his authority to enter the forthcoming investigation.

When I succeeded in reaching Carlson, I found that he had already received a report of the case. When I broached the object of my call he pleaded reluctance to use the power of his office to dominate the police department. However, I pulled some particular wires to good effect.

"Very well," he finally agreed. "But it will require some diplomatic handling. It will be to your advantage to make friends with O'Brien and Olsen."

Who were they? I asked. O'Brien was the inspector in charge of the detective force; Olsen was sergeant of the homicide bureau, I was told.

"They are on the way down there now—along with some of the homicide squad and McDougal, my assistant. By the way, you have met him, haven't you? Have him call me when he gets there," Carlson concluded.

As I turned from the telephone, McClennen came down the stairs.

"I have had a look at Snowden," he said, as we met in the hall. "He was killed by a blow that pretty well demolished the left side of his skull. It is doubtful if he ever knew what hit him."

I asked if he had seen Miss Donnay.

"No," he replied, "I didn't think it necessary to disturb her." He paused and smiled grimly. "But I called on my friend, Marshall. His nonappearance worried me."

"By George!" I exclaimed. "I had forgotten all about him."

"I found him a very sick man. The poor chap says he nearly died as a result of drinking that rum coffee of Snowden's; was violently nauseated all night." McClennen laughed silently. "There was abundant evidence in corroboration. And that reminds me," he went on, turning to leave me: "I had better send Simpson up to him."

At that moment the butler appeared at the end of the hall. He approached us and addressed my companion deferentially. "I am serving breakfast for you and Mr. Holt, Doctor; in the breakfast room, if you please, sir."

McClennen nodded. "I'll join you in a minute, Holt. I have some directions for Simpson"; and noting the butler's apprehensive glance: "Don't be so frightened, Simpson," he grinned sardonically, "they'll not hang you this time."

The butler seemed relieved. "Oh, I hope not, sir. I was only doing my duty as I saw it, sir."

McClennen shrugged. "Anybody back there to take care of Mr. Holt?"

"Yes, sir, Amelia is there," the man replied; and speaking to me: "The first door to your left, beyond the back stairway, sir, if you please."

The good-looking housemaid who had played a small part in the happenings of the morning was arranging the breakfast service. At my entrance she looked up, an expression at once inquisitive and eager on her pretty face. "Itching ears!" I thought, giving her my best smile. I could see that she was ready to talk.

"By the way, Amelia," I said, "did you by any chance see the party who brought the rum last night?"

She nodded. "Colleti, you mean? Yes; I was in the butler's pantry when he gave the bottle to Mr. Snowden out on the side porch. I heard Colleti say: 'Here's your Jamaica rum.'"

"And then he left, I suppose," I said, testing her story, for I knew he had not.

The girl was silent for a moment. She took my empty-glass and brought a dish from the butler's tray.

"No, he didn't," she declared, serving the bacon and eggs.

The rumble of McClennen's voice came from the hall.

The girl glanced at the door and spoke quickly in a low voice:

"Mrs. Randel—Mr. Harry's wife, I mean—came round the house, and they talked together a good five minutes."

"Did you hear what was said?" I asked.

The girl shook her head. "They talked too low. All I heard was what he said when he left—and that didn't make sense."

There was the sound of a footstep outside the door.

"What was it?" I demanded quickly.

Without replying, she again turned to the butler's tray. McClennen entered the room.

"Just let me have some orange juice and a cup of coffee, Amelia," he said, seating himself at the table; and to me: "They'll be here any minute now"; and to the maid, as she served him: "That will be all, Amelia; I'll ring if you are wanted."

Over his shoulder I caught the girl's eye. She must have seen something in my face that caused her to reach a sudden decision. She came and collected my used dishes. As she bent over my shoulder, she brought her lips close to my ear.

"'Three bells.' That's what he said," she whispered and left the room.

I glanced at McClennen. If he had noted the girl's action he gave no sign. He drank his orange juice and drained a cup of coffee; then lit a cigar and surveyed me through a blue cloud.

"I was just thinking," he smiled grimly, "how surprised they will be to find two corpses. As a matter of fact, Snowden's death should have been reported."

"It was reported," I said; and I told him of Jane Maxwell's belief in Harry's innocence, of how she had solicited my services, and of my arrangement with the district attorney. He heard me in silence, slowly puffing at his cigar.

"What damn nonsense," he commented when I had finished. "No disparagement of your capability intended by that remark," he hastened to add, "but, unfortunately, there can be no doubt of the boy's guilt"; and he favored me with a sardonic grin.

I found myself imitating his characteristic shrug.

"Well, don't you agree with me?" he queried irritably. "You heard what he said, didn't you?"

My noncommittal nod seemed to anger him.

"Why, man alive, what more do you want than an actual confession?" he snapped. "You believe your own ears, don't you?"

"Sometimes," I admitted; and then, catching the sound of a car passing round to the front of the house, I added: "Right now they tell me we are to have visitors."

"Sure enough," he agreed. "Here they are."

When we reached the front door we found a very frightened Simpson admitting several men. At the sight of the leader, Dr. McClennen advanced with outstretched hand.

"Good-morning, Inspector," he saluted the tall, red-headed fellow, indubitably Irish, who, having advanced three or four paces beyond the threshold, stood looking about the big hall. The two shook hands, the red-headed man continuing his scrutiny of his surroundings. When he spoke, it was a bass grumble that rivaled McClennen's deep voice.

"Morning, Doc. What's the trouble here?" He released the other's hand and gave me a sharp look.

McClennen didn't answer the question.

"Hello, Olsen," he greeted the man at the inspector's elbow. Then, turning to me, he introduced Inspector O'Brien and Sergeant Olsen. I also shook hands with the other two members of the outfit, respectively McGurn and Anselmo, the former a dapper, well-dressed young chap who looked more like a broker's clerk than a police operative; the latter a swart, heavy-set fellow who, so far as appearance went, might have been successfully cast as a Sicilian gunman. At our introduction O'Brien's manner warmed perceptibly.

"Mighty glad to meet you again, Mr. Holt," was his cordial expression as he grasped my hand; then, noting my look of inquiry, he added: "You know—the dinner for the big shot." He spoke to Olsen: "You were there, too, Howard, weren't you?"

It appeared that Olsen, who was several years his superior's junior, fair, stout, and prematurely bald, had been there.

"Sure," he nodded and gave me a friendly grin. "I remember the story the big fellow told about Mr. Holt."

I congratulated myself on this fortunate circumstance.

"Certainly," I assured them. "I remember you both, perfectly."

O'Brien touched my arm.

"And here's someone else you'll remember," said he; and, turning, I faced two men whom Simpson had just admitted. One, an undersized, anemic young man with straw-colored hair and pale blue eyes behind thick-lensed glasses, was a stranger to me. The other, a dark, thickset man of thirty, immaculately turned out, I recognized as McDougal, assistant to the district attorney. He greeted me warmly and introduced his companion as Dr. Burgher, assistant medical examiner to the police department. "Where is our friend Burnham?" McClennen inquired of the latter when greetings had been exchanged.

"The chief has a mild case of ptomaine poisoning," the pale young man informed us; and O'Brien laughingly added that we should have to get along as best we might with the understudy.

"Speaking of understudies, Inspector," I said, "if you have no objection I should like to cooperate with you in this case—keeping entirely in the background, of course."

He stared at me, astonished and not any too well pleased. However, I gave him no time to enter a protest. I told McDougal of my talk with Carlson and of his order that the assistant should call him. Also, thinking the time ripe for the announcement, I recounted my discovery of the defunct Mr. Snowden. O'Brien listened with interest, and when McDougal started for the telephone he spoke;

"Hold on, Mac; I'll go with you. I want a word with the D. A. myself."

Olsen said: "Just a minute; we'll make it three"; and to Anselmo and McGurn: "You two cover the outside till further orders; and keep an eye on that little Johnny Bull. He's liable to take it into his head to scram"; and he hurried after McDougal and the inspector.

McClennen's amused glance followed the trio.

"The pangs of professional jealousy!" he grinned maliciously. "Scared before they're hurt."

He laid a patronizing hand upon the shoulder of Dr. Burgher.

"Come, my honored colleague," he continued ironically. "Let us seek quarters more comfortable in which to await the return of the legal Achilles and his Myrmidons"; and, chuckling, he led the way into the living room. A newly kindled fire blazed on the hearth. We seated ourselves before it. I lit my pipe, McClennen was smoking a cigar, and, thus encouraged, Burgher somewhat diffidently produced a cigarette.

"You know," he said to McClennen, "Dr. Burnham's sickness throws quite a bit of responsibility on my shoulders. I never before had entire charge of a case of this importance."

"You may count on my help," McClennen promised; adding: "I suppose Carlson will insist on post-mortems?"

The little man nodded emphatically.

"Oh, most certainly. That, really, was what had me worried. If I can depend on your assistance it will be a great relief."

"Nothing to worry about," McClennen reassured him.

Burgher smoked thoughtfully for a time.

"I have asked no questions," he said at length. "I think it best that I see the parties first and form my own conclusions."

McClennen suppressed a smile. "Oh, quite so," he agreed; adding, as there came from the hall the sound of voices and approaching footsteps: "The august supporters of law and order return."

I was amused to note the changed manner of each of the three as they rejoined us. Inspector O'Brien was especially cordial.

"We'll be mighty glad to have you work with us, Mr. Holt," he assured me. "Of course," he added, after a momentary pause, "just like the D. A. says, it might be better if you don't figure too prominently; you know—with the newspaper boys and such."

Nothing was further from my wishes, I told him.

McClennen gave a raucous chuckle and flung the end of his cigar into the fire. O'Brien shot a quick look at the physician.

"What's the matter with you, Doc?" he asked gruffly.

"You make me tired—the lot of you," McClennen growled. "One would think you were called upon to solve the riddle of the ages. Let me tell you there is far more of misery than mystery in the occurrence of this morning. It calls for the ministrations of my profession rather than the activities of yours, Inspector."

O'Brien, unimpressed by this outburst, merely commented:

"That sounds like a riddle, too, Dr. McClennen. Suppose you let us have the answer."

"The answer is this," replied the physician, hotly. "The self-confessed murderer is the poor irresponsible boy who lies in his bed upstairs, hovering between life and death, a victim of his own madness. If you are looking for the criminal, go up to Piermont and find the one whose carelessness is answerable for Harry Randel's escape."

He paused for a moment; then, noting the blank faces that questioned him, he resumed:

"For the past three months Harry Randel has been an inmate of the Piermont Sanitarium, suffering from an acute neurasthenic condition. You may take it from me that he has been totally unaccountable for his actions. This morning he escaped. He came down here, climbed up to his wife's bedroom by way of the lattice on the rear porch. He killed his wife; and he killed Campbell Snowden. Then, in his retreat, he was shot by Simpson, who, naturally enough, took him for a burglar. A very terrible occurrence, but perfectly obvious and devoid of any mystery."

There was a short silence; then O'Brien said:

"You used the expression 'self-confessed.' Are we to understand that Mr. Randel told you that he did the killing?"

"Yes. In the presence of Mr. Holt, myself, and his brother, Tom."

O'Brien looked at me. "You heard him, Mr. Holt?"

I nodded.

The inspector and Olsen exchanged glances, and both rose.

"O. K.," said the sergeant. "Let's go up and look 'em over."

10

The body in the sportive dressing gown had been turned face upward, from which position the rabbit-like visage stared at us, open-eyed and with the dignity of expression which, I have often noticed, seems to be common to the great transition.

McClennen was not slow to take the reins. Addressing no one in particular, he said:

"I have already made an examination of the deceased, rather perfunctorily, it is true, but sufficient to satisfy me as to the cause of death." He bent over the body, running the tips of his fingers lightly over the side of the dead man's head. "You will see, Burgher," he went on, looking up at the little doctor, "there is a bad fracture here, at the point of suture, lower left parietal and upper left temporal region. See—I can lay two fingers in the depression."

Burgher knelt and brought his near-sighted eyes close to the spot indicated by the prodding forefinger.

"Feel there," McClennen told him. "Crushed to the consistency of a sponge."

"Looks to me as if it was the result of a blow from a heavy object with a rounded surface," Burgher commented, getting to his feet. "Well," he added, "I don't think we need look for any other cause of this man's death; though, of course, we'll check thoroughly at the autopsy."

"Exactly," grunted McClennen; and he, too, rose. "Do you want to make any further investigations here, or shall we go to the other victim?" he asked O'Brien.

"Just a minute," Olsen interrupted. "Before we go I'd like to know a little more about the finding of this body."

McClennen smiled deridingly.

"There you go!" he scoffed. "Looking for the thing that is not!" And he went on with bitter vigor: "Listen, Olsen; don't, I beg of you, inflict additional suffering and heartache on this unfortunate family by injecting the element of mystery into a case that is self-evident."

The sergeant scowled.

"That's all right, Doc; but, my God, man, you got to remember I have my duty to think of," he declared reproachfully. His tone was deprecatory, and I could see he had no wish to be at cross purposes with McClennen.

"Duty!" mocked the physician; and he added savagely: "It is your duty to get the madman who is responsible for this tragedy back under restraint as quietly as possible."

"Well," protested Olsen, "no need of all this song and dance. After all, I only asked how come this party to be found."

McClennen grinned at me.

"Ask your new confrere, Mr. Holt," he told Olsen.

Finding myself thus pushed to the fore, I once more recounted, and in detail, how Jeff and I had entered the room in response to the scream of Miss Donnay and had found her and Snowden.

"Well, well; that will all come out later," O'Brien interposed; and he turned to McClennen: "Doc, when we get through up here I want you to round up everyone who was in the house when this thing happened. We'll talk to them in the big room downstairs."

McClennen's reply was forestalled by the entrance of one of the two members of the homicide squad who had been assigned outside duty. It was the swarthy Anselmo, looking more than ever like a Sicilian bandit. With an indifferent glance at the body on the floor, he approached us. He wore a satisfied smile and carried something wrapped in a gaudy handkerchief.

"You'll be glad to get this," he said, and handed it to Olsen.

The sergeant unwound the handkerchief, disclosing nothing more impressive than a foot-length of one-inch galvanized iron pipe with an elbow screwed to one end. He raised it to the light for a better inspection. We all gathered round him, peering at the thing.

"I found that close to the side of the house, right by one of the posts of the back porch," Anselmo told his superior. "Turn it over, chief; look in the elbow that's screwed to the end of it."

A satisfied grunt attested Olsen's appreciation of the importance of the find. The elbow showed a crust of sandy soil which but partly concealed a thick smear of blood dried on the gray surface of the pipe.

"It's the goods, all right," declared the sergeant. "Look here," he went on, indicating with the end of a stubby little finger the thread spirals in the elbow. "Here's more dried blood, and plenty of it."

"If you don't mind," I apologized, reaching over his shoulder and taking the exhibit, handkerchief and all. I went over to the window for a better look. There was no denying the evidence. It was blood, beyond a doubt; and the coarse red hairs which I discovered adhering to the inside of the elbow—several of which I furtively abstracted—were undoubtedly from the head of the dead man. I surrendered the pipe to Olsen, who returned it to Anselmo.

"Take this down to McGurn and tell him to give it the once-over for fingerprints," he directed. "All right, Mike," he told O'Brien. "I'm satisfied here if you are. Let's go."

McClennen leading, we trooped up the corridor to come to a halt at a closed door. The physician unlocked it with a key taken from his pocket. Without so much as a backward glance he preceded us into the room.

As the door swung inward, a gusty draft tossed the curtains at the open windows and stirred the rose-colored eiderdown on the bed in a flutter of movement which might have been an eerie greeting from the slim form outlined by the coverlet. There came to me a suggestion of perfume, a fragrance of elusory significance, which I recognized as a potent attribute of Muriel's personality. Was it seductive—or was it repellent? Upon my word, I don't know.

We gathered round the bed, McClennen and the assistant medical examiner at one side, Olsen and I at the other, McDougal and O'Brien at the foot. In silence we stood awaiting McClennen's disclosures. There was a look of interested expectation on the face of each of the two policemen, but McDougal's cheeks were pale. I heard his quick intake of breath as McClennen bent over the bed.

The physician paused with his hand on the corner of the gayly colored eiderdown, which, drawn up closely to the headboard, concealed what lay beneath. He looked up at us, his eyes showing hard and gray over the gold rims of his spectacles.

"Gentlemen," he addressed us, "all here is as I found it, with the exception of the position of this counterpane. It was thrown over the foot of the bed. I used it to cover this."

He threw back the eiderdown.

Prepared though I was for a gruesome unveiling, my gorge rose at the sight.

From the aureole of tawny hair, her face marble-like in its pallid cast, Muriel stared up at us from beneath half-lowered lids which revealed the jade-green rims of eyes rolled backward by the contraction of the orbital muscles. The thin lips of the wide mouth had lost their carmine shade. Now of a leaden hue, they parted in two lines tightly drawn across the clenched small white teeth. The down-turned coverlet disclosed that the body was clad in an extremely décolleté silk nightgown, once pink in color, now reddened by a hemorrhage from a wound in the throat of the dead girl. Apparently it was the result of a single knife thrust, delivered from above and from the right, that had left the weapon buried hilt deep, the carved metal handle projecting from beneath the angle of the jaw.

There was a stifled exclamation from McDougal, and he went to stand at the open window. Olsen, one knee on the edge of the bed, leaned past me to put back the hair from the dead girl's face. He bent close above the corpse to scrutinize the handle of the knife.

"Not a chance in the world for prints here," he said, tracing with the end of a forefinger the arabesques on the carved metal. He spoke to McClennen: "Pull it out, Doc; let's have a look at the thing."

The physician had some difficulty in following the suggestion. It wasn't a pretty sight. At length he straightened up, the knife in his hand.

"No toy, this," he growled, wiping the blade on the sheet. "A good six inches of steel," he went on, surveying it critically; and I heard him mutter to Burgher, who was content to stand by, an interested spectator: "Probably the jugular and the right subclavian and carotid branches, well down into the arch of the aorta."

"The bed looks like it, at any rate," was Burgher's contribution. He took the weapon and after a quick scrutiny handed it to O'Brien.

"What's that stamped on the blade?" Olsen inquired, peering over the inspector's shoulder.

"You can search me," O'Brien admitted. He turned to me. "What do you make of it?" he wanted to know; and he handed me the knife.

My interest centered on the two lines of script lettering which ran lengthwise of the blade.

"French, isn't it?" O'Brien asked.

"Dago, most likely," Olsen hazarded; adding: "Them's the babies for the chives."

I studied the inscription:

"No me saques sin razon,
No me envaines sin honor"

I read it aloud.

"Humph!" grunted Olsen. "What kind of talk is that?"

There came a derisive chuckle from the other side of the bed, and I looked up to see McClennen regarding me with a malicious grin.

"'The Spanish cavalier,'" he hummed in his deep bass.

O'Brien and Olsen stared at him in blank astonishment; McDougal, at the window, showed a surprised face over his shoulder; and little Dr. Burgher snickered approvingly. McClennen seemed to enjoy the effect of his ill-timed pleasantry. He grinned at Olsen's puzzled expression.

"Even I can tell you what that means, Sergeant," he jeered. "You'll find that little verse embellishing a lot of toad-stickers in the hockshops up on Wylie Avenue. It's Spanish, my boy, and it means: 'Don't pull me unless some fellow treads on the tails of your coat, and then don't put me up till you've seen the color of his viscera.'"

I returned the knife to O'Brien.

"Anyhow, it shouldn't be hard to trace," he remarked. "It's sharper than Billy-be-damned," he added, fingering the blade. "Get something to wrap it in," he told Olsen.

The sergeant looked round uncertainly.

"Might take the lady's lingerie," he grinned, moving toward a low slipper chair over which was flung the dress Muriel had worn the night before, together with stockings and step-ins, just as she had discarded them before donning the pink silk nightgown. That was more than I could stand. I started after him, but McClennen forestalled me.

"Get a towel from the bathroom," he growled, nodding toward a closed door.

Olsen gave me a sheepish look and turned to obey. I stooped to pick up Muriel's slippers from where she had kicked them off at the foot of the bed, intending to add them to the other articles of apparel. Something lying under the chair caught my eye, and when I rose I held a bit of lace and satin ribbon, the dead girl's brassiere. And then I made a discovery which brought before me the vision of Colleti's rococo bedroom; I seemed to hear the man's triumphant: "By God, then you do have it!" and the girl's answering cry.

O'Brien had joined McClennen and Burgher at the window where McDougal, having conquered his queasy stomach, was examining the knife. I went over to them.

"What do you make of this, Inspector?" I asked, extending the brassiere.

He took it and for a time stood silently considering the torn chamois-skin pocket which had been secured by two safety pins to the inside of the brassiere and now hung by a corner from one of the fastenings.

"Where did you get this?" he asked at length.

I told him.

"Well, Mr. Holt," he commented deliberately, "I should say that Mrs. Randel carried something that she valued in this little bag. It might have been her rings, or money, perhaps. One thing sure"—he laid a finger on the flap of the pocket, which, torn across, hung by a shred—"whoever did this was in one almighty hurry."

"That suggests robbery, doesn't it?" said I.

O'Brien studied the pitiful relic in his hand.

"Might be," was his somewhat reluctant admission. "We'll have a look." He turned to McClennen. "Doctor, you knew Mrs. Randel well. How was she fixed for jewelry?"

"Muriel's taste didn't run to jewels," McClennen shrugged. "She wore three rings; the diamond engagement ring that Harry had given her, and her wedding ring; and on the little finger of her right hand she wore a carved gold ring set with a square emerald surrounded by small diamonds."

"I noticed last night that she wore a very fine little string of pearls," I said, thinking it well to jog his memory. I know something about pearls, and the ones which made up the string to which I referred, though neither large nor numerous, were particularly fine ones and had cost real money.

"That's right; so she did," McClennen grinned at me. "I had completely forgotten the fact. She seldom wore them. They were a memento of her days with Campbell Snowden. Cost the old boy twenty thousand dollars, so he told me. They are fully insured, by the way."

"Well, well," exclaimed O'Brien. "If there's anything of that value lying round, it had better be accounted for. Let's have a look."

Olsen had been prying about the vanity that occupied a position between the two windows.

"I think we're a day late for the fair," he said. "There's nothing but this"; and he held up an empty velvet case.

He was right. A thorough examination of the drawers of the vanity and an equally complete rummaging of the dresser failed to produce what we were looking for.

"How about the bed?" suggested Olsen. "Maybe it's there. We ought to see if her rings are gone, anyhow"; and he made a move to follow out his idea.

McClennen interposed peremptorily.

"We'll attend to that," he snapped; and, nodding to Burgher, who tagged after him, he went over to the bed.

There was a knock on the door, and Olsen admitted Anselmo and McGurn. The latter carried the piece of galvanized pipe and wore a broad grin. With a mere glance about the room he approached O'Brien. He had, it appeared, been successful in developing some very satisfactory fingerprints. He exhibited them with professional pride.

"Good work, Jimmy," Olsen commended; and he added: "Now get busy on the windowsills over there. And there's some marks out on the roof of the porch that might show something."

O'Brien returned the pipe to the operative.

"Take good care of that, James," he ordered. "And don't run off; we'll be wanting you to get the prints of a young fellow in the next room. Well, Doc, what's the good word?"—this to McClennen, who at that moment rejoined us, his dark face showing annoyance. A glance at the assistant medical examiner at his side convinced me that little Burgher was decidedly flustered. McClennen extended his hand; on the upturned palm were three rings.

"She hadn't removed them," he replied.

"Any sign of the pearls?" asked Olsen.

McClennen shook his head.

"No pearls, Sergeant. Nothing resembling pearls in that quarter," was his grim reply. "However," he rumbled on, "my friend Dr. Burgher has called my attention to a detail which I neglected to mention. Mere inadvertence on my part. Here, I'll show you." We followed him to the bedside. "I think I told you that I found this quilt lying across the foot of the bed," he proceeded, laying a hand on the eiderdown and eyeing us sharply over his glasses.

"That's right, Doc," Olsen agreed. "You said you used it to cover up things."

"Exactly," nodded McClennen; and with a quick turn of his wrist he unmasked the ghastly face. "Not a pretty sight, you will admit," was his grim comment. "However," he continued, raising the edge of the silk spread from beneath the dead girl's chin, "what, in the stress of the moment, I forgot to mention was that when I found the body the face was hidden by the sheet. It had been pulled up over Mrs. Randel's head before the death blow was struck."

"You mean that she was stabbed through the sheet?" I asked.

McClennen shot a quick glance at me.

"Even so, my perspicacious friend," was his ironical response.

"But we didn't see any sheet," Olsen interposed. "And there was the knife sticking in her. How come?"

Without replying, McClennen drew down the spread and lifted to our view the widely rent edges of the blood-stained sheet.

"You see," he went on, suiting the action to the word, "this covers the face. It was so when I first saw it, the handle of the knife protruding above it. When I took hold of the sheet, it parted against the edge of the knife. Just now Dr. Burgher, very properly, called my attention to this slit, reminding me that I had not reported the detail."

There were both humor and condescension in the look he directed at me; and he added: "I hasten to rectify my error of omission. Who knows? That trifle may prove to be a thread in the rope to hang the murderer. Any hypothesis, Mr. Holt?"

"None," I answered.

"Too bad!" he deprecated.

"I'll tell you how it looks to me," Olsen affirmed triumphantly. "The poor lady saw what was coming and covered up her head."

O'Brien nodded his approval, and McClennen brought his hands together with a smack.

"By Jove, Sergeant, I believe you're right," he avowed; adding, in an aside to McDougal: "Observe the superiority of the trained professional."

The sergeant and I exchanged glances; he smiled indulgently.

"How does that strike you, Mr. Holt?" he wanted to know.

"Oh," said I, "the trained professional, by all means."

"Aw, that!" he protested. "No, no; I meant about the lady here. Do you think she pulled the sheet up over her head?"

"Suppose we ask the doctor about the position of her hands when he found her," I suggested.

"That's right," O'Brien seconded me. "How about that, Doc?"

McClennen shrugged. "The right arm was extended along the body; the left arm was bent at the elbow, the forearm lying across the abdomen," he replied.

"As they are now, Doctor?" I asked.

"As they are now, Mr. Holt," he bowed.

Without further ado I reached over and stripped down the sheet. It was as McClennen had said. One slender white arm, streaked and bespotted, rested athwart the narrow form; the other, half concealed by the folds of her nightgown, lay stretched at the dead girl's side. I bent over the body for a closer examination, lifting a rimple of stained silk which hid the left hand. I touched the small fingers. Cold and rigid, they were extended in a clawing fashion which well might have been the result of a last clutching effort, cut short by a spasm of dissolution, which had drawn the arms to their present position. Later I was to know I had overlooked at that moment a most important piece of evidence, an unpardonable bit of stupidity on my part for which I, and several others, paid dearly enough. Now, however, I looked up to find McClennen's gray eyes fixed on me in steady regard.

"Well, Mr. Holt; any deductions?" he gravely queried.

"Olsen's theory might be tenable," I admitted.

"Oh, quite," he agreed; and once more he used the eiderdown to cover the dead girl.

We turned from the bed, and Olsen called to McGurn: "Jimmy, how about those fingerprints?"

Anselmo and McGurn left the window and joined us.

"Here's a funny thing, chief," said the latter. "We've been pretty well over everything—the windowsills and the porch roof and all—and, believe it or not, there's nothing doing. Out there on the roof I got one or two fairly good hand impressions, but nothing come out in the way of fingerprints. Looks to me like the guy had gloves on."

McClennen laughed derisively. He stood between Olsen and O'Brien, and now he laid a friendly hand on the shoulder of each in sudden bonhomie.

"Listen, you fellows," he admonished. "You're giving yourselves a lot of unnecessary trouble."

O'Brien didn't look any too well pleased, and Olsen indignantly protested: "My God, Doc! To hear you talk, you'd think this was a pink tea!"

McClennen ignored the interruption.

"As I told you in the first place, there is no mystery here," he proceeded. "In the name of common sense why look for more fingerprints? Your man tells you he has found them on one of the lethal weapons, and I'll tell you where you will find the fingers that made them. Safe in the bed in the next room. What's more, the owner of the fingers has confessed the killing."

I caught O'Brien's eye, and the inspector grinned at me.

"Well, that sounds convincing enough, anyway," he acknowledged; and, speaking to Olsen: "What do you say, Howard? Suppose we drop things here and check up on the young fellow, like the Doc says."

"O. K. by me," Olsen somewhat reluctantly agreed.

Passing through the adjoining bathroom to reach young Randel's bedchamber, we encountered a middle-aged woman dressed in the uniform of a trained nurse. She was engaged in washing a clinical thermometer, and she discreetly acknowledged our intrusion by a nod to McClennen.

"I came immediately I had your phone call, Doctor," she told him, adding that the patient, though still unconscious, seemed to be resting easily. McClennen merely grunted in reply, and we all filed into the room where Harry Randel lay. Whether he had been officially relieved by the coming of the nurse, or had deserted his post, Tom Randel was gone, the only sign of him being the disordered breakfast tray on the chiffonier.

The nurse followed us into the room. Olsen started his investigation by demanding to see the clothes Harry Randel had worn.

"I've seen no clothes of his," the woman tartly informed him.

"All right, sister, we'll have a look," retorted the sergeant, nowise abashed.

He opened the door of a closet and stood regarding a varied assortment of apparel which hung from the hooks. Seeing his dilemma, I went to his assistance. He cast a puzzled look at me.

"This guy had some wardrobe," he commented.

Someone had carefully arranged on a hanger the suit we had removed from the wounded boy, and when we had made a thorough examination of it we had only our trouble for our pains. Aside from a broken cigarette in one of the pockets of the coat, we drew a complete blank.

"What price pearls?" I said to Olsen.

He shook his head.

"Too bad we couldn't have frisked these duds before somebody else had the handling of them," he grumbled, returning the clothes to the closet.

Over at the bedside the other members of our party were gathered round McGurn, who, ink pad in hand, was taking a series of impressions from the fingers of the suspect. As I joined the circle, the operative triumphantly held up the result in a comparison with the fingerprints on the pipe.

"Surest thing you know!" he declared gleefully; and he looked up at Olsen:

"This is your man, all right, chief."

11

The ambulance from the Department of Public Welfare had arrived and had borne away the remains of Campbell Snowden and his ex-wife. Viewing the two coffin-shaped wicker baskets casually bestowed into the sinister and shabby conveyance, I had the grim thought that here they were, these two, taking their final trip together, Tragedy their starting point; their destination, Oblivion. A hideous simulacrum of a joy ride!

Now we were gathered in the big living room, the two medicos, the two policemen, McDougal and myself. The two plain-clothesmen had been assigned their duties. Anselmo was at the rear of the house, keeping an eye on things in general. McGurn had been left at the bedside of the wounded boy, a station he would occupy till young Harry's condition justified his removal to quarters more circumscribed.

Following the technique of the sergeant, we had already interviewed the less important members of the household. Olsen had duly badgered a frightened Negro boy; he had had his little game of cross-questions and crooked answers with the phlegmatic German woman who was the cook; and the diffident Irish lass who was the second housemaid. He had crossed verbal foils with the pretty Amelia, the little baggage proving herself no mean antagonist. We had learned exactly nothing.

"Well, that about clears away the small fry," said O'Brien, after Amelia had been dismissed with instructions to send in Simpson.

Olsen's expansive frontal was puckered in a speculative frown.

"Yeah," he commented moodily. "And I got a hunch that last floozy was holding out on us, at that. Come on in here, you"—this to Simpson, who appeared in the doorway. "Sit down there," he ordered, indicating a chair, as the little Englishman advanced to where we were seated before the big stone fireplace.

The butler sidled round the end of the davenport and sat down. He cast an appealing glance at McClennen, and the big man, grinning derisively back at him, mocked: "And now, Simpson, do you solemnly swear to tell the truth, the whole truth, and nothing but the truth, so help you God?"

O'Brien made an impatient movement. Olsen took the gibe seriously.

"That ain't necessary," he explained. "All we want you to do is just to answer the questions that are put to you." He stopped to refer to his notebook. "Your name is Simpson, and you're the butler here; is that right?"

"Quite, sir," the man nodded. "Given name, Alfred. I have been butler with Mrs. Randel for the past eight years. Previously I—"

"Never mind that," Olsen interrupted. "How about last night? Mr. Holt here was at your party, and he tells me that everything was jake and everybody accounted for up till the time he left, round twelve o'clock. And, by the way, you were upstairs about that time. How come?"

Simpson cast me a reproachful look.

"You see, sir, it was like this," he told Olsen—and there was something in his deliberate recital which made me suspect that he had carefully rehearsed the story: "Mr. Marshall makes it a nightly custom, just before retiring, to drink a glass of Ovaltine. It is my duty to prepare it for him and take it to his room, where, if he is not there, I leave it on the bedside table. Last night, uncertain what duties might later demand my attention, and having a few minutes' leisure, I prepared and took the Ovaltine to Mr. Marshall's room at a few minutes before midnight. That is how I came to be above stairs at that time."

"Any way to prove all that?" was the sergeant's query.

Simpson brightened.

"Oh, quite so, sir!" he eagerly affirmed. "Amelia can tell you. She was taking some refreshments up to Miss Svenson at the same time and accompanied me to the second floor."

At the mention of Amelia, the sergeant looked annoyed.

"Well, go ahead; you started up with the drink; then what happened?" he demanded.

"There was no one in Mr. Marshall's room, and I left the tray on the table. Returning through the corridor, I stopped when I saw Mrs. Randel standing in the doorway of Mrs. Harry's room saying good-night to Mrs. Harry. I wanted to ask her orders for the morrow, and after she had finished speaking to Mrs. Harry and

had closed the door and had started up the corridor, I followed close after her, down the front stairway, and waited in the rear while she bade Mr. Holt good-night. Then I spoke to Mrs. Randel and received the information I sought."

"Well," said Olsen, "we can check you up on that, anyhow. Mrs. Randel saw you, did she, up there in the second-floor hall?"

She certainly had, Simpson declared emphatically; and he went on:

"Mr. Marshall's room is on the third floor, opening on the mezzanine, and as I descended the stairs Mrs. Randel looked up and smiled at me; then she turned and said to Mrs. Harry: 'Here is Simpson, waiting to escort me back to my guests.' She paused to answer a question from Mrs. Harry, and: 'Oh, absolutely!' she laughed, and said to Mrs. Harry: 'Sweet dreams, dear.' Then she closed the door and, with another smile to me, started down the corridor. I followed, as I told you. Oh, positively, Mrs. Randel will corroborate all I have said. From that time until 1:30 I was engaged in my regular duties. Then the guests, Dr. McClennen and the young ladies and gentlemen, left. Almost immediately the others, Mrs. Randel, Miss Donnay, and Miss Maxwell, broke up their circle and ascended the stairs. Then I locked the doors and windows—the other servants had already retired—and went to my room and to bed."

"Where does the help sleep?" Olsen interrupted to ask.

The servants' quarters, he was told, occupied a wing which formed a right angle with the north side of the house. This part of the structure being at the rear and facing east, the windows commanded a view of the entire back of the edifice.

"All right," said Olsen. "You went to bed; and then what?"

"I went to sleep at once," was the ingenuous reply. "But I woke some time later feeling quite ill." Simpson paused to address McClennen: "If you please, sir, I think it was the result of drinking Mr. Snowden's coffee. As you are aware, it made Mr. Marshall horridly ill also. There is very little more to tell. It seems it all happened in a flash, if I may say so. Almost at once I heard a snapping of the tin that covers the roof of the veranda—you may have observed that it runs entirely across the back of the house. I lay still for a minute or so, and then I heard it again, a sort of a crinkling sound, if you know what I mean. I grasped the revolver I keep under my pillow, a .455 Webley, and went to the window. I put out my head and looked along the roof of the veranda, and there, crouched at the edge of the roof, was a man. I was so startled that I fired at once. Very reprehensible of me, I know, sir, but I only did my duty as I saw it."

He came to a stop and looked at McClennen appealingly. The physician merely shrugged; and Olsen barked: "You and your duty and your .455 Webleys! Well, go on. Did you hit him?"

Simpson flinched. "No, sir," he replied weakly. "I don't think I did, sir. At least, he scrambled to his feet. I thought he was coming at me. I fired again. He fell over the side of the roof. I heard his body hit the ground."

He stopped speaking and closed his eyes. He was white and shaking.

"Well, go ahead," Olsen pursued relentlessly.

Simpson made an effort to pull himself together.

"I was very much frightened," he went on, "but thinking that the shots would alarm the house and that the gentlemen would come at once, I took my electric torch and went down and out to where the man lay. I threw the light of my torch on him, and, to my horror, I saw it was Mr. Harry."

He came to another stop, visibly affected by the recollection.

Burgher took advantage of the pause to ask: "Mr. Randel was unconscious?"

Simpson threw a quick glance at the little man.

"Oh, quite so, sir. I feared that he was dead. I ran into the house to get Mr. Tom. He had been aroused by the shots, and I met him halfway down the second-floor corridor. He said, 'What the hell's wrong?' and I replied that I had shot Mr. Harry, mistaking him for a burglar. Our voices were raised, and immediately Miss Maxwell's door opened and she appeared. Mr. Tom said, 'Simpson has shot Harry.' I heard a cry, and I turned to see Mrs. Randel and Olga in the doorway of Mrs. Randel's room. We all went downstairs; and Mr. Tom told me to telephone for Dr. McClennen, which I did."

There was a short silence. Olsen took the towel-swathed dagger from his pocket and undid the wrapping.

"Ever see this before?" he asked, holding up the weapon.

The butler recoiled, his eyes bulging at the exhibit. He shook his head.

"Never, sir," he replied fearfully.

Olsen continued to regard him for a moment. Then he returned the knife to his pocket, and again I caught the glance that passed between him and the inspector; again there was the hardly discernible nod.

The sergeant turned to Simpson.

"Well, it looks to me like you get an out on this rap. Anyway, we ain't going to take you in now. But"—he shook a thick forefinger at the relieved man—"you want to stick round here close. Don't let me hear of you off the place till further orders."

Again he studied his notebook.

"Now we want to talk to Olga Svenson." He looked up at us, obviously amused. "This one must be a ski jumper, like me," he chuckled. "Send her in, you," he told Simpson.

I noticed McClennen pull up the neck of his pajamas, his Vandyke pointing at me as, with head tipped back, he fastened the collar across his wide throat. He caught my eye.

"Place aux dames," he grinned at me as he buttoned his coat.

And, indeed, I was conscious of my own nondescript get-up a minute later when our next subject for interrogation entered the room. Brief as had been my first view of her, and under circumstances not calculated to promote recollection, I knew her at once for the woman who had attended Mrs. Randel in the scenes of the early morning. She had left with me merely the impression of a white face and a cloud of crimson-hued hair. Now, as she stood before us, surveying our party with calm appraisal, I studied her with interest.

She was a tall young woman and well-formed, her short-skirted black dress defining a length of shapely limb. I was at once reminded of the Viennese type of feminine loveliness; the narrow, rounded hips; the somewhat short torso, with high-set, swelling breasts; the unbobbed, flame-colored hair drawn smoothly round the small head in a French twist at the nape of the white neck—none too sylphlike—which was set well back on splendid shoulders.

McDougal was on his feet, offering her a chair. She sat down and crossed a dainty silken pair of ankles. Of course it was Olsen who began the inquisition.

"Your name is Olga Svenson?"

She raised her gaze to meet his and gravely inclined her head.

"You will please answer, miss, when I speak to you," Olsen tartly informed her.

I thought I detected the flicker of a smile at the corner of her wide mouth.

"My name is Olga Svenson; yes."

The words came slowly, and at once I noticed the low-pitched, slightly guttural quality of her voice, the merest suggestion of foreign accent.

Olsen, studied the girl in silence for a moment; then, bending toward her, he spoke in his native tongue.

Again she bowed. "Naturally. But hadn't we better speak so the others can understand? Much better, I think."

There was something of a rebuff in the reply, and Olsen reddened. I looked for an added severity of his catechetical method and found it.

"Your full name?" he demanded, pencil poised above his notebook.

There was a trace of contempt in the sidewise look she gave him, her long gray eyes half hooded by the white lids.

"You have already said it—Olga Svenson." Her voice was deliberate.

I heard McClennen chuckle. Olsen made a pretense of jotting down the name.

"Age?" he gruffly inquired.

The answer came without hesitation.

"Thirty years. And," she proceeded leisurely, "that you may be spared the asking, I can tell you that I am—also you have said it—Swedish; at least, my father was Swedish; my mother was Austrian. I came from Karlskrona to this country eight years ago. I am a masseuse. Here I work at a sanitarium at Danville, New York, giving the massage. That is where I first met Mrs. Randel; when she is a visitor there, five years ago. When she leaves, I go with her as her personal maid. Is that what you would ask me?"

There came another chuckle from McClennen. He tossed the end of his cigar into the fire and got to his feet, extending his thick arms wide above his head.

"Seventh inning; all stretch," he derided.

No one paid any attention to the interruption. Olsen continued to regard the maid thoughtfully. At length his good nature asserted itself.

"Well, it's swell the way you bring things up to date, anyhow," he laughed. "You work so good without the force pump, suppose you go ahead and tell what you know about last night. Just in your own words. And don't skip any of the details, see? Begin with the party."

The girl considered a moment; then shook her head.

"Really I can tell you little of that," she replied. "I spent the evening in Mrs. Randel's room, mine—which is next to it, and separated by a bath—being assigned to Miss Maxwell. Throughout the evening I was engaged in sewing—reconstructing a dress for Amelia, one of our maids. At a little before midnight—about a quarter of twelve, I think—she brought my tea. She sat with me till we heard the guests leaving. Then we went out into the corridor and stood at the head of the stairway, looking down into the hall. Mrs. Randel and the young ladies, and Mr. Tom and Mr. Marshall and Mr. Snowden, were in a group. Mrs. Randel looked up and saw me. She knows I consider late hours bad for her health, and she smiled and nodded to me; then she turned to the young ladies, and I heard her suggest that they retire. Mr. Marshall said, 'That suits me'; and when Mr. Snowden said, 'Suppose you and I have a nightcap before turning in,' he replied, 'No more for me. Your damn coffee has upset my stomach.' The ladies joked Mr. Snowden about that; and then, laughing and talking, they all came up; and Amelia left me.

"At the head of the stairs the gentlemen said goodnight. Mr. Snowden turned into the hall leading to his room. Mr. Tom and Mr. Marshall went down the corridor. Mrs. Randel and the young ladies stood talking for a few minutes. Then Miss Donnay said good-night, and she also went down the corridor to her room. I followed my mistress and Miss Maxwell into Mrs. Randel's room, where Miss Maxwell left us almost at once, going through the connecting bath to her room. I helped my mistress prepare for the night; then I undressed and lay down on the davenport."

"Any idea what time that would be?" Olsen broke in.

She nodded. "I wound my watch just before lying down. It was twenty minutes past two."

"And you hadn't heard anything out of the usual? Nobody moving about, or the like of that?"

"Nothing till the shots; and then Simpson and Mr. Tom shouting at each other. But the doors in this house are heavy; you can be in one room and not know what is going on in the next, if the door is shut."

"Yeah, I noticed that," Olsen agreed. "Well, you were saying you went to bed. Go ahead."

"I am a poor sleeper," the girl continued, "and my bed was a strange one and not comfortable. I don't think I closed an eye during the night. I was in the bathroom when I heard the two shots. I went into the bedroom and found Mrs. Randel awake. Almost at once we heard Simpson and Mr. Tom. Mrs. Randal got up, and we opened the door just in time to hear Mr. Tom tell Miss Maxwell that Simpson had shot Mr. Harry. My mistress was terribly distressed. She would pay no attention to me and insisted on following the others downstairs. I stopped to get Miss Maxwell's coat and a wrap for my mistress, and then I went down to where they were gathered round Mr. Harry."

She came to a pause, and her slow glance swept our circle.

"That is really all I can tell you," she concluded.

Once more Olsen produced the dagger.

"When did you see this last?" he asked, suddenly extending his hand, the blade lying across the upturned palm.

The girl's leisurely glance went from the lethal instrument to Olsen's face and back to the knife. The long gray eyes behind the heavy lids were calmly incurious; the delicate line of the dark brows lifted in what might have been contempt for the policeman's stratagem. She bent slightly forward, the better to scrutinize the thing.

"You intimate that I have seen this before?" she suggested and stretched put a long white hand. "May I take it?" she asked, again lifting her eyes to Olsen's.

"Sure, take it; and take a good look at it," he told her, looking rather set back.

And take it she did, balancing it in her hand, holding it, I noticed, not in the usual way, but as a swordsman holds a foil.

With the tip of a long forefinger she traced the carving of the handle.

"Foreign, I think," she commented, and once more her inscrutable gaze turned to Olsen's face, and she handed the dagger back to him. "No," she told him, "I never saw it before."

A short silence followed, broken by O'Brien:

"In your position here you would see quite a bit of young Mrs. Randel and her husband. What seemed to be the relation between them? Friendly?"

There was, I thought, a hint of venom in the reply.

"Which husband? She had two, you know."

"I think you know which one I mean," O'Brien told her sternly.

She raised her fine shoulders in the least of shrugs.

"Mr. Harry? Oh, aside from his excessive jealousy, I should say they were much as other couples."

There was a general pricking up of ears. I looked at McClennen. He had lighted a fresh cigar, and he sat noncommittally, smoking in slow puffs and watching the blue cloud rise. There was a suspicion of a smile about his eyes.

"Oh; jealous, was he?" cut in Olsen. "And who was he jealous of? Campbell Snowden?"

But Miss Svenson evaded this as a leading question.

"You mustn't ask me." She inclined her head toward McClennen. "Ask him. He can tell you much more than I."

Olsen glanced at the physician.

"How about that, Doc?"

Without removing the cigar from his lips or changing the back-tilted position of his head, McClennen took his eyes from the slowly rising smoke wreaths and gave the sergeant a humorous consideration.

"What do you think?" he asked dryly. "From what you have seen, I should imagine you might have a fairly good idea."

Olsen turned back to the maid. "What did you ever see to make you think Harry Randel was jealous of Snowden?" he demanded.

The girl was thoughtful for a moment.

"If I must say so," she replied, with apparent reluctance, "I heard Mr. Snowden mentioned in several quarrels between Mrs. Randel and her husband. For one thing, Mr. Harry very much resented his wife's refusal to return to Mr. Snowden a string of pearls he had given her. That was the cause of frequent disagreements between them."

Olsen sat up sharply.

"And those would be the pearls she wore last night and that are missing now!" he exclaimed.

Before any comment could be made on this observation, there came from the direction of the rear of the hall an outcry of loud and angry voices.

12

Olsen looked up in annoyed surprise.

"Now what the hell?" he demanded.

The next instant we were on our feet. I, being nearest the door, was first in the hall. Back at the foot of the rear stairs what appeared to be rough-and-tumble fight was progressing. Two men—they were so closely intertwined that recognition was impossible—were entangled in eager conflict, while a young woman in street attire was belaboring with impartiality and an overnight bag either of the two battlers who chanced for the moment to be the nearer. The girl was Lea Donnay, and the two warriors, who, as we hurriedly advanced upon them, separated and, breathless and disheveled, stood glaring at each other, proved to be Tom Randel and the plainclothesman, Anselmo.

Olsen stepped between the two men.

"What's coming off here? Who are these people?" he inquired angrily of his subordinate,

Anselmo was tentatively fingering an eye which was rapidly entering the first stage of discoloration.

"You can search me who they are, chief," he answered morosely. "All I know is they're fixing to make a getaway, and when I tell them there's nothing doing, this guy here steps back and takes a smack at me."

Young Randel was still full of fight. "Certainly I did," he jeered. "Did you think I'd stand for you laying your filthy hands on me?"

Olsen, with a restraining forearm across the willing Anselmo's chest, considered young Tom with strong disapproval.

"Say, mister, just who do you think you are?" he drawled.

Once more it was McClennen who stepped into the breach.

"Allow me to introduce these two young persons, Sergeant," he suggested; and he did so, including O'Brien, McDougal, and Burgher in the formality. For the moment the tenseness of the situation was lessened by the big man's savoir-fairé. O'Brien's smile was tolerant. He seemed mildly amused at the incident. Olsen alone retained a semblance of hostility.

Then Tom Randel's arrogance overcame his diplomacy.

"There is no earthly sense in running things in this autocratic fashion," he berated. "My God!" he continued, turning to O'Brien, "Is this the Spanish Inquisition? This young lady has nothing to do with what happened. She is unhappy and wants to go home. I offered to drive her out there, and then this roughneck stopped us." He glared at Anselmo, and Miss Donnay dramatically added her quota:

"It is impossible that I remain here. I demand that I be allowed to go."

"Well, I'll be damned!" Olsen marveled.

O'Brien's smile faded.

"Mr. Randel—and you, too, young lady—you ought to know better than to make this kind of a break," he rebuked, wagging his head at the two culprits. "There has been murder done in this house, and, though we have got the one who did it, nobody can leave here till there's a general check-up."

"Yes," added Olsen, "and you two can step into the front room right now for your part of the program."

I think Tom Randel would have given them an argument on that, but McClennen laid a hand on the boy's arm.

"Just as a matter of form, Tom," he conciliated; and he added, grinning at O'Brien: "Merely to roll up a little departmental red tape. These gentlemen have to turn in a report, you see."

"It won't take long to tell all I know," Randel remarked. He took Miss Donnay's hand. "Come on, Lea."

As McClennen and I entered the living room, Jane Maxwell joined us.

"I think you should see Ann," she told the physician, anxiously. "She doesn't answer when I speak to her; and she's not asleep—just in a sort of lethargy."

"A lot you know about lethargy!" he smilingly derided; and laid a hand on the girl's arm, impelling her across the threshold. "You may as well face your judiciary ordeal. Here are some gentlemen who would speak with thee. Come, let us join the hallowed circle."

The others had resumed our former position at the big fireplace. Olsen was speaking to Tom Randel.

"And you say you wound up the evening in a card game?"

"It was this way," Tom explained. "Miss Maxwell, Uncle, and I had left Campbell and the rest of the bunch in the dining room. The three of us came out together just as Mr. Holt was saying good-night to Mother. When he went she joined us, and almost at once she and Uncle got into an argument over a system of force bidding. Uncle insisted that we play a rubber, so Mother and I played him and Miss Maxwell"—he smiled at Jane. "And we beat them, too. That's all gospel, isn't it, Jane?"

The girl nodded soberly.

"And that went on till Doc and the others left, did it?" Olsen inquired.

"That's right," Tom told him.

There was a short silence while the sergeant referred to his notebook; then he queried: "Now, after you and Mr. Marshall left the ladies, you both went up to your rooms, eh?"

They had, he was told. Their rooms, with an adjoining bath, were on the third floor, opening upon the mezzanine.

"I was out of cigarettes," young Randel continued. "I went into Uncle's room with him and he gave me a box. We talked for a minute or so; then I went to bed."

"What time would that be?" Olsen interrupted.

"About two o'clock; a trifle earlier, perhaps. I didn't notice. I was all in; asleep as soon as I hit the bed. Later I was wakened by Uncle in the bathroom. The old boy was deucedly sick—sick and noisy. I got up and went to him. After a bit he was better, though still pretty bad. I saw him back to bed. Then I turned in again. The shots woke me. Feeling nervous about them, I got up and went downstairs. The lights were turned on in the lounge—the second-floor hall, you know—and I met Simpson coming to call me. He told me he had shot Harry. Then the women came out, Mother and Jane and Olga, and we went down to Harry. I told Simpson to phone for Dr. Mac." He came to a sudden stop. "And that's all I can tell you," he concluded.

There was another short silence, broken by Olsen: "Now just one more question, Mr. Randel. From your observation, what would you say was the condition between your brother and his wife?"

I heard Jane Maxwell at my side draw a quick breath. I glanced at Miss Donnay. Gracefully reclining in a big chair, her black bobbed head in its little toque pillowed in the silver-fox fur draped across her shoulders, her eyes fixed on the ceiling in meditative aloofness, she had maintained an attitude of disdainful tolerance. Now, however, she sat up sharply, and her glance went swiftly to young Randel. Surprised by Olsen's question, for the moment he was silent. His face paled, then flushed darkly.

"You must remember that I only recently came here," he said at length, his voice low and well controlled. "My brother was removed to the sanitarium very shortly after my arrival." He paused and took a few puffs on his cigarette then added, with returned confidence. "Really I had little opportunity to form an opinion which would justify a reply to your question."

Whether the answer satisfied Olsen, he pressed the matter no further. He turned his attention to the girl at my side.

"Who would this young lady be?" he wanted to know; and after I had introduced Jane, he once more thumbed his notebook.

"Well, miss," he said at length, "I see here that you left Mrs. Randel and the maid, Olga Svenson, in Mrs. Randel's room. What did you do then?"

"I went to bed at once," Jane told him.

Olsen fixed a stern eye upon her.

"Were you out of your room during the night?"

He shot the words at her with the staccato effect of machine-gun fire. There was, I thought, the barest hesitation before the answer.

"Certainly not," Jane declared indignantly. "At least, not till I heard Mr. Randel and Simpson out in the hall."

Olsen's manner changed with disconcerting suddenness. A smile chased the stern look from his face, and he favored Miss Maxwell with an encouraging nod.

"Now, Miss Donnay," he proceeded, turning to that young woman, "it appears that you ought to be able to tell us something interesting. You left the other ladies at Mrs. Randel's door. What then?"

The spotlight of attention thus focused upon her, giving her, so to speak, the center of the stage, Miss Donnay turned her dark eyes from their gaze of affected disregard to widen them at the sergeant in theatrical solemnity.

"Oh, the horror of last night! Shall I ever forget it!"

The low-pitched timbre of her trained voice vibrated in melodramatic tremolo.

"Sure you will," the practical sergeant told her; and he added: "Now just you go ahead and tell us what you know."

Divested of its histrionic wrappings, Miss Donnay's story was as follows: She had been wakened by the shooting. For a time she had lain in a state of trembling apprehension. She had seen the reflection of the glow from the porch lights, had listened to the sounds which came to her through her open windows—sounds of comings and goings, of voices raised in excitement and grief, the sound of an arriving automobile. At length, her curiosity having mastered her fears, she had risen to investigate.

Aware that the adjoining room opened upon a balcony which commanded a view of that part of the premises whence came the sounds of disturbance, and with the determination to avail herself of this vantage point, she had made her way through the connecting bathroom into the apartment aforesaid. She had turned on the lights and had seen, as she neared the glass door to the balcony, the foot of a man whose inert form, a second glance had shown her, was stretched on the floor. Promptly she had screamed and fainted. Her next impression had been the sight of two strange men bending over her.

Olsen seemed content. He and O'Brien and McDougal proceeded to get their heads together in a conference. As though by common consent there was an immediate pairing off. Tom Randel went over to Miss Donnay to bend above her chair in a whispered colloquy; McClennen and

Burgher were cheek by jowl; and Jane Maxwell touched my arm.

"Have you decided yet who did it?" was her ingenuous, though flattering, query.

"Now look here," I told her. "All this inquiry this morning doesn't mean a thing. Simply routine formula. Of course, they are perfectly satisfied that Harry Randel killed Muriel and Snowden; so, 'Why bother a lot?' say they. Now wait," I hastily added, seeing the corners of her mouth droop. "Our time will come later"; I might have said: "If at all," but I hadn't the heart to.

The trio came out of their huddle, and Olsen nodded to me. I excused myself to Jane and joined Burgher and McClennen as they foregathered with the representatives of the law.

"I don't believe there's anything more we want to do here, Mr. Holt," O'Brien told me. "We all agree that Harry Randel is the only one responsible. We'll leave McGurn in charge of him till he's ready to be moved. I think we'll let it go at that."

There remained two members of the household to be interviewed, McClennen reminded him.

"I don't see it's any use to disturb the poor lady," O'Brien replied. "You tell me she's all shot to pieces, and that old Marshall is a pretty sick man, too. That's right, isn't it?"

"True enough," McClennen assured him.

"Well, we'll not bother them," decided the inspector; he turned to Olsen: "What do you say, Howard?"

The sergeant readily agreed. "Besides," he added, tapping the notebook in his vest pocket, "I've got all the dope I want on them. And there's no good holding these people"—he turned to them: "Mr. Randel," he called, "you folks can go now, if you like."

"Does that mean that I may take Miss Donnay home?" Tom asked.

"That'll be O.K.," Olsen returned. "But she'll have to stay where we can get hold of her if there's an inquest or the like of that." He glanced at Miss Maxwell: "And that goes for everybody."

Jane cast an imploring look at me, and I went to her. In their exit, Tom Randel, with Miss Donnay very much under his wing, brushed by us without ceremony. Evidently not the only conference that morning had been carried on in the big living room.

Poor Jane looked pretty blue. I knew that work was the best thing for her.

"Well, Miss Maxwell," I asked, "is it to be 'business as usual' today? Aren't you going up to the shop? Nothing to keep you, you know," I added, as she regarded me rather doubtfully.

"I suppose I might as well," she admitted. "I have a Ford coupé out in the garage."

"Good," I told her. "I'll get your car while you pack your bag."

She gave me a grateful look. "That will be sweet of you; and I won't be five minutes. I don't think I'll bother Ann."

She was as good as her word. By the time I had gone out to the garage—where I found a still frightened Negro boy in charge—and had backed out Jane's car, I saw her waiting on the steps of the rear veranda.

"When am I going to see you again?" she asked, as I helped her into the coupé.

I rubbed the bristles on my chin.

"I'll tell you," I said. "I want a bath, and a shave, and a clean shirt. Then, after lunch, I shall want to smoke a few pipes and think things over. Then I might run up to your place for a call, if it's all right with you."

"That will be fine, and I shall be looking for you," she told me; and off she drove.

I turned to reenter the house and met McClennen and the others coming out. Just then the police car, driven by Anselmo, came round from the front of the house; it was followed by little Dr. Burgher in his sedan. O'Brien paused, with a foot on the running board of his car.

"Everything run to suit you?" he wanted to know, extending his hand in farewell. I shook hands and gave him the assurance that, in my opinion, the proceedings had been conducted in an eminently fitting manner.

Olsen, too, shook hands cordially.

"If there's anything we can do for you any time, Mr. Holt, you know where to find us," was his parting remark as he followed the inspector. They drove off, and after McClennen and Burgher had made an appointment for the gruesome task which later in the day was to be theirs, the little assistant medical examiner and McDougal took their leave. We watched the car out of sight; then McClennen laid his hand on my shoulder.

"Too bad, Holt, that you and I had to meet under such untoward circumstances." His deep voice was very friendly. "Here's hoping that our acquaintance may ripen under happier conditions."

I trusted so, I assured him. He got into his car and with a flourish of his hand left me. I turned my eyes from the disappearing coupé to see Jeff at the kitchen door, over at the bungalow. And once again I was glad to turn my back on the big house and take my way down the path through the hedge.

13

"A person would be wondering sometimes at the things that happen," remarked Jeff, getting out of his chair to put a log on the andirons.

Outside, the lingering mists of the gray morning had turned into a cold, autumnal drizzle. Through the windows I could see, beyond the tracery of the bare branches of the sycamores which bordered the Hammond grounds, the foggy outlines of the locks down at the edge of the river. On the farther side of the broad Ohio the blurred masses of the hills showed unsubstantial and indefinite in the moisture-laden air. Though but late afternoon, a twilight murk was gathering over the scene. Since lunch my man and I had sat before the fire in the bungalow living room, going over the events of the morning. Partly to satisfy Jeff's curiosity, partly to strengthen in my mind the pictures of the scenes, I had accurately recounted each circumstance.

"But," continued Jeff, reseating himself, "if Mr. Randel admits the killing, what are you to do about it?"

"You have the wrong angle," I told him. "What I have undertaken to do is to show that he's innocent."

"In the face of his confession?"

"Why, yes; that has been done, you know."

My man continued to look doubtful.

"And why would you not be telling them of this Colleti man?"

"Time enough for that," I said. "Innocent or guilty, Harry Randel will stay safely in bed for some time to come. In the meantime I don't want the police to annoy Colleti."

Jeff wagged his head at me.

"It will be leaving he will be. Faith, I will wager that tomorrow's morn will find him stole away."

"Not if he isn't frightened off, he won't," I asserted with conviction.

Jeff grinned knowingly.

"I could be telling them why you did not speak Colleti's name. It would be for the reason that you are satisfied he did not do it at all—that it was the young Randel chap, and it is not a laughing-stock you would be making of yourself."

"Perhaps; and then maybe you are not as keen as you fancy," I said with some amusement. "However," I went on seriously, "for the purpose of my investigation, in spite of his admission, I intend to consider Harry Randel as the victim of false appearances. If you are to be of any help you've got to feel the same way."

Jeff's Irish loyalty immediately asserted itself.

"Mr. Holt, sir," he declared solemnly, though there was a twinkle in his eye, "from this minute young Mr. Randel is as innocent as an unborn babe."

"All right," said I. "That leaves Colleti from the angle of an outside job. Now to consider the possibility of the thing having been done by a member of the household. I think we can leave the servants out of it. I am not including Olga, Mrs. Randel's maid, under this head. That young woman is deep. She knows more than she told us. Of the remaining inmates of the house, several have perfect alibis. It could not have been Mrs. Randel. The check-up on her movements is complete. Miss Maxwell, however, is not quite as satisfactory. From the time she left Mrs. Randel and the maid, her movements are unaccounted for until the time of the alarm."

"If it is the women you are checking into, how about the girl we found along of the dead man?" queried Jeff.

I knocked out my pipe, filled and lit it before I replied.

"I am free to confess that is a phase of the business that has me puzzled. One thing sure—Snowden went into that room of his own accord. Why? You tell."

Jeff's whimsical look was slightly contemptuous.

"And it is surprised I am at your innocence. A ten-year-old lad could answer that."

"Are they so precocious where you hail from?" I jeered. "Oh, yes! An assignation, say you. With Miss Donnay?" I shook my head. "Not in a thousand years."

"And would you be telling me why?" Jeff questioned, his manner a trifle less confident.

"Her face," I told him. "Her face. Did you notice it? Think a minute."

He did; and his expression became blank.

"God be merciful to us," he said at length; "I mind it well, now you speak of it. An inch thick in goose grease it was, with plasters at the corners of her mouth and between her eyes."

"She never went into that room to meet Snowden," I contended. "Her get-up is her best alibi."

Jeff considered a moment.

"How about the talkative old gentleman?"

"Old man Marshall?" I shook my dead. "No doubt he would have liked to—on account of Snowden's rum coffee. However, that cause would also act as a preventive. As a matter of fact, he was sick as a dog all night from having drunk it. Ever sick to your stomach? Is a man in that condition going around assassinating people?"

"Faith, then," asserted Jeff, "the answer is quickly come at. It is the brother it would be, and he the only one left."

"It was a man's job," I admitted. "It took a bit of a blow, shrewdly placed, to crush Snowden's skull. Also, Tom Randel's alibi leaves something to be desired."

"A man's job," I repeated to myself. Surely no woman could have struck those blows. And I damned the logic which bade me remember Jane Maxwell's powerful white wrists.

I got to my feet and stretched, working the kinks out of my muscles; and to Jeff I said: "Get me out the car, you long Irishman; I am going for a drive."

Jeff stared; but my order automatically placed us in the position of master and man once more, and he rose. I followed him out into the hall, where at once I became aware of a most delectable aroma. I sniffed rapturously. Jeff observed me and grinned.

"And do you not know what that is at all?" he asked.

"Faith, and I do," I mocked. And, indeed, I did. Chicken paprika it was, cooking slowly in an earthen casserole, and made in the Hungarian style which I myself had taught Jeff to prepare. I was inspired with an idea, and when Jeff had brought round the Buick I said to him as I got into the car:

"Don't be surprised if we have company for dinner"; and I drove off, leaving him wondering.

Up the lane, then north over the state highway, I drove through the misty drizzle, until at length, coming into the village, I was on the lookout for the brave little shop with its shining brass sign and the intriguing nightie in its window. As before, the place was untenanted when I entered, but at once the velvet curtains in the rear parted to disclose, not her I came to find, but a diminutive handmaiden clad in decorous black, save for the frilled white apron. She regarded me doubtfully.

"Would you be another of the newspaper gentlemen?" she asked, before I had a chance to speak. "Because, if you are, Miss Maxwell has gone for the day."

I disclaimed any connection with the press. "Holt is the name," I told her; and added that I had an appointment with Miss Maxwell.

"Oh, in that case, Miss Maxwell is in," she smiled and held aside the curtains for me to enter. I followed her into a side hall and up a narrow stairway to the second floor, where I was ushered into a tiny living room. In the rear wall there was a closed door upon which the girl knocked.

"Yes?" I heard Jane's voice.

"Mr. Holt is here," the girl announced.

I heard a movement beyond the door.

"Ask him to sit down; I won't be a minute," came the reply.

I nodded to the little maid; without further word she left me. I heard her high heels go clicking down the stairs. There was a sound behind me, and I turned to see Jane's face at the crack of the door.

"Hello, there," she greeted me. "I'll be decent in just a minute. There's a bottle on the mantel and cigarettes on the little table in the corner"; and the door closed.

A glance at the bottle showed a Johnny Walker label, and a taste of the contents satisfied me that if it had not come from the same stock to which Muriel had referred when we had visited the Cambridge Arms, it nevertheless fitted her description of the tipple, I lit a Rameses and sat in one of the easy chairs, taking stock of the room.

It was a cozy little retreat, made cheerful by bright chintz-cushioned wicker furniture and two tall lamps with colored shades, and warmed by a shining gas burner installed in the fireplace beneath the old-fashioned, elaborately carved wooden mantelpiece. There was a combination radio and phonograph in one corner, in another a well-filled bookcase with glass doors. On the walls were half a dozen reproductions of Ludivico's coaching scenes; a bright one-toned rug covered the floor.

With my eye on the bookcase I said to myself: "Tell me what you read, and I'll tell you what you are"; and I was rising to investigate when Jane appeared. She wore an ankle-length wine-colored silk negligee, loose but clinging, that revealed the curves of her beautiful figure and made her seem very tall, after the short-skirted dresses in which heretofore I had seen her.

"Hello!" I said, taking the capable white hands she offered. "Certainly my suggestion was a good one. You're looking charming."

"It's a wonder if I do," she replied, taking the big chair I had vacated. "I've been through a lot since I saw you."

I stepped to the mantel, got the bottle of Johnny Walker, a siphon of soda, and two glasses.

"I feel entitled to that," Jane said, as I poured the whisky and squirted the soda. She took the glass and waited for me to serve myself. It had been, she informed me, a strenuous afternoon, what with curiosity seekers calling under the pretext of business, to say nothing of several newspaper reporters, voracious for information. Finally she had abandoned the shop to her assistant and had sought refuge in her apartment.

"I took a couple of aspirin tablets and went to bed," she concluded.

"Well, here's to you, my dear," I said, and we drank.

"I had no idea you lived here," I added, taking her empty glass.

"I don't, really," she told me. "My home is with a maiden aunt, out in the East End. But sometimes that is too much of a trip. And, besides, Auntie and I get on each other's nerves occasionally. So I maintain this little apartment for emergencies. It is just this living room, and my bedroom and bath, and a kitchenette. And that reminds me"—she made a movement to rise—"I must put on the tea kettle."

I was seated on the broad arm of her chair, and I laid a restraining hand on her shoulder.

"Wait a minute. It's all fixed. You're to have dinner with me and Jeff. Jeff is my general factotum. You'll like him. And do you fancy chicken paprika, Hungarian style?"

"I'm crazy about it," she assured me, enthusiastically.

I got to my feet and drew her up after me.

"Fine!" I told her. "Now you take off this tea gown and put on that orange sport suit I like so much and we'll be off."

She shot me a quick look.

"You're a darling to think of a lonesome girl," was her low-voiced comment.

I felt a renewed stirring of my protective instinct.

"Get your dress on," I told her, impelling her gently toward the bedroom.

Through the open door we continued to talk as she made the change. Had I progressed in the investigation? she wanted to know.

"Suppose we don't speak of that till after dinner," I suggested, "Then you and I and Jeff will hold a council of war."

She was silent for a little; then:

"Just what did Dr. Agnew—he's the physician in charge of Piermont, you know—have to say about Harry's escape?"

"He talked to McClennen," I replied. "I heard no details."

There was another short silence; then Jane came in to me where I sat smoking one of her cigarettes before the gas burner. She was wearing the knitted sport suit with a beret to match and carried a golf cape. I took the wrap from her and arranged it about her shoulders, and after she had reduced the room to darkness we descended to the street. Despite the inclement weather, it was pretty well thronged with the cars of Saturday-night shoppers.

And even after we had left the town, and were plugging through the fog along the state highway, we continued to encounter a succession of headlights of incoming cars. It wasn't hard to guess tonight's main subject of gossip. By this time news of the tragedy would be widespread. I think that thought was in Jane's mind. I felt the shoulder close to mine stir in a little shiver. The hand she laid upon my arm seemed to petition sympathy. I was bound to make her snap out of it.

"Do you know what I am thinking about?" I said, speaking in a loud voice to make myself heard in competition with the noisy engine of the Buick.

"No. What?" Jane replied, bringing her face nearer to mine.

"Why, about our dress. It should have reached Boston before this. Probably my young namesake is wearing it tonight."

"Your namesake?" she laughed. It did me good to hear it.

"Namesake is right," I insisted. "Merely substitute an 'e' for the 'i' as the penultimate letter."

"Oh, I see. And how do they differentiate when there's the two of you?" She laughed again.

"She is 'Fannie,' and I am 'Frank,' you see. That makes it easy for all."

I felt a pressure from the hand that rested upon my arm.

"I wish you'd call me Jane, instead of Miss Maxwell. It would be ever so much more friendly."

"It shall be done," I assured her.

While we had talked, the going had progressed from bad to worse, the foggy outlines of roadside hedge and fence being scarcely discernible in the powerful rays of our headlights. Indeed, I should have missed the turning completely but for Jane's better knowledge of the locality.

"Ours is the next crossroad," she warned me.

I slowed down and, seeing an opening on our right, I gingerly swung the car into what fortunately proved to be the approach to our destination. Down the lane we crept in second gear, past the big Randel house, which loomed larger than life through the vagueness of the fog, with lights showing hazily in but two or three of its many windows, until at length we cautiously made the turning into the Hammond grounds and came to a stop before the front veranda of the bungalow.

I assisted the girl to the ground and turned to see Jeff outlined in the brightly lit doorway. We entered, Jeff stepping aside with the little bow he reserved for moments of ceremony. I took the boy by the arm, ignoring his attitude of self-effacement.

"Miss Maxwell," said I, "allow me to present to you this long Irishman, Jeffries, better known as Jeff, who is the friend, companion, and comforter of my declining years. And, Jeff," I went on, grinning at his look of embarrassment, "this is Miss Maxwell, of whom you have heard and whose allies we are."

Jeff showed a serious face as he confronted the girl; he repeated his formal little bow.

Jane put out her hand.

"I'm delighted to know you, Jeff," she smiled at him.

He bowed over the hand; then dropped it and straightened up to look at me, his inherent sense of the fitness of things asserting itself.

"I will be serving the dinner at once, sir," he said and departed kitchenward.

Jane pulled off her beret and tossed it and her golf cape upon the hall rack. We went into the living room. She sat down in the judge's big leather chair before the fire, and I stepped to the windows to draw the curtains against the night. In the bay which faced south I stood for a moment, a heavy curtain in either hand, my face close to the glass, peering at the ill-defined outline of the big Randel house, a shadow of a shade in the fog-enshrouded scene. The prospect was cheerless enough. I thought of her who had so recently made her final exit.

Somehow, there came to my mind the lines of an ancient Scottish dirge:

> *"Fire, and sleet, and candlelight;*
> *And Christ receive your soul. . . ."*

Finding myself for the moment unduly depressed, I retreated to the warmth and brightness of the pleasant room. In her big chair Jane had half turned and was regarding me with a look of speculative interest.

14

Dinner was finished and Jeff was bringing in the coffee when we were broken in upon by the jingle of the telephone. It was a feminine voice that saluted me.

"Is that you, Mr. Holt?"

"Speaking," I replied.

"Well, this is Miss McCarthy. Do you get me?"

"Miss McCarthy?" I returned uncertainly.

"Yes; you know—Kitty; down at the Cambridge Arms."

The vision of the blonde cashier rose before me.

"Oh, yes," said I. "How do you do?"

"I'm swell." There was an instant's pause; then: "Say, Mr. Holt, can you fix it to see me tonight? It's important. I have some inside dope to slip to you about Snowden and Muriel."

Something prompted me to say: "I don't know that I am interested."

There was another momentary silence. I got the impression that the transmitter at the other end had been suddenly covered. Then came a little chuckling laugh.

"Quit your kidding," I was admonished.

"Kitty," I laughed, "you have been drinking again."

There was an inebriated giggle. "Sure I have. Ain't it Saturday night—and my night off? I'm handing you the straight goods just the samc."

Half drunk already, I told myself. Probably this call was simply an alcoholic vagary.

"Meet me tomorrow up in the city; I'll buy your lunch," I suggested.

"Nothing doing," was the prompt response; and she went on quickly: "You'll see me down here in the jungle tonight, if you want the dope I can hand you. Of course"—the voice took on a contemptuous tone—"if you haven't the guts to come, after the Houdini you pulled the other day, you can stay where you are."

"Listen," I told her. "I'll come down; and if what you have to say doesn't mean anything, I'll take you over my knee."

She laughed at that.

"It's the real McCoy, dearie," she assured me. "It'll mean the hot seat for somebody if you handle it right."

"Where shall I find you?" I asked, preparing to hang up.

"In the take joint downstairs," she told me. "If you don't see me, ask Tony."

Wondering what I had let myself in for, I returned to the dining room.

"Our evening is wrecked," I said; and explained why I must leave.

"I'll tell you," put in Jane. "We'll all go. Oh, you needn't look shocked. I've been to the Cambridge Arms several times. We'll throw a little party."

"A likely story!" I laughed at her.

"Oh, please, Frank," she begged, getting up to come to me. "Be a good sport. Let's all three of us go."

I looked at the pleading face and felt myself slipping. After all, why not? There was no particular reason why she couldn't accompany us, and it would be a shabby trick to take her back to the loneliness of her apartment.

"Very well," I agreed somewhat dubiously.

She gave a delighted little cry.

"Wait till I powder my nose," she commanded and hurried from the room.

When, my brief preparations completed, I went out to the car, I found that the weather showed little improvement. Not quite so foggy, perhaps, but colder, with an occasional big wet snowflake in the drizzle. Jeff was seated at the wheel, impatient to be off. I got into the rear seat with Jane and felt her welcoming hand tuck itself under my arm. She settled herself down in the seat, happy as a kid going to her first party.

"I know something exciting is going to happen," she declared, prophetically jubilant.

I found myself wondering if this could be the same girl who, plaintive and sorrowing, had that morning solicited my aid. Had I, by any chance, overestimated the value of Miss Maxwell's depth of feeling? Wanted excitement, did she? I might have reminded her that there had been enough excitement crowded into the past twenty-four hours. However, I merely answered by a pressure of the hand as we swung out of the lane and took a skid on the greasy surface of the highway.

"Watch that heavy foot," I cautioned Jeff, as we straightened out and, ignoring the uncertain going, he began to work the car up to speed.

However, as we proceeded there was a lessening of the obscurity. A rising wind from the west that drove raindrops and soggy flakes of snow against the windows of the sedan dissipated the fog, and before we had reached the borough limits the single lighted street of Glen Athol showed a luminous line ahead of us.

We had passed through the town, lively with its Saturday-night activities, and once more were traveling the dark highway, when the mirror reflected the headlight of a pursuing car. It was coming up fast. At once Jeff pulled over to the right, giving it all possible room. It passed us with a roar. I had a glimpse of a small coupé with a single occupant. The red tail light disappeared round a curve, and when again the road lay straight before us it was barely discernible, a crimson dot in the distance. Suddenly it winked out of sight.

"Doing sixty or better, that chap," Jeff called back over his shoulder.

"He'll come to grief," I predicted; and two minutes later: "There!" I exclaimed. "What did I tell you!"

We had topped a rise beyond which the road descended a long, gentle slope in an undeviating line. Some five hundred yards distant the headlights of two stationary cars shone diagonally across the highway.

"Tried to pass a truck and sideswiped it," I added, as we came to a stop within fifty feet or so of the scene of the accident.

It was a big black moving van with which the coupé had apparently collided. The little car, seemingly none the worse for the meeting, rested across the road, its front wheels at the edge of the gutter. Beyond it the black length of the truck combined to block our progress effectually. Several dark figures moved about the two cars, evidently in an effort to restore order. It seemed an impasse for us.

"Let us see if we can help," I said to Jeff, and we got out.

"What's the trouble?" I asked, moving forward in the glare of our headlights, Jeff alongside of me.

The answer came with startling suddenness. A man stepped from behind the coupé, a slim young figure, nattily attired in a double-breasted blue overcoat, the brim of his tan-colored soft hat pulled down over his eyes.

"No trouble. Just stick 'em up as high as you can," he said pleasantly enough, but the menace of the sawed-off shotgun that he trained upon us belied his tone. I promptly obeyed.

"Do it," I said to Jeff, fearing he would make a break for his gun. I had been through this kind of thing more than once. I knew it would be folly to resist, especially with Jane in line with the sawed-off shotgun. However, if I thought that young lady would frighten, I was wrong. There was the slam of the door of the sedan, and at once Jane was at my side.

"What do you think you're trying to do?" she indignantly demanded of the fellow with the gun.

"Listen, lady," the chap replied. "You're excess baggage in this party. We didn't bargain for you. Behave and you won't get hurt."

"If I may lower my hands I'll give you what money I have on me," I dissembled; adding: "The lady has nothing of value. Can't she get back in the car?"

The fellow laughed.

"Do I look like a chiseler, mister? It's not peanuts we're after. Keep up the mitts." He waved the blunt muzzles threateningly. "O.K., boys; snap into it," he called, never taking his eyes from us.

Immediately there was action. The engine of the van started with a cough of the self-starter. The big vehicle, quickly backing in a short arch, again stood facing the bare line of wet highway. A man hitherto concealed in its shadow sprang forward to open doors of the van. A screech of the siren, and from a clump of bushes at the roadside some fifty yards ahead there materialized into the illumination of the headlights an armed figure which rapidly approached us. At the same time I was conscious that from somewhere in the darkness at our rear we had been joined by another member of the gang. A well-planned ambuscade, I told myself; blockade, pickets, the whole bag of tricks. At least five men in the party. In a scabbard under my left arm I carried an army automatic that held eight cartridges, and I knew that Jeff would instantly back up any move I might make, but the odds were too heavy. I stood there in the drizzle, my hands above my head, feeling a trifle foolish and not a little alarmed.

All at once Jane seemed to understand that we were in a bad fix. Suddenly realizing our position, she had recourse to the usual feminine device under duress. She screamed at the top of her lungs. The effect was electric. Jeff made a hasty movement which brought him a blow on his head, delivered from the rear by the fellow who had come in from guard duty. The same man threw an arm round Jane's neck, effectually stifling further outcry. For my part, I found the snub nose of the sawed-off shotgun shoved tightly against my abdomen.

"Make a move, guy, and I'll cut you in two," I was told.

The young fellow had a nice voice. He didn't seem at all excited. At close quarters I had a pretty good look at his face. He appeared to be a mere boy.

"Well," said I, "you're bossing the job. What shall I do?"

"Get in," he replied, indicating by a jerk of his head the black maw of the van.

As I obediently moved forward I glanced over my shoulder. Jane's scream had instantly drawn to us the three other members of the outfit. Now two of them were lifting Jeff from the ground; the chap who had come in from advance sentry duty stood at one side, a vigilant figure, the short barrel of a Thompson automatic resting across his arm; Jane remained quiescent in the grasp of her assailant. To turn my back on my two companions, and one of them a girl, was a bitter thing to do. The knowledge that my first resisting move might be the signal for the elimination of the three of us didn't make it any easier.

My captor brought me to a halt before the open doors of the truck. "Hold it," he ordered; and I watched them bestow the unconscious Jeff into the dark interior; then Jane was bundled in. At a dig in the ribs from the muzzle of the shotgun, I followed. The doors were slammed. I heard the snap of the lock. In the pitch darkness I sprawled on the rough floorboards. My extended hand encountered the smooth roundness of a silk-stockinged leg.

"Are you all right, Jane?" was my low-voiced and anxious query.

The roar of the engine as the truck started in violent motion was my only answer. At once I was aware that we had made a right-hand turn, the roughness of our progress showing that we had left the highway. I got to my knees and lit a match. In the brief illumination I discovered Jane seated on the floor, her back against the padded side of the van. With her skirt pulled high above her knees, her beret cocked jauntily over one eye, she looked for all the world like a little girl undergoing punishment by being made to sit in the corner. Beyond her was Jeff, apparently none the worse for hard knocks. From where he lay on the broad of his back, his clasped hands behind his head, he grinned up at me reassuringly. The match flared out. I settled myself beside Jane, slipping an arm round her; and so we continued for the next half-hour, pretty well shaken by the rough going.

At length, after we had covered a particularly uneven stretch of road, the truck came to a stop. From, the cab beyond the forward wall of our prison came the faint rumble of voices. There was a grunt from Jeff as he got to his feet.

"Is it ready to start something they are?" was his growled query.

"You have your gun," whispered Jane. "Couldn't you shoot them by firing through the back of the cab?"

I drew my cramped legs under me.

"Let's try to hear what they're saying," I said; and crept to the foremost limit of our narrow quarters.

All this time from up in the cab there had come to us the sustained growl of low-voiced conversation. Now, as our whispered colloquy ended, there was, I thought, in that monotonous rumble a snarling note of dissension.

The partition which divided the cab from the body of the van was, like the side walls, overlaid with canvas-covered padding. This covering acted as an effective silencer, but when I had torn loose a corner of the pad, and had an ear to the rent, the conversation beyond was no longer inaudible.

There was a nasal whine:

"Naw; you got the wrong slant on the proposition. Anyhow, there it is, buddy; take it or leave it."

A gruff-voiced burst of profanity outlined the first speaker's maternal origin, his characteristics, habits, and probable finish.

"Wait till you go to the mat with the boss. I'd hate like hell to be in your shoes then," the gruff voice declared.

The first voice drawled:

"You two are just plain dumb. Me and the boss'll not tangle over this. He never expected the broad to show up. That makes the whole damn play go sour."

"Did Nick say so?" demanded number two.

"No, Nick didn't say so," mocked the other; and continued: "That torpedo wouldn't give a damn anyway. But, at that, he wasn't hep to who the dame is. Knocking off this other party is taking chances enough. He's wired-in with the U. S. Secret Service. We're liable to have the federal crowd get busy. But this dame is a friend of the Doc. We'd have him on our backs, and I'm here to tell you I don't want no run in with that bird—and the boss don't neither, if you ask me."

A short silence followed, broken by a boyish voice.

"Well, you two guys make up your minds what's doing. I got to get this scooter up the line, and I'm late now."

"I'm all set to go ahead," rumbled the bass voice. "If you think I'm going against orders you're crazy as hell.

You try double-crossing the boss! Try it! You'll last about as long as a shot of hootch."

"Listen, sap," was the nasal admonition, "I know the boss as good as you do. If he says the word, why, it's ok with me. But he won't. He'd be the first to say lay off for tonight. Now here's what we'll do. Jerry can go ahead with the scooter, like he says. You hold the three of them here while I beat it back to see the boss. It won't take over an hour. Then we'll be all jake for the next move. See? How does that strike you after thinking it over?"

"That ain't a bad idea at that, Larry," commented the boyish voice.

There was silence for a moment. Then came a deep-toned exclamation of disgust and a bass growl: "All right, wise guy; have it your way."

The voice that had argued for delay in the proceedings said:

"Atta boy, Larry. Come on; we'll take them in the house."

There was a sudden stirring beyond the partition, and the sound of the opening cab door. I turned to my companions.

"Here they come," I whispered.

15

I heard Jeff's belligerent grunt as he got to his feet. I pushed him aside to grope for Jane. My hand met hers as she reached for me in the darkness. I felt her tremble as she clung to me.

Then the doors swung open and we had a surprise. Our prison was invaded by a dazzling glare of light that half blinded us. I blinked uncertainly at the figures silhouetted against the illumination from the headlights of a car drawn up in our rear.

The chap with the nasal accent hailed us.

"Come out, folks; you're stopping here for a while," he called. His voice, I thought, was not unfriendly. Then, as we maintained our position, dazed by the sudden brightness, he added:

"Hey! You with the dame. Get her out here. We're in a rush."

I helped Jane to the muddy ground. Jeff jumped out after us, and there we stood in the windy drizzle, awaiting the pleasure of our abductors. It was, a glance showed me, a narrow lane in which we had halted. I surmised we had left the side road. To the left of this by-path ran a stake-and-rider fence, beyond which I could distinguish a dark mass of trees and undergrowth. To our right, and bordered by a tumbled-down stone wall, was a clearing, with the barely discernible outline of a house which stood some distance back from the lane.

Upon our descent from the van our captors had withdrawn to a position slightly to the rear. As I had judged from the voices taking part in the conversation to which I had listened, the original party of five had shrunk to three. They stood just within the radiance cast by the headlights. The nasal voice spoke up.

"You two guys take the lady up to the house," he ordered Jeff and me, pointing a directing finger.

"And don't try to pull no fast one—without you want me to open up on you," added the big fellow with the bass voice.

"Come on," I said to Jeff and Jane. We splattered through the mud and passed between the stone pillars which marked the break in the decadent wall where once there had been a gateway. Then, indifferent to orders: "Stop a bit," I said to Jeff, at my heels; and I came to a halt to peer into the obscurity ahead.

Now that we had passed beyond the range of the headlights, the outline of the house was more clearly defined. Seemingly the place was quite deserted.

"Any idea where we are?" I asked Jane.

The answer came from the big fellow. Unobserved by me, he had approached to close quarters. Now, with one of his smaller companions, he was at our heels.

"Never mind where you are, mister. Just keep right on ahead," he ordered; and as we moved toward the house the nasal voice added: "To your right, round to the back."

I took Jane's arm and led the way. There was the sound of the departing truck.

At the rear of the house they halted us while the smaller of our captors unlocked a door.

"All set, folks; in you go," he told us, rejoining his companion. I noticed that he took good care not to come between us and the sub-machine gun in the hands of the big fellow.

Again I led the way, stumbling down three or four steps to a cement floor. Then my two companions were shepherded in after me. The little chap lighted an old-fashioned oil lantern, and I saw that we were in a windowless cellar some thirty feet square. Many shelves, ranging from floor to ceiling, extended around the walls. In one corner there was a great pile of five-gallon tin cans. A rickety extension table and half a dozen kitchen chairs supplied the furnishings.

Now, while the big fellow continued the menace of the deadly automatic, the smaller gangster quickly placed three chairs against the wall. He set the lantern upon the table and turned to confront us.

"There you are, folks; take your weight off your feet," he said, indicating the chairs by a wave of his hand. Again, it seemed to me, his voice was friendly. "The big boy here," he went on, with a jerk of his head toward the burly figure in the rubber coat, "will keep you company. He'll treat you good—as long as you behave. Don't pull nothing foolish, or that little baby he's holding is liable to start talking."

I laid a hand on Jane's arm. The three of us moved forward and seated ourselves. The big man kicked a chair in place and sat down facing us, resting the machine gun on the table, its muzzle directed toward us, its stock cradled in the crook of his arm.

"I'll be seeing you," promised the other, starting for the door.

Well, there we were; and there we continued to sit amid a silence that was absolute. I had taken the middle chair, Jeff rubbing elbows with me to my right, Jane equally close at the other side. The girl was behaving beautifully. And it required nerve to sit there quietly, contemplating that somber figure at the opposite side of the wide dining table, with his deadly Thompson automatic.

For the next fifteen or twenty minutes I studied the fellow, watching for some sign of lessening vigilance which might be my opportunity. As for a view of his features, with the raised collar of the rubber coat forming a black band across his face, and his cap pulled down over his eyes, he might as well have been masked. Silent and motionless he sat there, his left arm extended upon the table, his hand supporting the short barrel of the machine gun. My eyes grew tired in the strain of my scrutiny. Of the least evidence of wavering alertness on the part of our guard there was none. I had the feeling that those invisible eyes were fixed on me. I feigned an apologetic cough and raised my hand to my mouth. The muzzle of the machine gun lifted slightly, steadied itself, and remained motionless.

As though my action had been her cue, Jane began to fidget uneasily. I heard her occasional deep inhalation of breath, noted the ensuing pause followed by the fluttering sigh. She was, I became aware, fast approaching the limit of her self-control. Seemingly the contagion of the girl's agitation attacked Jeff. He, too, squirmed in his chair. I heard his low growl of restrained unrest.

This was all very well, so long as these manifestations were judiciously moderated. Though of insufficient portent to cause our watchdog to bite, the slight movements of my companions undoubtedly disturbed him. For the first time, I thought, he showed a trace of nervousness, as, bending a trifle forward, he made the snub nose of the automatic travel slowly across our front. I grinned to myself; and with a half-formed plan beginning to play about in my mind I settled back in my chair, administering a cautionary jog of an elbow to either of my companions, whereupon they became quiet.

Never allowing my eyes to center on the gunman, I simulated a sudden interest in what lay behind him. I did this cannily, proceeding slowly with my act, progressing from merely staring intently at an imaginary object above him to a series of guarded movements of head and shoulders as I pretended to spy at something that moved in his rear. For a time my histrionic efforts produced no effect. The somber figure sat motionless. With infinite caution I persisted. At length I thought I could detect a spirit of unrest entering our keeper. In little tentative movements he turned his head, inclining an ear now over this shoulder, now over the other. Suddenly he shifted uneasily in his chair; now he sat stiffly upright, his head raised as though he listened intently.

The time had come for me to play my trump card.

For the past ten minutes I had been nerving myself for a coup, to accomplish which demanded perfect timing, an exact coordination of mind, nerves, and muscle. My arms hung at my sides, in the just sufficient space between my chair and those occupied by my companions. Between the thumb and the index finger of my right hand I cuddled a silver half-dollar. Now, as the gangster's action told me that, momentarily at least, his nerve had failed him, I flipped the coin high above his head and beyond him. My hand had scarcely moved; in the half-light of the lantern the coin in its passage through the air was invisible. It struck the piled up five-gallon cans and rebounded to the cement floor with a sound incredibly loud in the dead stillness of the room.

As for the gangster, his nerves already keyed to the breaking point as a result of my byplay, the threat of this unseen menace from the shadows behind him drove all else from his mind. We were forgotten for the moment. Half rising, he turned to confront a danger unknown, and therefore the more greatly to be feared. And now,

I went into action.

With the flip of the coin I had laid hold of my companions' chairs. As I lurched to my feet I carried them with me, spilling my friends to the floor and out of danger of a fusillade. That effort brought me to my knees. As I went down I glimpsed the big fellow's instant reaction as he rounded on me, his weapon poised. The split second by which I anticipated him decided the affair. My pistol, snatched from its spring scabbard, was in my hand when I hit the floor. From where I knelt I threw two shots across the table, under the arm that swung the sub-machine gun to bear on me.

In the blast of my gunfire the flame of the lantern flared up. By its flicker I saw the black figure slump forward upon the table, twist half over, and slip to the floor. For the moment I knelt motionless; but I knew he was finished. I snapped on the safety catch of my Colt and returned it to its holster.

All this happened so quickly that Jeff was just getting to his knees from where I had thrown him. He grinned at me approvingly. I turned to Jane. She sat on the floor, leaning back upon her supporting arms, staring at me in bemused surprise.

"It's all right," I told her. I got to my feet and helped her to rise. She looked round her, half dazed.

Jane's arm tightened about me. I felt her tremble.

"Where is he?" she whispered.

I patted her shoulder.

"You should worry," I temporized; and I said to Jeff: "Come on, let's go"; and I took the lantern and led the way outside.

We emerged into the same infernal brand of weather we had escaped when we had entered the house. If anything it rained worse than before. I pulled up the collar of my coat and wrapped Jane's cape about her.

"Here," she said to Jeff, cool as you please now that she thought we were out of the woods, "tie that over your head"; and she gave him her scarf to replace the hat he had lost in the fracas.

"Do you know where we are?" I put the question to her for the second time that night.

Yes, I was told, she did know, perfectly.

"This is the clubhouse of the old Leesdale Hunt Club—that was more than five years ago," she informed us; and she added: "We're not more than a couple of miles from Campbell Snowden's place."

By the light of the lantern I looked at my watch. It lacked a few minutes of ten o'clock. As nearly as I could guess, we had been in the house about forty-five minutes. I remembered that the nasal-voiced sportsman had promised to return within the hour.

"You say we're not far from the Snowden home?" said I, itching to be off.

"Not more than a couple of miles."

"And can you find it in the dark?"

She thought she could, she said.

"Then that is our next stop," I declared. "At least, they'll probably send us back home."

They would do much more than that, Jane insisted.

We followed a continuation of the gravel path for a hundred yards or so, passing some dilapidated outbuildings, to another stretch of tumbled-down stone wall. Beyond, rising out of the obscurity, there appeared a skyline of bare branches.

"There," said Jane, coming to a halt. "We go through those woods and climb the hill on the other side. From there we can see the Snowden house."

Jeff took the lantern, and I helped the girl over the wall.

We had gone the better part of half a mile—we never could have done it without the lantern—when there began to be a thinning out of the trees. Then it wasn't long till we were out of the woods entirely, standing in a narrow, rutted road that cut our course at a right angle. Beyond the road was a bare hillside that rose sharply. And a long and a toilsome climb it was, over turf slippery with rain. We crossed the stretch of level ground at the top of the hog's-back and stood in a chilling wind looking out across the valley.

"There it is," said Jane, and she pointed to a half-dozen pinpoints of light. All we had to do now, she went on, was to follow the golf course that ran along at the bottom of the hill and we would come out directly behind the house.

The rest was easy. Within the next twenty minutes we came to a macadamized driveway that disappeared to our right, around an edifice of ample size, constructed of stone and of the chateau type.

"Here we are," said Jane; and we followed her along the drive, past a dimly lit conservatory of impressive extent, and an oversize garage, brightly lighted and most imposing, with a display of shining cars visible through the several glass doors. And so we came to a halt at last under the overhang of an arched doorway. Jane, with the manner of one quite at home, tried the knob, unsuccessfully.

"They must be getting scary," she said; and she pushed the bell button vigorously and struck the door a knock for good measure.

Suddenly we found ourselves inundated by a flood of light from a lamp above us.

"Here they come," said Jane; and the door opened to disclose a brightly illuminated interior which formed a background for a stocky fellow whose evening clothes didn't prevent him from looking like a middle-weight pugilist gone to fat. At sight of us his face took on a look of surprised disapproval, which at once cleared to the blank expression typical of the well-trained upper servant. Jane hailed him familiarly.

"Hello, Jenkins; can we come in?"

The man stepped back, opening the door to its widest extent.

"Certainly, Miss Jane," he replied with a perfect manner.

We stepped inside, and the fellow closed the door. Jane said to me: "This is Jenkins, Mr. Snowden's butler. And"—turning to him: "This is Mr. Holt, who is occupying Judge Hammond's place"; she waved a hand toward Jeff in the background: "Also Jeffries, Mr. Holt's man."

The butler's bow included both of us, and Jane went on: "We have had a series of adventures and find ourselves stranded out here without a car. Do you think you can take care of us?"

"Certainly, Miss Jane," he said. "Please come into the living room." He paused as he turned to show the way. "You will have company," he added; and with that he conducted us through the hall that led to the front of the house from the side door by which we had entered. We followed into a living room as big as the whole first floor of the Hammond bungalow. The walls were lined in modern pine, slightly colored and given a wax finish, as were also the matched wide oak planks of the floor; the roof timbers were of natural oak, broad-axed. A gigantic stone fireplace took up most of one end of the imposing apartment, which was, I thought, over-furnished and in keeping with the ostentation of the departed master of the house. However, these details did not at once attract my attention.

At one side of the great room was an offset formed by the sloping timbers of the roof into a spacious recess furnished with a long refectory table and half a dozen tapestried armchairs. The light in the room came from the glow of the logs on the hearth and three or four small wall fixtures; also there were a couple of tall wax candles in silver holders at one corner of the refectory table. They shone upon silver and crystal, upon white napery and delicate china, a dainty little supper service for two. And seated there, and looking very much surprised at our appearance, were Lea Donnay and Tom Randel.

16

Tom Randel hurriedly rose, an embarrassed smile on his handsome face. Miss Donnay sat motionless, staring at us, her dark eyes opened wide. Jane, slightly in advance of me, had come to a halt at the sight of the young couple.

"Well, of all things!" she exclaimed. "Who would have thought to find you two here!"

Tom's smile broadened. A second look showed me that the boy was a trifle tight.

"One might say the same of you," he returned. "And, if I might add without offense; you all look like you had been swimming the river." He paused to laugh foolishly. "And, oh, look at that one!" He pointed at Jeff, a comic figure with the draggled scarf twisted turbanwise around his head.

"You needn't try to be witty," Jane retorted indignantly. "Wait till you've heard what we've been through."

I had no mind to make public the details of our experience.

"Yes," I put in, laying a hand on Jane's arm. "We are walking home from an automobile ride." I gave the arm a warning squeeze.

Young Randel stared at me doubtfully.

"You don't tell me!" he gravely returned. "Well," he added, with a wave of his hand, indicating the two chairs which the butler had drawn up to the corner of the table, "you might sit down and have a little drink with us—unless that also is against your principles."

But Jane said: "I'm soaked to the skin. Jenkins, where is Mrs. Hubbard? I must ask her for some dry clothes."

I retained my hold of the girl's arm.

"You see, it was this way," I told them, wanting Jane to hear my version of our adventure. "About two miles from here we were held up by a couple of hoodlums. They turned us out and went off in the car. We took a short cut over the hills and stopped here to see if we could get a lift back home."

Then, before anybody could make a comment, Jane began to cry. Suddenly she was trembling all over. Lea Donnay quickly rose and came to us.

"You poor darling! What a terrifying experience!" she gushed and magnificently took the weeping girl, wet golf cape and all, in her arms.

The butler intervened. If the young ladies would come with him, he would lead them to Mrs. Hubbard, he assured them. So, when they had left the room—and Jeff, at a nod from Jenkins, had followed—I joined Tom Randel. He had reseated himself and was removing the wires from a quart bottle of champagne. I took a chair at the corner of the table, watching him skillfully open the wine and send it creaming into two wide glasses. He handed one to me.

"I'll bet that will taste good to you," he grinned.

I swallowed the excellent wine with less deliberation than its admirable vintage merited.

"Rather amazing to run into you like this," I said, holding out my empty glass to be refilled.

Young Randel glanced at me owlishly. Pouring the wine, he replied: "That's right. The last you saw of me I was headed for the East End, wasn't I?"

I nodded.

"Well," he went on, "it was this way: I spent the afternoon at Lea's—had dinner there. This is the cause of our being here."

He produced a gold cigarette case from his pocket and tossed it upon the table.

"Lea gave me that—in Paris. Today she noticed I wasn't using it. I had to admit I'd left it here when I played golf with Campbell last week. Lea was sore. She declared I'd never see it again, with a lot of strangers overrunning the place now that Campbell is gone. So tonight we decided to drive down and get it."

I picked up and examined the monogrammed gewgaw.

"Very nice," I commented. I might have added that I had noticed it when he had offered a cigarette from it to Miss Winans, the night before; but: "No," thought I. "Let him lie about it, if he wants to."

Then it came my turn to prevaricate. Young Randel was full of curiosity concerning our adventure, and he asked a lot of questions. He had nothing to say about the happenings of the morning. His indifference to Muriel's tragic death and the impending fate of his brother surprised me. They were, I told myself—and I was forced to include Jane in the same category—a pretty hard-boiled crowd. Last night at this time we had been watching Muriel as she spun the roulette wheel, and now . . .

It wasn't long till Jenkins appeared with a message from Miss Donnay. Would Mr. Randel come upstairs for a moment? The boy shot an angry glance at the butler and got to his feet.

"I was expecting something like this, Shylock," was his cryptic comment; and none too steadily he went out of the room.

"Now what in the world did he mean by that remark?" I asked myself. I took out my pipe and started to fill it. If

I preferred a cigar, or cigarettes, he would be glad to fetch them, the butler assured me.

"I'd rather have my pipe," I told him; and asked about a car to take us home. He leaned over my shoulder, got a tall cloisonné lighter that stood among the things on the table and snapped it on.

"I think Miss Donnay intends to speak to Mr. Randel about all of you remaining here for the night. I understand Miss Maxwell has contracted a severe chill," he informed me and held the flame to the bowl of my pipe.

I made no reply. He began to clear away the remains of the supper. The sight of the cigarette case lying among the dishes gave me an idea.

"Very likely to be forgotten again," I said, holding up the case for the butler's consideration.

"Quite likely, sir," was the ready answer. "I was glad to have it safe when Mr. Randel came looking for it tonight."

No doubt that had been very gratifying, I told him, rising to go to the window at the end of the long room.

A fine, sleety rain was beating against the panes. When I peered between cupped hands set close to the glass I couldn't see a foot beyond. A dismal prospect indeed. I felt myself chill in my damp clothes. Turning to go to the fire, my attention was attracted to a number of photographs enclosed in a single big frame that took up most of the wall space in an alcove to the right of the window. They were, I saw, likenesses of celebrities of the stage, in costumes of their best-known characters. What caused me to stop for a second look was a large portrait of Campbell Snowden which occupied the place of honor at the center of the collection. It showed him in the guise of a Bedouin sheik, wearing aba, agal, and kuffieh, and armed to the teeth—an eye-filling spectacle. Knowing something of these gentry I was immediately struck by the ignorance Snowden had displayed in the selection of weapons to go with his costume. His rifle was a long, muzzle-loading Afghan juzail; a curved scimitar hung from his girdle, which supported a long flintlock pistol and a sheathed dagger. At the sight of the latter weapon my amusement changed to wonder. Doubting the evidence of my own eyes, I continued to scrutinize the thing. The detail of the unique handle showed very clearly. I could even recognize the arabesques, and the carved pomegranate that formed the end. It was, beyond all doubt, the knife that had been used to kill Muriel.

I went to the fireplace and stood warming myself, thoughtfully studying the complicated design of the Shiraz rug underfoot; which intriguing example of Eastern symbolism was no more intricate than the puzzle in hand, I unwillingly admitted.

The butler, having cleared the table, had disappeared. For a while I continued to absorb the warmth of the fire, devoutly wishing that Jeff and I were back where we belonged. Now there came footsteps in the hall, and Tom Randel entered. He was followed by a wizened little old fellow, very spruce in a dark cutaway coat and striped trousers, with black Ascot tie and high winged collar a mile too wide for his shrunk and corded neck. He came to a sudden halt at Tom's heels, as the boy paused at sight of me, and ran a thin, veined hand back over his sparse gray hair, his watery blue eyes taking me in with evident curiosity.

"We've been putting your young lady friend to bed," Tom informed me waggishly and kissed his fingertips toward the ceiling. "It's like this: Jane has caught cold as a result of your ramble in the rain. Says she's a sick girl and can't go on. Lea refuses to leave her, and it looks as though you and I were elected to stay here for the night. Any objections?"

I couldn't see any necessity for me and Jeff to intrude, and I said so.

"Intrude, hell!" Tom Randel scoffed. "You don't know this joint. Besides, it isn't every day you get access to a cellar like Campbell's. We'll have Jenkins in the role of Ganymede. You and I will be jocund with the fruitful grape and drive away dull care."

The little old man put in a word.

"If you will allow me to mention it, Mr. Holt, you will be most welcome," he assured me, bowing with old-fashioned courtesy; he was, he smilingly added, taking good care of my man.

Tom Randel laid an affectionate hand on the old fellow's shoulder.

"This is Rodgers, friend of my youth. 'He hath borne me on his back a thousand times!' That's right, Rodgers, isn't it?" he went on, gently shaking the thin shoulder. "You've been with Mr. Snowden thirty years or more, haven't you?"

"Nearly forty years," was the reply. The words came slowly; the voice was subdued, and the faded old eyes continued to regard me gravely as he added: "I have a message for you, Mr. Holt, from Miss Jane. She would like to see you before she sleeps, if you will be so good."

I was at Miss Maxwell's service, I said. Again he bowed and turned to lead the way. Leaving Tom Randel to his own devices, I followed down the length of the main hall and up a Jacobean staircase that was truly a noble piece of work—out of keeping with the character of the house though it was—to an even nobler gallery. Crossing this, we entered a dimly lit corridor where, after traveling half its length, we came to a stop before a closed door. My guide turned to me.

"I think Miss Jane wishes to speak to you privately, sir. You will find me waiting here when you have finished," he whispered and knocked gently. A voice said: "Come in." I entered and closed the door behind me.

Jane lay in bed. Big girl though she was, she looked appealingly small in the great four-poster with its high tester.

"Is that you, Frank?" she said at once. "Come over here. There is something I want to tell you before Lea comes back."

A white arm emerged from concealment and was extended to me.

"Sit down," said Jane; and under the coverlet the shapely body turned to make room for me on the side of the bed.

"Where is Lea?" I asked.

Jane smiled despite her evident anxiety.

"As a favor to me, Mrs. Hubbard decoyed Lea to visit her sitting room. Frank, I'm afraid of that girl. It's about her and Tom Randel that I want to tell you."

I told her to go ahead.

"First promise that you'll stay here all night," she demanded.

"Without benefit of clergy?" I grinned at her.

"You know what I mean, Frank," she pleaded. "Honestly, after what I have overheard, I'm afraid to sleep here unless you are in the house."

"All right," I agreed, matching her mood, "I'll stay. Now tell me what the trouble is."

She wrinkled her white forehead in a perplexed frown, looking up at me through troubled eyes.

"Frank," she asked suddenly, "do you think Lea could have killed Muriel and Campbell?"

Here was a poser.

"Do you?" I asked noncommittally.

"Oh, I don't know what to think. It is all so mixed up."

"What put that idea in your head?"

She raised her fine shoulders in a quick shrug.

"It's been there from the first. For one thing, she had reason enough—real or fancied."

"You don't mean the spat she and Muriel had over the roulette game, do you? That is ridiculous," said I, egging her on. I had to smile to myself to see the way she bridled up.

"Oh, she has you fooled with all the rest. But I know her! She's as revengeful as a red Indian. She would do anything, once she got started. Besides, that was only one of many things."

"There was something more, was there?" I asked, thinking how perfectly she expressed the dead Muriel's opinion of the girl whose hand I was holding.

There certainly was, I was told.

"She was fighting to keep Tom. You knew Muriel was in love with him, didn't you? Well, if you're looking for a motive—there it is."

I shook my head. Somehow, I resented her evident determination to convince me of Miss Donnay's guilt.

"If every person who has a motive to kill should follow the inclination, there would be an epidemic of homicide," I reminded her pointedly.

It may be that she sensed the inference of my remark; perhaps she was merely irritated by my response to her suspicions. At any rate, her fingers tightened on mine in a grip of astonishing power. I learned something of the strength of those round, muscular wrists and large capable white hands. I had declared that the killing of Muriel and Campbell Snowden had been a man's job. I found myself doubting the soundness of my deduction. The girl flung away my hand impatiently.

"If she hadn't anything to do with killing Muriel and Campbell," she demanded, "why did Jenkins threaten her and Tom that he would tell something to the police unless they gave him a thousand dollars?"

"So!" thought I; and I asked her how she came by that knowledge.

"I listened," she confessed. "Tom called Lea out into the hall. They looked at each other so queerly I thought something was wrong; so I got up and went to the door. They were talking to Jenkins. I heard Tom say: 'There's a check for your lousy thousand dollars. Now hand over the letter this little fool wrote, and we'll get out.' And Jenkins said: 'The letter is safe. I'll hold it till I cash this check.' 'That check is O. K.,' Tom told him; and Jenkins answered: 'You two came here at my orders, and you'll leave the same way, unless you want the police to know who killed Snowden and your brother's wife.' I couldn't hear what they said after that. I was frightened. I got back to bed. When Tom and Lea came in, they looked at me as though they suspected that I had overheard their talk. That frightened me worse than ever. Then Rodgers brought me a hot drink Mrs. Hubbard had made for me. I managed to have a word with him. He is a dear old soul, as smart as can be. He fixed it with Mrs. Hubbard to get Lea away so he could bring you."

She laid her cheek against the hand she had repossessed, and for a time neither of us spoke.

"I wanted you to know what I had heard. I wasn't going to stay here for the night unless you promised not to desert me," she said at length, smiling up at me.

"All right," I told her. "I'll stick."

When I left her I found Rodgers waiting for me. If I was ready to retire, he would be happy to show me to my room, he assured me, his old face lighting up pleasantly. That sounded good to me, for I was pretty well played out and ready for bed; however, I had other plans.

"Rodgers," said I, studying the kindly wrinkled face that was turned to me, "you have been an inmate of this house for a long time. No doubt you know the history of many of the things it contains?"

The reply came without hesitation.

"That is true, sir. I was more than a valet to Mr. Snowden—I was his confidential servant as well, with a watchful eye over his belongings. There is not much in this house that I don't know about."

"Fine!" said I. "Now, down in the living room there is a framed collection of photographs; among them is one of Mr. Snowden in Arab dress. What do you know of it?"

"I can tell you all about it," Rodgers promptly assured me.

He went on to explain that the photograph had been taken some ten years before and showed Snowden as he appeared in a production of an amateur theatrical organization of the valley. "Why, sir," the old chap concluded, a kind of eager sadness in his voice, "I dressed Mr. Snowden for the part. Oh, yes; well do I mind that night."

"Let us go and have a look at it," said I, greatly pleased.

When, having found the big living room deserted, we stood before the photograph of the dead master of the house, I congratulated myself that in this ancient retainer I had the one of all others best able to furnish the information I sought. The items of the costume, I was told, had been selected by Mr. Snowden from material ready to his hand.

"This was part of a collection my master had made at various times. He was greatly interested in such things," my companion dolefully explained, pointing to the caricatured Bedouin.

"And the gun, and the pistol, and so on—what of them?" I asked.

"All part of the collection, Mr. Holt."

"And are they about the place now?"

The old man nodded emphatically.

"Oh, certainly, sir."

I pointed to the dagger.

"And this knife—do you know where it is?"

There was forbearance in the old chap's smile.

"Of course, sir. If you care to see it, I'll show it to you."

I should, I told him. He opened a door at the right of the alcove. We entered a room beyond, and he snapped on the light. Apparently this was where Snowden had conducted the business of his considerable estate. There was handsome office furniture, a great carved table desk, filing cabinets, and so on. The place had quite a commercial air, save for the really splendid trophy of arms above the mantelshelf. And there Rodgers went at once.

"Here it is, sir," he said; and stopped with hand extended to an empty hook which projected from the black velvet background. He turned to me, a look of surprise on his face.

"Why, it's gone!" he exclaimed in shocked astonishment.

"I see it is," I told him. "And since when? Do you know that?"

The old man wagged his head in absolute certainty.

"Positively, sir. I could swear that it was there no longer ago than ten o'clock yesterday morning. Mr. Snowden had sent for me to come to the office. As I stood and talked to him, my eye was on the collection of weapons. I remember one of the guns was hanging a trifle out of line. It was immediately above the dagger. It so attracted my attention I failed to reply at once to a question Mr. Snowden asked me. The man with whom he was transacting business laughed and asked if I was thinking of turning gunman."

"What's that!" I exclaimed. "You say there was someone else—an outsider?"

Startled by my sudden vehemence, the old man regarded me with a look of blank surprise before he replied:

"Why, yes; there was, sir. A young man who furnishes us with liquor; name of Collcti."

17

It is not to be supposed that I hadn't from the first considered Colleti as a logical suspect in the murder of Muriel and Campbell Snowden. As a matter of fact, I had not been particularly concerned as to the identity of the killer. My problem was to establish the innocence of young Harry Randel. However, on that Sunday morning when, having left Tom Randel and Miss Donnay at the Snowden house, Jane, Jeff, and I were passengers in one of the Rolls-Royces, speeding back to Glen Athol, I carried the knowledge which promised to enable me to serve a double purpose.

We had the chauffeur drop Jeff and me at the bungalow before proceeding to the East End, where Jane was to spend the day with her aunt. Left to ourselves, each wrapped in his own thoughts, we were unusually silent and preoccupied. To make matters worse, the weather continued to be beastly. What with the cold drizzle, and the slow drip from the bare branches of the trees, and the infernal fog so thick you couldn't see across the river, it was gloomy enough. Jeff was stiff and sore from his experience of the previous night. I spent most of the afternoon and evening seated before the log fire in the living room, with a book and my pipe and a bottle of the judge's excellent rye. And so, early to bed.

I woke to find that a night of rain had given place to bright sunshine. From downstairs came the sound of Jeff's whistling. A whiff of coffee and frying bacon got me out of bed at once. I was tying my tie when Jeff beat his tattoo on the gong down in the hall.

At breakfast I like to glance over the newspaper headlines. Naturally, this morning I was more than usually eager to see what was going on. The city papers were late, and I was reduced to the *Valley Herald,* a two-sheeted local product. Among the mixed news items and advertisements which formed its make-up there appeared a name which instantly centered my attention. The name was in an advertisement, and the advertisement was this:

> LOST—AIREDALE DOG
>
> Strayed or stolen from the premises of The Piermont Sanitarium, Saturday morning, October 24, large male Airedale; brass collar with name "Buster" and address; reward. A. B. Agnew, M.D., Piermont Sanitarium.

I read it a second time, and gradually there came to me the belief that I had laid my finger upon one of the threads of the tangled skein I had set myself to unravel. I pocketed the paper.

"Call the station and have them send up a taxi," I said to Jeff and hurried through my breakfast.

The shiny Ford sedan which responded to Jeff's call made little of the seven-mile drive to Piermont. We turned in between the iron gates and proceeded up the hill to the big red-brick building. I told the taxi driver to wait, and ascended the steps with the feeling that such places always engender in me.

A white-uniformed nurse seated at the reception desk looked up from her writing. Could I see Dr. Agnew? I asked, and gave her my card. She pressed a button, and an athletic male attendant materialized with startling promptness. He departed with my card. I took a seat, prepared to twiddle my thumbs; but he returned in a minute or two and nodded to the nurse.

"You can go in now," she told me, and I followed the young chap down the length of the hall and into a well-lighted room that was half office, half library. A big fellow of fifty or so, red of beard and pompadour, broad-shouldered in his double-breasted blue serge coat, was seated at a table desk. With outstretched hand he courteously rose as I approached. He gave me a bone-crushing grip, and his big greenish eyes took me in most I thoroughly.

"I suppose, Mr. Holt, you have called in relation to the unhappy occurrence of Saturday morning," he said, plunging into the subject without preamble.

I took a chair beside the desk.

"That is so," I admitted and asked how he came to connect me with the affair.

He had turned to an open card-index file which stood at his side, and before replying he found what he wanted and studied it for a moment.

"I was talking to Inspector O'Brien, yesterday," he said, suddenly rounding on me. "He explained your status in the case. Naturally, I was expecting a call."

He paused for a moment, and his eyes went back to the card in his hand.

"I have here," he resumed, "our record, as of Friday, October 23rd, of our patient, Harry M. Randel. There is nothing out of the usual routine during the earlier hours of the day. At three o'clock in the afternoon he received a caller, who remained twenty-five minutes. After this visit the patient was silent and morose."

Again there was a momentary silence, during which Agnew continued to study the report; then he went on:

"There seems to be nothing further which might interest you, till three-thirty, Saturday morning, when Randel was encountered in the upper hall by one of the nurses, to whom he satisfactorily accounted for his presence. That was the last seen of him. His absence was discovered when he failed to appear at breakfast."

He stopped speaking and glowered at the record; then, returning the card to the file: "That is all there is to tell," he growled; adding as an afterthought: "Except this: We are having some repairs made to our plumbing, and the workmen have been able to assure me that a short end of galvanized pipe is missing from their stuff left in the upper hall. No doubt it was carried off by young Randel and used to kill Mr. Snowden. Where in the world he ever got hold of that knife is a mystery, though. Have you looked into that?"

All this didn't interest me particularly, I took the newspaper from my pocket and pointed to the advertisement.

"I see you have lost a dog," I replied irrelevantly.

He stared at me, his face taking on a look of amused surprise. He reached for the paper and read the advertisement.

"That's right," he said, handing it back to me. "If it is the reward you're thinking about, Mr. Holt"—he chuckled—"I'm afraid you'll be disappointed. You see, we found poor old Buster, dead as a mackerel, in a clump of blackberry bushes down by the road."

"What have you done with him?" I asked.

"Buried him, I suppose. Why? What difference does it make?"

"Well," I told him, "it may make a lot of difference. I'd like to have a look at him."

"We'll see," he said and pressed a button under the edge of his desk.

The same young fellow who had ushered me in made a quick appearance. From him we learned that the body of the Airedale was in an outhouse, awaiting burial; and he added: "Old Jim is going to make a coffin for him. He thought a lot of that dog."

"We all did," Agnew said, getting to his feet. "Come on; we'll go to him."

We went out to a greenhouse in the rear. There we found the carcass of the late Buster lying in one of the big wooden trays used to carry potted plants. When Agnew had removed the burlap sack that covered the remains, I saw the body of a fine big Airedale, a grizzly brown in color and weighing perhaps sixty pounds. In life he must have been a formidable fellow. I stooped and examined the head. Repeated blows had reduced one side of it to a blackened gory mass. From the uninjured side I got some hairs. I straightened up and handed them to Agnew, who had been watching me curiously.

"Now," said I, "you can swear, if need be, that these hairs came from your dead dog, can't you?"

He nodded. "I could, certainly; but I must say I don't see what the object would be."

Without replying I produced the envelope containing the hairs I had taken from the bloodstained bit of pipe found at the scene of the murders.

"You see this envelope?" I said. "Now be prepared to testify, if called on, that you saw me take these hairs out of it."

When we had compared them with those I had taken from the head of the Airedale—and found them identical—I explained how I came by them. I also told how young Randel's delirious mutterings had been accepted by all of us as a declaration that he had killed Snowden.

"Evidently," I added, "he was literal in his remark; he meant a four-legged cur—though he was libeling poor Buster here."

"And that was the clinching argument of the police in deciding that he was the killer, wasn't it?" asked Agnew.

"That and the bloodstained pipe," I answered. "Both of those points can now be combated."

A hopeful look came to Agnew's face.

"My God!" he exclaimed. "If you can prove the boy innocent, it surely will lift a load of responsibility from my shoulders."

"I think I shall drive up to the city," I told him, looking at my watch. "My first job is to submit these hairs to some expert whose evidence will go in court. Then I'll call on Inspector O'Brien. We'll see how amenable to reason he is."

Agnew nodded. "That is your course, undoubtedly. And I can tell you the very man to go to."

He took an envelope from his pocket and wrote an address on the back of it. "There," he said, handing it to me. "Go to this old fellow, Mueller, on Second Avenue. Hair Doctor, he terms himself. An old German—half crank, half wizard. He diagnoses most amazingly from a sample of hair. The police know him well. You'll find that his opinion will carry a lot of weight."

I thanked him, and we started for the taxi out front.

"There is one thing bothering me," I told Agnew. "What was young Randel's reason for wanting to get back home in the night that way?"

"I've asked myself the same question," he replied and said no more till we had reached the car.

"I'll tell you what you might do," he proceeded, as he gave me a good-bye shake of the hand. "As I said, Randel was a changed man after his visitor left. If we knew the topic of conversation during the call, perhaps that would throw some light on that phase of the mystery. Why don't you talk to Miss Maxwell? You've met her, of course—she was at the inquiry at the house, I understand."

"Miss Maxwell!" I exclaimed. "Yes; I've met her. Have a talk with her, you say? Why?"

It might be a good idea, Agnew insisted. "You see, she was the caller young Randel received Friday afternoon."

"Oh, yes," said I. "You hadn't mentioned the name. A good idea. I shall have a talk with her."

After I had promised to let him know the result of my efforts, I got into the Ford and we proceeded on our way. During the ride to the city I had plenty to occupy my mind.

Arrived at the address given by Agnew, I found a narrow old dwelling of red brick sandwiched between a Chinese food shop and a Turkish coffee room. My pull upon the shining brass knob of the old-fashioned doorbell was answered by a little old woman, indubitably Teutonic. I spoke to her in German. Was the *Herr Doktor* at leisure? She gave me a smile that broke up the wrinkled face alarmingly and replied by a series of quick nods.

At the end of a dark and narrow hall, which smelled of cabbage soup and mustiness, I was ushered into a nondescript room, at once office and laboratory. There I found myself confronted by a remarkable figure.

He was a thin little chap, his abnormally large head, bald for the most part, supported on a long and scraggy neck. Behind thick-lensed spectacles prominent dark eyes looked out of a sallow face, which was cut across below the great aquiline nose by a walrus mustache of noble proportions. I introduced myself. In a flabby grasp he took the hand I offered, and nodded silently.

"I have, for the *Herr Doktor's* analysis, two specimens of hair," I began, my story ready-made; and he followed me over to the window and I laid the exhibits before him. "There seems to be no difference," I went on, "but, as a matter of fact, in one instance they are from the head of a sexagenarian, the others are from a much younger and more vigorous man. My object is to determine which is which."

The old fellow laid the hairs on the palm of his hand and poked at them with the end of a bony forefinger. At once a broad grin overspread his sallow face.

"Jokes, you make with me, my friend," he chuckled.

"Jokes, *Herr Doktor!*" I said, feeling rather a fool.

"Ach ja wohl!" he gargled, nodding vigorously. "'Hairs from head of old man; hairs from head of young man,' say you. Hairs from a dog, say I. *Nicht wahr?"*

"Well, maybe so, *Herr Doktor,"* I admitted, glad to have him take it in such good nature. "However," I assured him, "you must not imagine I was joking when I had you make the test. You have settled an important point and served a serious purpose."

He looked pleased at that.

"Listen, my friend," he went on eagerly. "These hairs come all from one dog. The animal is what you call—Airedale."

"The *Herr Doktor's* science is unique," I returned; and I handed him a bill which he pocketed without so much as a glance.

I left the strange little man standing on his doorstep and got into the waiting Ford, feeling much elated at the result of my inquiry.

"Police headquarters," I told the driver.

When we reached headquarters, I was fortunate enough to find O'Brien in his office. He seemed glad to see me.

"What good wind blows you here?" he wanted to know.

"Maybe you'll think it an ill wind, before we're through," I told him.

"How's that?" he asked, looking surprised.

"Well," I said, "I'm going to knock the props out. from under your theory that you've got the murderer of Mrs. Randel and Campbell Snowden. I'm afraid that means more trouble for your department."

"You'll have to go some to do that," he asserted, though, I thought, he showed less surprise than my boast warranted.

"In the first place," I began, "if you don't mind, just mention the premises that lead to the conclusion that Harry Randel is the guilty party."

O'Brien gave me an amused glance.

"That's easy," he grinned. "First and foremost, there's his own word for it."

I shook my head. "Without evidence to prove it, the law would not accept his confession. You know that as well as I do."

"In this case there happens to be plenty of corroboratory evidence," O'Brien insisted somewhat defiantly.

"For instance?" I grinned, pleased by this sign of uneasiness.

"For instance, the motive," O'Brien returned.

I laughed in his face.

"Poppycock! If jealousy were a motive which infallibly led to murder . . . However—the motive, say you. Go on from there."

"Also there is the weapon that was used to kill Snowden, with Harry Randel's fingerprints on it," the inspector triumphantly pointed out.

"And that is where you jump to conclusions. That bit of iron pipe was not used by the murderer. What is more, it was never in the house till carried in by your man."

O'Brien laughed derisively.

"That's right," I told him. "Harry Randel was shot as he climbed on the roof of the porch. He didn't enter his wife's room. What is more, I shrewdly suspect that you have your doubts on that point. How about the absence of fingerprints on the windowsill? What have you to say about those marks of gloved hands on the porch roof? Where are

Mrs. Randel's pearls? If young Randel killed his wife and stole her pearls, what did he do with them?"

Inspector O'Brien had listened to this with an air of patient tolerance, a smile of forbearance on his big florid face. Now he turned to me, a suggestion of finality in his manner.

"Anything further?" he inquired blandly.

"Why, yes," said I. "One might wonder where he acquired the quite remarkable knife that we found in Muriel Randel's throat—for it was a very extraordinary weapon, you know, despite Dr. McClennen's jokes concerning it. Also, a smart lawyer would stress the impossibility of the boy's walking seven miles, breaking into a house, killing the woman, enticing the other victim into another part of the house, murdering him, secreting the string of pearls, and be making his escape, all in less than an hour and a half. Young Randel was shot before five o'clock. It can be proved that he was safe and sound up at Piermont at half-past three."

O'Brien shot me a quick look.

"Aha! You've been checking into that, have you?" he asked, grinning at me.

"Yes," said I; "and I think you'll agree with me that Randel was shot when he was trying to get into the house—not when leaving it."

He wagged his head at me, and his face became serious.

"Very pretty, Mr. Holt; very well thought out, indeed—but for one thing that knocks your argument into a cocked hat."

He came to a pause, a glint of amusement in his eyes. I knew what was coming, but I kept a poker face.

"You see," he went on, "unfortunately for your deductions, there were several hairs from Mr. Snowden's head found on that bit of bloodstained pipe that bore Harry

Randel's fingerprints. That rather fits in with the young man's confession, doesn't it?"

He leaned back in his chair to shake with silent laughter as he regarded me triumphantly. I saw that he was enjoying himself, and I let him have his laugh out.

"There certainly were hairs of some kind sticking to the pipe," I observed at length. "You see, I noticed that, and I took the liberty to appropriate several of them."

O'Brien sat up sharply. "What's that!" he exclaimed.

I held up my hand. "Yes, I did," I admitted. "And now," I went on, "I'll tell you another one"; and I proceeded to recount the story of Buster, described my call at Piermont, and told of my interview with Agnew. "So," I concluded, "when Harry Randel uttered those words: 'I settled that damn cur,' he referred to one of the canine variety."

During my account, O'Brien's face had changed from gay to grave, and when I had finished the recital he looked sober enough.

"All very well," he said grimly, "but those hairs may have come from Snowden's head, after all."

Then, of course, it was time to uncover my ace in the hole, and I told of my visit to Mueller. At the mention of that name, I saw that Agnew had told me truly. It was evident that the little German was well and favorably known in this quarter.

"Well, I'll be damned!" was O'Brien's comment at the conclusion of my account.

"Probably," I laughed. "And wouldn't the newspaper boys love to hear that the police can't tell the difference between hairs from a millionaire and those of an Airedale!"

The inspector held up his hand.

"Don't rub it in," he growled. "What do you want me to do?"

"Do!" I echoed. "Why, I want you to take the rap off that poor kid. Give out the word that something has broken to remove suspicion from him. And, first of all, I want you to call off that gorilla who is standing guard."

That was reasonable enough, O'Brien agreed; it should be taken care of at once. I got up to go. He laid a hand on my arm.

"Thank you for calling. As you see, I'm mighty glad to cooperate with you. By the way, all this is just between the two of us, I suppose?"

"Absolutely," I promised. "Say hello to Olsen for me."

"Humph! Dog hairs! Wait till I throw the hooks into that big Swede!" he growled.

So, laughing, I left him.

18

It was well toward evening when I found myself headed for Glen Athol. Darkness had fallen in the valley, though the afterglow showed red above the hilltops, when we pulled up to the front porch of the Hammond bungalow. I paid the taxi driver and hurried to the telephone. Repeated calls of Jane's number failed to get a response. Disgruntled, I hung up and went into the dining room where Jeff was putting dinner on the table.

"Anybody phone today?" I asked, thinking Jane might have called.

He grinned at me and set down the steak platter and the dish of fried potatoes before he answered.

"No phone calls; but there was a lady to see you."

"Miss Maxwell?"

Jeff laughed. "Not a bit like her. Sure it was the red-headed woman from next door."

"Mrs. Randel's maid?"

"The maid, as ever was," he chuckled.

That silenced me for the moment. We took our places at the table. "Well," said I, carving the steak, "what did she want? Go on, tell me about it."

"Sure," Jeff asserted, with an air of mystery, "there was that going on this afternoon at the big house that had me wondering. First it was the laddie-buck that was policing the sick man. I am outside, raking off the lawn, when I see a cab drive up next door. I know the car—a taxi from down at the station it is. Pretty soon out comes the policeman, and with him is the red-headed girl; and for a while they talk. Then into the taxi he gets and away.

"In about twenty minutes another car comes down the road—like a bat out of hell. It turns down the lane and drives in at the big house. I know it, too. It is the Cadillac coupé belonging to the big doctor. Out he gets and into the house. The rush he was in made me wonder if the sick man was worse. 'Maybe it is dead he is,' says I to myself. 'Maybe that would be the reason for the police leaving.'

"After a while, out comes the doctor—and the red-headed maid is with him. Before he leaves, maybe for five minutes, they stop there—talking. Twice the girl points over here, and I see the big fellow shake his head—like it is an argument they are having. Then away he goes in his car.

"Later on—maybe an hour afterwards, and I am out in the kitchen, paring these potatoes—the bell rings. When I go to the door, there is the red-headed woman, like I tell you.

"'Can I see Mr. Holt?' says she, opening her big eyes at me.

"'He is out, miss; and I am not knowing when he will be back,' says I; which I did not—you leaving so quick this morning, without saying a word."

"I'll tell you all about it when you've finished your story," I laughed. "Did she say what she wanted?"

"Devil a word did she say," Jeff grinned. "Just pulled her shoulders up to her ears, like the foreign body she is, and made off, swinging her fine shape. Back she will be, I am thinking."

"Probably she carried a message from Mrs. Randel," said I, believing I perceived the reason for the call. And with that I began to recount my activities of the day.

"So you see," I said at length, "each of the incidents of your story has a logical explanation."

Jeff appeared unimpressed by my inference.

"It sounds like enough, the way you put it, sir; but it was not that way it seemed to me at all"; and after we had eaten for a time in silence he went on; "There is something else one would be wondering about. This Colleti man. Why would you be shielding him now?"

"Shielding Colleti?" said I.

"Sure and does it not amount to that? Never a word to this inspector fellow today about him—how he waylaid us and carried us off; nor of how he stole the knife from Mr. Snowden—nay, sir, you need not shake your head. You believe that as well as I do. Nothing have you said of him murdering the poor little lady and the old gentleman. Shielding him, I call it; and would you be telling me why, sir?"

My man had become quite earnest.

"You're wrong, Jeff," I told him. "I'm not shielding Colleti."

He seemed to grasp a meaning not implied by the words. The expression of his face changed.

"By the piper that played before Moses!" he exclaimed, grinning at me. "It is saving Colleti for your own little cup of tea you are!"

"There seems no doubt that Colleti killed Muriel and Snowden," said I, musingly, "and yet, somehow, I can't feel sure about it. At any rate, it is the job of the police to track down the criminal. If Colleti had seen fit to keep his hands off me, probably I should have minded my own business. However, he did not. He made it a personal matter between us—a challenge, if you like. And so, just for that, we are going to give him a run for his money."

"Aye; and we will get him, too," affirmed Jeff, all aglow at the prospect of conflict. Suddenly his face fell.

"Will it be forgetting you are the word of the butler man, Jenkins—and him saying Miss Donnay did the deed? And young Mr. Randel paying him hush money?"

"Forget it," I told him. "Whatever cock-and-bull story Jenkins may have used to blackmail that young pair will never connect Lea Donnay with the murders."

"But the letter?" Jeff reminded me.

"Probably a tomfool effusion written by that scatter-brain. Nothing to be taken seriously, except by a pair of scared young ninnies."

This confident assertion left my man still unsatisfied. We had finished eating, and, pipes alight, were enjoying Jeff's superlative coffee. For a time we smoked in silence. There was a frown on my companion's usually good-natured face.

"Well, now," said he at length, "that, as you may say, narrows the circle of inquiry."

"How's that?" I asked, smiling at his choice of words.

He knocked out his pipe and refilled it before replying, the doubtful pucker still between his heavy black brows.

"I mind you said that if it was an outside job, this Colleti man would be the killer. Now you say, no, you do not believe him the guilty one. Was it an inside job, then? And if the brother and his young lady—just two scared young ninnies, you call them—are both of them innocent—and with alibis for the two old people and the red-headed maid—who does that leave at all but Miss Maxwell. Is it her you would be suspecting?"

"Nonsense," I replied, discomfited by his logic.

"Well, then—and who?" he persisted.

"Didn't I say it was a man's job?" I reminded him. "Can you imagine any woman—Miss Maxwell least of all—clubbing an old man to death; not to mention cutting a woman's throat?"

"Who then?" he repeated doggedly.

"Why, Colleti—obviously. Everything points his way. I didn't say I thought him innocent; just an odd sort of hunch I had. He's our man, depend on it; and we'll get him—as you say."

"Well, and that is good hearing, anyhow," Jeff commented; and for a while he smoked in meditative silence, broken at length by his amused chuckle.

"I am thinking this Colleti man will be in no good humour with us—and you serving his man, Larry, as you did. Sure it was a surprise that lad was for them, when they came back to settle with us."

"You haven't heard any complaint from him, have you?" I grinned. "No legal summons, or anything of that kind?"

"Devil a complaint; and as for a legal summons—you and I know that is not the way of such as Colleti. Sure the summons such as he would be serving is for the bar of final justice on high, delivered from the mouth of a machine gun!"

"Hear! Hear!" I cried with mock enthusiasm, vastly amused by this outburst. "'Thoughts that breathe and words that burn!' Who said the Irish weren't a race of poets!"

Jeff was in nowise put out by my ridicule.

"Laugh away, if you will, sir; but depend on it, it is not the last of him we have heard," he prophesied darkly.

There was, I was forced to admit, ample grounds for his opinion; though, when ready for bed, I grinned at the caution that prompted me to extinguish the light before I raised my bedroom windows.

My rest that night was broken by a series of bad dreams, which accounted, perhaps, for my rising in a particularly ill humor, surprising poor Jeff by my irascibility at breakfast. Till lunchtime I dawdled around the place, unable to set myself to anything. To my chagrin I caught myself listening for the ring of the telephone that would mean a call from Jane. I listened in vain. Confound the girl, at length I decided. If she didn't think it important enough to call me she could go hang.

At lunch, shamed by my man's unfailing good nature, I managed to snap out of my fit of bad temper; and then, as though to reward my return to normality, we hadn't been at table more than ten minutes when the telephone bell sounded.

"There she is now," I said to myself; and, with a momentary return of perversity, I told Jeff to take the call.

He came back on the broad grin.

"And I will give you three guesses who that was," he chuckled in high glee.

"Miss Maxwell?" I hazarded.

Jeff shook his head. "It was not, then; sure it was the police, at the Northside headquarters. Had we lost a car? they wanted to know. 'As ever was,' says I; 'and us just missing it out of the garage and about to report it.' 'Come and get it, then,' says the lad, 'for it is here we have it, safe and sound.' And I thanked him kindly and said I would do that."

"Fine," said I, glad to hear the good news, and pleased by Jeff's finesse. "That means a trip up to the city for you this afternoon."

Later, having seen Jeff depart in the same taxi that had carried me on the preceding day, and finding myself mooning dejectedly about in a state of oppressive loneliness, I clapped my hat upon my head, slipped into my Burberry, and, with a good ash-plant stick in my hand, set out for a walk.

I reached the top of the lane and paused at the intersecting state highway, which on either hand disappeared in the distance, a straight and narrowing ribbon in the hazy autumnal sunshine. To my right was the way to the city; to my left, three miles down the road, was Jane's little shop. I looked at my watch. I had, I saw, plenty of time for the six-mile walk and a word with Jane before Jeff would have dinner ready. Maybe, I told myself, if Jane was particularly nice I would suggest that she might drive me back home and take pot luck with Jeff and me.

However, arrived at my destination, I found myself the victim of a trick of fortune. When the mauve curtains parted at the sound of my entrance, it was the assistant who greeted me.

"How d'you do, Mr. Holt?" she said, recognizing me at once. "Miss Maxwell isn't here today. They phoned from her aunt's that she's in bed with a bad case of flu."

I was sincerely grieved to hear that, I told her.

"Yes; I'm sorry, too," declared Miss Pert; and she added, brightening: "Anyhow, I've got to go out to see her tonight; I'll tell her you were here."

Suddenly it occurred to me that I could send Jane a piece of news that would do her more good than all the medicine they were giving her.

"I wonder if you will do me a little favor," I asked. "I should like to send Miss Maxwell a note. Would you deliver it for me?"

She smiled at me knowingly and said she would be "charmed."

"Well, that is very nice of you," I thanked her; adding that, if she would supply me with the necessary materials, she would increase my obligation. From some place of concealment in her scanty costume she produced a key.

"Here," she said, handing it to me. "You can go right upstairs. You'll find everything on the desk."

So once more I entered the tiny living room. All was as I had last seen it. The glasses and the siphon and the bottle of Johnny Walker still decorated the mantelshelf; the tray with the ashes of the cigarettes I had smoked still rested on the wide arm of the chair. Apparently nobody had entered the room since Jane and I had left it Saturday night.

I snapped on the light and sat down at the desk. I found paper and envelopes; I had a fountain pen. I wrote the message which I trusted would carry happiness.

As I blotted the address, I looked up, and my eye fell on the bookcase in the corner. I recalled the impulse which had prompted me to go to it the last time I had been in the room. Jane's entrance had forestalled my inquiry. Now I slipped the note into my pocket and went to consider what was to constitute for me the sounding rod of the character I had already, I believed, pretty well plumbed. I ran my eye over the titles of the books before me. I looked and I marveled.

"Well, I'll be damned!" I muttered aloud.

At best this assortment of trash was the work of writers catering to a poverty of intellect—to a clientele of fatuous femininity. At worst it emanated from less worthy sources, successful through exploitation of salacious eroticism.

In the right-hand corner of the upper shelf was a thick, calf-bound book bearing in gold lettering the words "Shakespeare's Complete Works." Truly an oasis in a desert of inanity!

Instinctively my hand went to the volume. At once I was aware of another book, flattened against the back of the case. It was, I discovered, an illustrated copy of Boccaccio's *Decameron*. I cast an ironic glance at the books so frankly displayed on the shelves—conglomerate bawdry, masquerading as smart sophistication. I compared them with the volume in my hand. Distorted modesty, I thought, to consider this bald portrayal, depicted by the master, as an obscenity to be hidden.

"Clandestine titillation!" I grinned wryly; and I was returning the *Decameron* to its place of concealment when my hand encountered a little bundle that was pushed back in a corner of the shelf.

Slipping Boccaccio to one side, I drew forth this new find. A lady's handkerchief it proved to be—Jane's, for at once I saw the monogram "JM." Its four corners were tied, concealing the contents. Something made me drop the volume of Shakespeare and carry my discovery to the desk light. My heart misgave me as I untied the knots. I had a pretty good idea of what I was going to see. I unfolded the handkerchief, sensing a reminiscent perfume that seemed to materialize Jane at my side. However, the tenderness of that association was embittered with resentment; and when I had uncovered what was hidden, my premonition was verified; for there, softly gleaming in the lamplight, was the missing string of pearls.

19

The variety of feelings which assailed me as I stared at this direct evidence of Jane Maxwell's culpability almost at once gave place to the single emotion of anger. The knowledge of the girl's duplicity, the belief that from the first she must have laughed in her sleeve at me, made me squirm. However, by the time I had replaced the pearls in the handkerchief and returned them to their hiding place I was able to make use of a philosophy which empowered me to grin at my disillusionment with derisive cynicism.

So I tore up what I had written and dropped the fragments into the waste basket.

I had changed my mind about the note, I told the assistant when I returned the key. The girl showed surprise. Well, anyhow, she would tell Miss Maxwell I had called. I thanked her and set out for home.

In my state of mind that three-mile walk was anything but a pleasant stroll. I was glad to reach, the lane leading down to the bungalow. In the drive by the back porch the judge's Buick loomed large in the dusk. At any rate, I wouldn't have to replace the car. Smiling grimly at this comforting thought, I went into the house. Jeff and dinner were waiting for me.

"I was fearing the Colleti man had got you—me coming back and finding the place deserted," my man greeted me.

"You have Colleti on the brain," I retorted grumpily, getting out of my coat. "He's becoming an obsession. To hell with him. I'm sick of the sound of his name."

Though the look he shot at me registered surprise, Jeff heeded my humor. Throughout dinner the conversation ranged on other matters. Jeff proudly showed me a police model Colt revolver, purchased that afternoon to replace the weapon lost to the gangsters, insisting that I admire its smoothness of trigger pull and beauty of finish. Furthermore, he had, he told me, found the Buick in the Northside police garage. Aside from two flat tires and an empty gas tank the car, though plastered with mud, was none the worse for its temporary lapse into the underworld. The police had found it on Sunday, abandoned in an out-of-the-way Northside street.

"What with my troubles and all, getting the old bus respectable once more, sure it was myself who was saying, 'To hell with Colleti,'" said Jeff, grinning at me.

Seeing where he was steering the talk, I grunted my disapproval, and he discreetly altered his conversational course. Later, however, when he joined me in the living room, where I sat smoking, deep in rumination as I stared into the fire, the forbidden subject cropped up again. Jeff had brought in a tray bearing a bottle of Haig & Haig, glasses, and a siphon of soda, and as he set it upon the table he gave me a quizzical look and went in at the deep end.

"Speaking of that Colleti man—saving your presence," he chuckled—"will you be telling me, sir, if you have changed your plans regarding him?"

"Plans?" I growled. "What plans?"

My man evinced indignant surprise.

"Why, to gather him in for the murdering scut that he is."

I shook my head, ready to wash my hands of the whole affair. After all, I said, I doubted the importance of Colleti's role in the tragedy of Saturday morning. As to the personal issue between us, considering that I had caused him to lose a valuable assistant in the person of the probably defunct Larry, I was more than quits with him. Why bother further?

That made my man sit up.

"Sure and that is not like you—if I may say it, sir—to blow hot and cold in that fashion," he reproached me.

I ignored his criticism, smoking in silence, staring into the lire. I felt his keen gray eyes studying my face.

"And can it be that something has happened—something that I do not know at all—to change your mind?" he asked at length.

I reached for the whisky bottle and poured myself a drink.

"See if a little good Scotch will help your logic," I told Jeff, pushing the bottle toward him. And thus fortified against the hazards of sophistry, he heard the story of my visit to Jane Maxwell's apartment.

"So you see," I finished, "we play no further part in the proceedings. I don't suppose you want to see Miss Maxwell with a rope round her neck, any more than I do."

"And is it that little faith you have in her at all?" demanded Jeff indignantly.

"Faith!" I jeered. "The belief in things unseen. Beautiful!"

Jeff shook his head. "Sure that kind of talk is too deep for me. But—begging your pardon, sir—I think you have seen so much of life that it is overlikely you are to doubt truth when you do see it."

We were silent for a while. Though I hated to admit it, I felt the need of moral support. I wanted Jeff to agree with me that it was best for us to drop the whole proposition and everyone connected with it.

"You think," I said at length, "that because Miss Maxwell is an attractive girl she had no hand in this business.

I ask you to consider the facts of the case against her. In the first place, she had a motive."

Jeff shrugged. "You are meaning that she was in love with Mrs. Randel's husband?"

"Yes. She had been engaged to him. She had reason to believe that if Muriel could be eliminated, Harry would return to his first love."

"It is more than a motive you will have to show to prove her the guilty one."

"You are right," I agreed. "The mere motive counts but little without the opportunity. When Miss Maxwell told Olsen that she hadn't left her room before the alarm, I noted both embarrassment and hesitation in her manner. As a matter of fact, she lied. She must have left her room to obtain the pearls. In other words, she had the opportunity to commit the crime."

"But it was yourself who said no woman did it—that it was a man's work," Jeff insisted.

"So I did," I acknowledged. "I based that assertion on the belief that a woman would lack the necessary strength. However, I have found that Jane Maxwell's power of hand and arm is equal to that of a man—and a strong man at that. So now we have motive, opportunity, and ability to commit the crime, with the evidence of the string of pearls to link the chain of testimony. What do you say to that?"

Jeff got to his feet and stood, his back to me, knocking out his pipe on the andiron. When he turned, his black brows were drawn down and his jaw was firmly set.

"I am telling you it is damn nonsense you are talking," he affirmed grimly.

As though to add emphasis to his assertion at that moment, from the window overlooking the front veranda there came the sound of a light tattoo. Someone was tapping upon the pane. When we went to the door, Jeff pistol in hand, we found the someone to be no other than Reuben Marshall.

"Good-evening," he greeted us. "I heard you talking in there, so I didn't ring the bell."

"Come in," I told him and led the way into the living room. Jeff followed us, put his revolver upon the table, and assisted our visitor out of his overcoat. The old chap silently turned to the fire, holding his hands to the glowing logs, and shivering—though the room was overwarm. I poured some whisky into a glass and gave it to him.

"Here," I said, "try some of this; you seem cold."

At that he turned to me, and I was shocked to observe his changed appearance. The ruddy countenance which I had known was pale but for the dark pouches under the terror-haunted eyes, the sagging muscles of the cheeks flaccid and pendulous. Apparently the man had aged years since I had last seen him. He drank down the whisky gratefully, though he distorted his face and a little shudder hunched his shoulders as he handed me the empty glass.

"Thanks," he said, his voice a kind of gasp, and he sat down in a big chair by the fire, again extending his hands to the warmth from the logs.

"This is a terrible state of affairs, Mr. Holt," he said at length, sinking back in his chair and turning his head to look at me.

It was terrible; I agreed and said no more.

My visitor fidgeted a little, then took out one of his big cigars. He was looking a trifle less ghastly.

"I understand that you were instrumental in having the guard removed from our house," he said, looking up from trimming the Corona to regard me shrewdly.

"Your nephew never should have been placed under surveillance," I replied.

He lit his cigar and sank back in the chair.

"Of course," he assured me, "we are very grateful to you. Speaking for myself, I have not for a moment believed Harry guilty of this awful thing. However, sick as I have been—all as the result of drinking that devil's brew poor old Campbell concocted—I couldn't take as active part in the investigation as I should have wished."

"No need to worry about that. Dr. McClennen and Tom Randel explained to the police what your condition was."

"That is not the point," said he, giving me a knowing look. "I should have been of great assistance. I could have told them things, I warrant you."

I bowed politely.

"Even now it is not too late," he went on ponderously. "If you will allow me to collaborate with you, I believe we might succeed in bringing the guilty one to justice."

Here was a surprise. In spite of myself, I grinned in his face.

"What do you know that might help us accomplish that?" I asked.

He gave me a sly look.

"Confidence for confidence," he bargained. "You must have already gained some important clues, otherwise the police wouldn't have released Harry from custody. Suppose you tell me just what you have discovered."

This time I laughed outright. "Why come to me? You should go to the police."

The police, he said, had bungled the affair from the first; he would much prefer working with me—"collaborate," he expressed it. Every now and then I caught him eyeing the whisky bottle, keen for a drink and ashamed to make it known. Hoping to learn something from his chatter, I pushed the bottle across the table to him. He promptly reached for it, putting aside Jeff's revolver, which lay in the way; then he filled his glass to the brim and rose, none too steadily, to his feet. I suppose he had taken my proffer of the bottle as a seal upon our union.

"Here's to our success. Drink deep, and, no heel taps," he mouthed, regarding me wisely; and he poured a good two-ounce drink of neat whisky down his throat. It might have been so much water. There was a chuckle from Jeff, who all this time had sat in the background, self-effacing as usual in the presence of company.

"Now suppose you tell me what you know," I suggested, hard put to it not to laugh at the old chap's technique. He wagged his head at me.

"Not till I hear what you have discovered," he grinned. I saw there was nothing to be learned from him.

"On the whole, I think you had better carry your information to the police. Probably they need it," said I.

He looked surprised.

"Does that mean you refuse to accept me as an associate in the solution of your problem?" he demanded, speaking slowly and with pompous dignity.

I lost patience with the old bore.

"'He goes farthest who travels alone,'" I reminded him sententiously.

The quotation seemed to tickle his fancy. He smiled and nodded thoughtfully, his eyes all the time on me. Then, allowing his glance to stray, with a sigh and a shrug he dismissed the matter. Immediately, following one of his erratic conversational digressions, he was off on a new subject.

"You mustn't suppose that the object of my call is to foist my services on you," he protested.

That was perfectly all right, I assured him.

"No, but it wasn't that at all," he insisted, wagging his head at me. "I'm here commissioned to deliver a message."

He came to a stop, and as our eyes met I knew that the same thought had come to both of us.

"As you were the first time you came to see me," I said gravely, feeling sorry for the old codger.

He nodded. "Exactly; and again it is an invitation from Ann."

He uttered the words in a broken voice and fell silent for a moment; then he cleared his throat loudly and proceeded: "My sister asks you to attend Muriel's funeral. We bury her tomorrow—from Lamson's Funeral Home, up in the city."

"No," I said to myself. "I'll not go." Aloud, and as gently as possible, I said the right thing.

A moment ago on the verge of tears, our visitor now veered off with disconcerting abruptness on another tack.

"Well, that's that," he remarked, making a little flourish with his empty glass; and he stepped forward to set it upon the tray, "Aha!" he exclaimed brightly. "Now this is a handsome weapon"; and he picked up Jeff's new revolver.

"Better be careful, sir; the gun is loaded," cautioned Jeff; and, in his alarm forgetting his good manners, he got to his feet.

Marshall, the revolver poised, turned smilingly to confront his adviser.

"Not much use else; is it?" he laughed. "Don't fear, my fine fellow. I am accustomed to firearms."

He aimed at a stuffed pheasant on the bookcase, squinting along the barrel, one eye tightly closed.

"Bang!" he ejaculated and grinned at me. "Right through the heart!"

I had been stretched out in the judge's morris chair. Now I sat up. The farce had gone far enough.

"Fine, Mr. Marshall," I said; and not knowing what the old fool might do, I added: "Better let Jeff have his gun now."

"Give it me," growled Jeff, extending his hand.

I was on my feet now, about ready to forget my role of host.

"Why, my good fellow," snickered Marshall, turning to Jeff, "I'm a graduate of B.M.I.—a sharpshooter; no need for you to be nervous."

His eyes were on Jeff, but I saw his finger slide within the trigger guard; I saw the black muzzle of the gun as it swung to cover me; and, as I jumped at him, I saw the hammer of the revolver begin to rise; then I had the weapon by the barrel, its muzzle over my shoulder, and there was an explosion close to my head which for the moment left me stunned. My action had been intuitive.

The thing was over before I had time to think, and I found myself holding the hot barrel of the gun in my scorched hand, watching Jeff pin down our obstreperous guest, the poor old chap being violently ill all over the judge's nice Chinese rug.

I tossed the gun upon the table and got Jeff by the collar.

"Here!" I said. "Let loose! Remember the man's age—and that it was an accident."

He got up reluctantly.

"Accident!" he snarled, fiercely resentful, his eyes showing green as a cat's. "Accident! Hell and damn it, it was for killing you the old spalpeen was!"

"Nonsense!" I told him. "That old stuffed shirt? He wouldn't hurt a fly. Help me get him onto the davenport before he ruins everything."

When we had the old boy stretched out, and a bit less unsanitary, he continued to shudder and retch in the most alarming manner. For a while it seemed touch and go whether we were to have a dead man on our hands.

"It's his heart," I said. "The shock was too much for it."

"From his heart, was it? Sure his stomach I was thinking it was," grinned Jeff, his anger forgotten.

Probably he had a weak stomach, I agreed.

Jeff chuckled. "Weak, is it? Sure it is fine it works. Would a bit of a drink be helping it at all?"

"He has had too much already," I said; and asked if there was any aromatic ammonia in the house.

Jeff didn't know of any. "There's a good big bottle of the other kind, out in the kitchen," he told me.

I sent him to get it; and when we had held it under the nose of our visitor, the long whiffs he took at it seemed to do him good. Soon he appeared better, though his better was very bad indeed. At length, however, he was sufficiently improved to be able to open his eyes and stare at us in dispirited vacancy.

"You're all right now, Mr. Marshall," I said, leaning over him.

He nodded weakly and made an effort to take my hand.

"We'll have you over in your own bed in no time," I went on. "Once you're safe there, we'll telephone for Dr. McClennen."

His lackluster eyes widened at that. The sound of McClennen's name seemed to put new life in him. He was holding my hand, and his fingers closed over mine in a quick pressure.

"No!" His utterance of the word was at once weak and decisive, and he shook his head resolutely.

"You don't want the doctor?" I asked.

He continued to shake his head. "Don't send for him," he begged; and, his voice becoming stronger as he proceeded, he babbled on: "He must not hear of this. I don't want him—don't need him. I'll be all right, if you will give me a little time."

He made an effort to rise, and, with my help, managed to get his legs over the side of the davenport and sat, his elbows on his knees, his head in his hands, a dejected picture indeed.

"Get his coat," I said to Jeff. "The sooner he is in bed the better."

Evidently Marshall agreed with me. He raised a haggard face, looking about him. I took the hand he extended and helped him to his feet.

"Thank God, you escaped unhurt," was all he said as we bundled him into his coat. During the next ten minutes, while we got him over to the big house, he didn't open his mouth. Arrived at his front door, I asked him if Simpson could help him to bed. We looked at each other in the light from the front hall. His face wore an expression of helplessness near to tears. At this time of night the servants would all be abed, he told me. As he made no suggestion that we should attempt to arouse them, I assumed that he was just as well satisfied to escape their observation. Willing to humor him, I turned to Jeff.

"I can manage here alone," I told him. "Get you back to the house. I am not keen about leaving it deserted tonight."

I had the old fellow put his arm across my shoulder, and so supporting him we ascended the wide staircase to the lounge. Down it we proceeded to the iron-railed stairs that led to the mezzanine. We negotiated these easily enough, and now I found myself in strange territory. Though the light was not overbright I could see three doors along the wall of the gallery.

"Which is your room?" I asked Marshall.

It was the one entered by the first of the three doors, and we went into a big, airy bedchamber. I deposited my burden upon the bed.

"There," said I. "Now I'll do a bit of valeting and have you between the sheets in no time."

No sooner had I started to undress him than he began to thank me fulsomely for my good offices; and when I tried to shut him up by making light of the occurrence, he refused to be silent, continuing his disjointed monologue under the plea of alibis for his tomfoolery. All this interspersed with sighs and groans and little shuddering cries.

"You see," he concluded, "my experience with revolvers has been confined to single-action weapons. I know nothing of the double-action variety. When— simply by the pressure of my finger on the trigger—the pistol fired, I thought I should have died from fright! I became nauseated—invariably I do when overwrought. That, and your man's attack, placed me in a somewhat undignified and ridiculous position."

I begged that he would forget it.

"Where are your pajamas?" I asked, having him ready for them by this time.

I left him a few minutes later, prepared to acknowledge that I was puzzled. Was this loquacious elderly fop the guileless old fogy he seemed? Tonight, betrayed by his verbosity, he had let slip a word or two which caused me to wonder. The recollection of what Miss McCarthy had told me didn't lessen my uncertainty.

Stopping at the foot of the stairs, I looked up and down the long corridor. Nearly opposite to where I stood, forming a black rectangle in the shadowy monochrome of the wall, was the open door of Muriel's room. To my left, at the dead end of the corridor, was the closed door of the room in which we had found the body of Snowden. I pictured to myself the latter scene, recalling McClennen's dogmatic attitude—with pliant little Dr. Burgher to humor it; I remember O'Brien's easy concurrence with his subordinate; how Olsen, satisfied with the evidence of the bloodstained pipe, had abandoned further search. From that moment the police had limited their efforts to merest routine. Without a dissenting voice the matter of young Harry's guilt had been settled.

Thinking of all this, suddenly I had a mind to view again the room which—presumptively, at least—had been the scene of Snowden's murder. Impelled by that motive, I slipped down the corridor and tried the door. It was unlocked. The room was pitch dark. However, I knew the location of the switch, and when I had stepped inside and had closed the door behind me, I snapped on the lights. Then, as I turned to take stock of my surroundings, fortuitous chance played its part. My glance encountered a handsome mahogany table, with drawers and ornamented with satinwood inlay, which stood upon square tapering legs of Hepplewhite style to the left of the door. From where I stood I could see clearly the objects upon it. A moment later I was making a closer scrutiny.

The articles were not numerous: a half-dozen late novels between bronze book ends; a silver box, containing cigarettes; a service tray, also of silver and bearing a lighter and ashtrays. Also there was a bronze statuette of a boy. I recognized it as a reproduction of the standing figure of the Christ Child by Andrea del Verrocchio. I picked it up to examine it. Including the base, the statuette was some eight or nine inches in height and surprisingly heavy, weighing, I judged, between three and a half and four pounds. I was replacing it when my glance took in a detail the sight of which caused me suddenly to suspend my hand in the act.

In Del Verrocchio's portrayal of the Christ Child, the figure stands relaxed, the weight supported by the right leg, the left leg slightly bent; the right arm is half extended, the hand at the level of the right shoulder; the left arm hangs gracefully at the side, the hand open and palm outward. Now I saw in the middle of the little out-turned palm a tiny spot that showed red in the lamplight, I knew at once what it was, though to make assurance doubly sure I proceeded to verify my belief. With the point of my knife, and with infinite care, I transferred a particle of the reddish stain to the moistened corner of my handkerchief. The result was unmistakable—blood it was, beyond a doubt. What was more, further scrutiny disclosed several other small stains, and no less than four short, grizzly hairs; the latter, oddly enough, adhering between the ripples of the bronze tresses of the Christ Child.

"Now," said I to myself, never doubting that I held the lethal instrument, "if we can get a fingerprint or two perhaps we shall know who gave friend Snowden his quietus"; and I carefully wrapped the statuette in my scarf.

Well, I was ready to call it a night and get back to Jeff with my news. I started to leave the room. My hand was extended to snap off the light. A faint sound, out in the corridor, brought me to a full stop, my finger on the switch, my eye on the door. And as, motionless, I continued to look, slowly the knob began to turn. Then, not caring to be caught like a chicken thief in a hen roost, I stretched forth my hand and laid it upon the knob.

"Won't you come in?" I said and opened the door.

Naturally I didn't know whom I was to see. It wouldn't have surprised me to find Tom Randel or McClennen; even Colleti himself was a possibility. However, it was Mrs. Randel's maid, Olga Svenson, who stood there, regarding me steadily, her manner quite assured, though she was clad only in a thin silk nightgown.

"Oh, good-evening," I said, brusque in my affected nonchalance.

She smiled and raised a hand.

"Not so loud," she cautioned in a husky whisper.

She moved a step toward me and laid a hand on mine.

And when I remained silent, merely looking at her, once more she smiled her inscrutable smile and, extending one white arm behind her, closed the door.

20

And so for the moment we stood, each looking into the face of the other. She was, as I have mentioned, a tall girl, and her eyes, narrowed under the heavy white lids, were on a level with mine. She was so close I could feel the warmth of her.

"You'll catch your death of cold in that rig-out, you know," I told her.

At that she shrugged her fine shoulders, milk white in the light of the lamps.

"I do not fear the cold—I am hot-blooded," she returned indifferently.

Suddenly her smile widened.

"And you are astonished to see me. You say: 'No; this is not Olga, that lady's maid!'"

The low-pitched timbre of her voice deepened to a throaty little laugh, instantly suppressed. Her assurance and poise in our somewhat grotesque situation amused me, and—without rhyme or reason—it nettled me, too.

"Doubt the substantial presence—when so confronted by the naked truth?" I laughed and ran my eye over her. "Never, my dear; why, Olga, I knew you at first blush."

She shook her head at me.

"You make fun of my costume? If you are a gallant gentleman you will say, at least, it is nothing if not charming."

"It is both," I told her bluntly.

She continued to shake her head.

"So; you do not like me so?" she smilingly asked; and with easy grace she moved into the room and picked up my Burberry. "There"—drawing the coat about her—"that is more—proper, is it not?"

"Less danger of pneumonia, at any rate," I growled, seeing my departure postponed by this trick of hers.

She gave me an odd glance and seated herself in a corner of the chaise longue by which we had found the body of Snowden.

"And now, Mr. Holt, explanations are in order, is it not so?"

"Very properly so," I agreed. "Suppose you tell first why you are snooping around this way in the dead of night."

"I like your nerve!" she exclaimed, her faint accent and slow, husky voice giving the words a charm. "However . . . If you will be good enough to fetch that silver box from over there"—she pointed to the Hepplewhite table—"I will show you the cause of my snooping."

"Oh," said I. "It was cigarettes, was it?"

Olga leaned back in the chaise longue, stifling her laughter. She looked up at the ceiling knowingly, a little devil of mockery in each gray eye.

"And he talks of 'snooping!'" she jeered. "Yes, Cigarettes! I was sleepless. I said, 'I will smoke'; then I found no cigarettes. I knew there were some in this room; so—you see?"

"That was how it was, eh?" said I, not believing a word of it. "Of course, you had no idea anyone was here?"

She shook her head.

"I was scared stiff when you opened the door."

"You red-headed liar!" I thought. It was humanly impossible for anyone unprepared to find the room occupied to have acted as she had.

"Here are your cigarettes," I said, and I gave them to her and held a match. She blew a cloud and nodded her thanks.

"Now it is your turn," she said, looking up at me.

I ignored the pat by which she indicated a place beside her, and sat down in one of the big chairs.

"Just doing my daily good deed," I told her; and explained how I happened to be in the house, though I didn't mention the shooting.

I could see that my story left her skeptical. But why had I entered this room? she wanted to know.

"Morbid curiosity," I declared. "I felt the urge to visit the scene of Snowden's murder."

She nodded thoughtfully. Some people, she admitted, were like that; though, for her part, she couldn't understand such unnatural interest.

"Evidently the room has no terrors for you," I commented dryly.

It hadn't, I was told. She had seen too much of death to be so affected.

"Now that I have found you here," she went on, "I have something to tell you."

"That's right," said I, reminded of her call. "You were over to see me, weren't you?"

She nodded and sat up and crushed out her cigarette, regarding me steadily. I remained silent. She leaned back in her corner, drawing my coat about her. There was a thoughtful pause while she continued to study me.

"You are working with the police, aren't you?" she suddenly demanded; and when I started a reply she stopped me.

"No; don't deny it—I know you are. From the first I have thought, 'He is blind, like the others.' You are all the same. You talk, talk, talk; you seek for fingerprints; you nod your heads, and you look, oh, so wise! You arrest a poor sick boy and set one of your policemen to watch him. Oh, yes! He is the guilty one! And then—no, you are wrong! It is not the boy, and you take away that tiresome policeman. Now you will guess some more. But all that time the one who killed is right there, in your hands—and all of you too blind to see her!"

She had shot this at me in a burst of low-voiced vehemence that for the moment left her breathless.

"Hello!" said I. "So it was a woman, was it? And you know her?"

She made an angry gesture.

"I am telling you—I do know; but it will be for you to prove it." She paused, eyeing me, and added, her voice sinking to a low guttural: "It is that girl, Lea Donnay!"

Somehow, I had expected to hear that name.

"Now what do you know about that!" said I, without much enthusiasm. My lack of surprise seemed to disconcert Olga. Didn't I believe her? she demanded.

"It doesn't sound so hot," I told her frankly. "Why should she want to kill the girl?"

"To retain her hold on two men who were important to her—one her lover, the other her meal ticket," she informed me spitefully.

"Well," I laughed, "that is plain talk, anyhow. I assume the lover was Tom Randel."

"Yes; and about to desert her for his own sister-in-law—that incestuous little pervert!"

"And that's strong talk!" said I.

"Strong talk, indeed," she sneered. "Though not strong enough by half—if you knew the truth of it. Muriel Randel was man crazy—anything in trousers, it was all one to her. Snowden divorced her—and immediately was after her again. She was playing fast and loose with him—and one or two others—when Tom came back from France. The moment she laid eyes on him, there was no one else for her. He had a lucky escape."

"I am wondering that the husband and the mother-in-law would tolerate her, if Muriel was the character you paint her," I remarked.

"Listen!" protested Olga ironically. "I thought you had seen enough in your time to know that in a case of this kind the persons most interested are the last to grasp the situation."

"Harry grasped it, at any rate," I reminded her.

"He did—finally! And the knowledge put him in Piermont. As for my mistress, she is an angel—the last person in the world to believe evil of anyone. Never would she hear a word against that creature. Even now she thinks that robbery was the motive of the murders."

"And you say not, eh? Well, go on; tell how Miss Donnay played her part. You haven't said why she wished for Snowden's death."

My apparent lack of understanding annoyed her.

"You don't seem to get the idea," she told me impatiently. "Here"—a white arm emerged from the fold of the coat—"give me another cigarette, and I'll tell you about it."

When she was back in her corner she blew a cloud upward, her eyes on the ceiling, and laughed maliciously.

"She didn't want him dead. You see, he was the meal ticket I spoke of a minute ago."

"You mean he was putting up for her?" I demanded bluntly.

Olga's frankness matched my own.

"I mean just that," she returned instantly. "The girl had been his mistress."

"You say 'had been'?" I suggested.

"Before he sent her to Paris. It was at that time he began chasing after his ex-wife. To get Donnay out of the picture he had her go over there to finish her musical studies."

"And in Paris she runs into Tom Randel and they proceed to fall in love?" I chimed in, beginning to understand.

"Exactly. With Snowden doing the financing," she laughed. "Word of their affair got to him, and at once he tightened the purse strings. Then Tom came over here on a visit, so there was the poor girl without her lover, and with very little money."

An unfortunate situation, I agreed.

"Unfortunate situation!" she returned indignantly. "I should say it was! Men have no idea what we poor women have to go through. Well; she had the price of a ticket, anyway. She came back here to see what she could do with Snowden. Not only does she find him dancing attendance on Muriel—and very shy when the subject of money is mentioned—but also she sees herself in a fair way to lose Tom. To make matters worse, there is that little wanton to twit her at every opportunity—always rubbing it in. You can see how desperate she must have been."

Once more I assured her that she was right.

"Well, now you know why the Donnay girl killed Muriel. Once she was out of the way, there was every chance both Tom and Snowden would forget the little devil and return to Lea."

"But why kill Snowden?" I persisted. "Would she kill the goose that laid the golden eggs?"

The red-haired woman gave me an odd look, an appraising regard, as though my question had brought to her mind a subject outside the scope of our talk.

"Self-protection," she slowly replied. "She had to kill him—to stop his mouth."

She paused and took a few deliberate puffs on her cigarette.

"You see, it was like this," she presently resumed: "As you know, I was with Mrs. Randel all during the night. I was ready for bed when I noticed the tray Amelia had brought up. I opened the door to put it out in the hall. It just happened that I looked toward this room. It wasn't that I heard anything. It was perfectly still—not a sound. I had put the tray outside the door, and I was straightening up, when by chance—or fate, perhaps—I looked down the hall just in time to see someone go into Muriel's room."

Again she paused, looking at me to see how I was taking it.

"And it was Miss Donnay, was it?" I queried.

"It was Miss Donnay," she declared calmly.

"You could be sure of that? At that distance? It's a good fifty feet; and the lights were low."

"There was plenty of light for me to see that she was tall. There were two women of that height in the house that night—Miss Maxwell and the Donnay girl. Miss Maxwell, I knew, was safe in the next room."

"Wonderful!" I acclaimed. "Your power of deduction is marvelous! And now for Mr. Snowden, for I suspect he is in the offing."

She nodded.

"It wasn't two minutes later that I saw him go into the same room. It was this way: Of course I knew how Donnay felt towards Muriel. The sight of her going into that room—and at that time of night—surprised me. I waited, expecting there would be a row. Then my mistress spoke to me, and I had to shut the door. I was curious to know what would happen—those two getting together like that—so I made an excuse of putting out some wilted flowers and opened the door again. When I looked down the hall, sure enough, there was somebody—Snowden, tiptoeing down the corridor. I watched him go into Muriel's room. I held my breath. I was sure there would be a rumpus. There wasn't a sound. I didn't want to worry my mistress with the knowledge of what was going on, so I shut the door and went to bed."

"And heard nothing more till you were roused by the alarm?" I suggested.

That was so, I was told.

It sounded convincing enough, but it left me cold.

"Why didn't you tell all this to Olsen on Saturday morning?" I asked her.

She didn't like him, she replied; adding, with a shrug and a shake of the red head: "He is fresh."

I smiled to myself, recalling how the sergeant had first spoken to the girl in their native tongue. That bald-headed Swede!

"He would have eaten up your story," I told Olga. "As for me, I can't see that it proves Miss Donnay a murderess. Maybe Snowden killed Muriel."

"And then came into this room and knocked himself on the head!" she retorted, disdainfully sarcastic. "Why, it is all perfectly clear. And you call yourself a detective!"

"Even so, that doesn't give one the power of clairvoyance that seems to be yours," I defended myself. "Go on; tell what happened when the triangle was joined in Muriel's room."

It was, she insisted, as plain as daylight. Lea had entered Muriel's room; she had found her rival asleep and had eliminated the menace to her prosperity and happiness in the most effectual way. Snowden, entering at that moment, had surprised his one-time girl friend *flagrante delicto,* and the two had retreated to confer in the big room at the end of the corridor. There had followed accusations, recriminations, and threats; and finally, to avert further betrayal by Snowden, the girl had killed him by striking him over the head.

"And what did she hit him with?—the well-known 'blunt instrument?'" I asked, solemn as a judge; wondering, nevertheless, what Olga would say if she knew what I had wrapped in my scarf.

That was for me to find out, I was told. How did she know?

"Well, anyhow," I said, getting to my feet, "you have been most entertaining."

There was a wistful look on the face turned up to me. Somehow the sudden change of countenance touched me.

"What is it, Olga?" I said, moved to earnestness.

"You place no faith in me—no belief in what I have told you," she replied pensively.

It wasn't that, I hastened to assure her; and, softened by her woebegone expression, I foolishly indulged in a half-confidence.

"You see," I added, "I happen to know that, whoever did the killing here the other night, it wasn't Lea Donnay."

The instant the words were out of my mouth I regretted them. Her face took on a stony hardness which indicated no wasted sympathy for the one she suspected.

"Oh, it is tiresome!" she exclaimed, breaking a short silence; and discarding my coat, she rose from the chaise longue, extending her arms wide in a gesture of weariness.

With the light of the lamp behind her making a transparency of her single flimsy garment, she might, to all intents and purposes, have been without it. For a moment she held that revealing pose, the very abandon of her action calculated to disarm the suspicion that she consciously flouted propriety. Consciously? An inarticulate instinct whispered there was method in this disregard of convention. I studied her curiously as she let her arms fall slowly to her sides and stood motionless before me, looking at me with innocent unconcern. Damn the girl! Such conduct was outrageous!

"Better keep that coat on while you're in this cold room," I told her, ignoring the display; and I reached for the discarded garment.

She took a quick step, interposing herself between me and the chaise longue. Once more we stood face to face. Again I knew her warmth and the scent of her freshness.

Presently—and when she spoke it was in a lowered voice, and with a return of the slightly foreign accent and manner which had been absent in our late talk—she said:

"You are—the limit! And yet—I cannot think of you as an old fogy!"

She was laughing, and I grinned back at her.

"No? Well, I'll tell you a secret—I'm not."

"Just—careful?"

"Just—politic."

She touched the lapel of my coat, tracing a stripe in the pattern with the tip of a white forefinger, her eyes downcast.

"I did not think any man was like that," she whispered.

"It is an acquired art," I told her and reached for my coat.

She watched me slip it on, her face alight with mockery. However, indifferent that in her eyes I must cut a sorry figure—and having gotten her out in the hall, the lamps extinguished, and the door closed behind us—I convoyed her in silence up the corridor to her room. She opened the door and stood on the threshold, outlined by the light beyond.

"Good-night," she whispered, bending toward me; and at once I found her in my arms—to be more accurate, I was in hers—her lips on mine.

"Be careful of the night air!" she whispered in my ear; and with this she twisted away and was in her room, with the door closed, leaving me with an impression of smooth firmness under the thin nightgown.

"Now, I wonder what you are playing at," I muttered half aloud; and I went down the wide staircase and out into the chill of the starry night, racking my brains for an answer to my question. I didn't believe that it was for myself that I had been subjected to the allurement of this handsome lady's maid.

Later, lying in my bed, waiting for the sleep that was slow in coming, I continued to puzzle.

21

At breakfast I told Jeff the story of the night before. Hearing the part Olga had played, he grinned knowingly.

"And was I not telling you?" he reminded me.

We found a powerful reading glass, and a closer examination of the spots on the statuette convinced me that they were indeed bloodstains.

"Agnew shall have a look at this," I said. "With his facilities he should be able to develop fingerprints—if any. He will send the hair to Mueller, of course."

It was after lunch before Jeff got away, dispatched with the statuette and a note to Agnew. For the remainder of the afternoon I was engaged at my neglected work, my thoughts of things far away from Glen Athol. Time flew, and it was only when the waning light blurred the written words that I looked up to see the sun low over the hills beyond the river. The clock on the mantel showed five-thirty. Considering the short distance he had to cover, and the nature of his errand, Jeff was certainly taking his own good time. Thinking perhaps he had slipped in quietly and even now might be preparing our dinner, I relinquished the pen from stiff fingers and went to investigate.

But the kitchen showed dusky and deserted. The quiet and the neatness of the place gave me a feeling of foreboding. Where could the fellow be? I asked myself. I made up the fire and put on the kettle. Then, still uneasy, I went to the telephone and called Piermont.

"Yes," said Agnew, when I got through to him, "your man was here. I thought we had better get a quick report on the hair, so I sent him on up to Mueller with it."

"What time was that?" I asked.

About one-thirty, I was told. "It looks as though you had found something important," Agnew went on, Jeff's whereabouts immaterial in comparison with the greater consideration. "I shall have a detailed report to give you tomorrow or next day."

"Right now I am more concerned to know what has become of my man," I said, somewhat shortly. "It would take more than a thirty-mile drive to so delay him. He should have been home hours ago."

"Probably he has gone to a picture show," laughed the doctor.

I knew better than that. I looked for Mueller's number in the telephone directory, and, speaking to the eccentric German, learned that Jeff had been there—at two-thirty, declared the odd little man, precisely definite. I hung up in a quandary.

Back in the kitchen, finding the kettle on the boil, I made tea and opened a can of soup. It was a dismal meal. I ate from habit, not because I was hungry. I kept telling myself that any one of a hundred unimportant things might have delayed Jeff. Perhaps the car had suddenly gone out of commission. Maybe, right now, Jeff was tinkering with it in some repair shop. But arguing thus was small comfort. I knew gangdom's code of reprisal. Leaving out of the question the reason for our attempted abduction, the defeat of his plan—the more or less damaged Larry being an additional slap in the face—would inflame Colleti to renewed activity.

As the evening dragged on, my uneasiness increased. Nine o'clock came and found me jumpy as a cat, my hot pipe going like a furnace, my throat parched by too much smoking, and more certain than ever that Jeff had been made the recipient of the attentions of the suave Colleti. I said to myself: "If he doesn't show up within the next hour, I'll go down there and check into things." Then, so little faith had I that my man would arrive, I made my preparations for the excursion; and so to sit in the living room, my eye on the clock, watching the intolerably slow progress of the minutes.

By the time the half-hour had struck I had formed only the most sketchy of plans beyond the determination to confront Colleti. Once we were face to face, I would put the cards on the table, holding the Italian personally responsible for Jeff's safe reappearance. . . . And then, waiting for that interminable half-hour to pass, I found myself assailed by doubts.

"After all," I pondered, "am I giving undue importance to Colleti? Isn't it probable that I am looking for a mare's nest when I attribute Jeff's absence to a result of the Saturday-night escapade?"

I smoked one pipe after the other, alternately staring into the fire and watching the slow-moving hands of the clock, and when the three-quarters struck I was almost persuaded that I was an alarmist.

But my hunch would not down. At the back of my mind was the conviction that Jeff was in trouble. All the time I was arguing with myself I knew that I had a trip down the river cut out for me that night, and when finally that lagging minute hand stood upright, I counted the ten silver strokes and then got to my feet, glad that the time for action had come.

I went to the telephone and was lucky enough to catch the taxi owner who had driven Jeff and me on our trips to the city. Arriving within the next quarter-hour, he hailed me as an old and valued friend.

"Hello, there," he sung out cheerily. "Where do we go this time?"

I asked if he knew the location of the Cambridge Arms.

"You bet," he assured me, pleased, I could see, at the prospect of a profitable night.

"That's got to be quite a place," he volunteered, after I had told him our destination and we were ascending the lane to the highway. "A lot of the live bunch up in the city are playing it lately."

I asked who owned the place.

"Oh, it's a stock-company proposition," was the reply, "I guess old Doc McClennen owns the big end of it."

Naturally I pricked up my ears at that.

"Funny stunt for a doctor," I dissimulated, seeing a chance to learn something.

My gossip laughed.

"He don't do so much doctoring any more—since he's in the dough—mighty near a millionaire. He cops off plenty from this joint we're going to—and, of course, he's in politics. You knew that, didn't you?"

"No; that's news to me."

"Oh, he ain't what you'd call a speechmaker, nor a handshaker, but he's wired-in good at headquarters, you bet. That's how they get protection down at this dump we're talking about."

I asked if McClennen's interest in the Cambridge Arms was a matter of common knowledge.

It wasn't, I was informed.

"And, brother," the fellow went on, suddenly becoming familiar, "all this is strictly on the q. t. I wouldn't have said anything, only you being a visitor and not liable to talk. If the Doc ever got word that I was broadcasting, the least I'd get would be to lose my license."

"Not a word," I assured him; and asked if he knew Colleti.

"Gus Colleti?" He uttered the name in a tone which showed me at once how he regarded the Italian. "Sure, I do! Why, mister, more than once I've carried him— right in this car."

"I hear he is quite a fellow," I suggested tentatively.

He was all of that, I was told. The head outlined against the windshield wagged emphatically.

"He's a perfect gentleman—without he happens to have a few drinks in him, or maybe something goes wrong to steam him up. The kind of a guy that never wants to know, 'How much is it?' Gus'll just throw you a bill—a ten spot, maybe—and say, 'Okay, kid.' He's the big finger down at the Arms—didn't you know that?"

Before I could answer he was off again.

"But Gus is a bad hombre to cross. Not long ago there was a lot of talk about him being mixed up in a killing. He went through the third degree with the police and the district attorney. The D. A. has it in for Gus, and he'd have sure burned him if he could have got the goods on him. But there was no evidence—nothing but talk. Gus walked out on them, grinning like a possum."

I made no comment. My lack of interest must have offended the hero worshiper, for he said no more. I had plenty to occupy my thoughts, and for a long time we sped down the highway in silence. Then the glow of the big electric sign of the Cambria Bridge Company showed ahead. Soon we were passing the jerry-built cottages on the outskirts of the town. It was eleven o'clock by this time. However, Main Street opened up before us under a dazzle of colored lights, with many cars, the sidewalks well crowded.

We threaded our way through considerable traffic and pulled in at the open space before the Cambridge Arms.

As we slowed down I had a surprise, for there, sedately parked in a line of cars, was the judge's Buick. Of course, there was no sign of Jeff; I didn't need to look a second time to be sure of that. However, now I was pretty certain I knew where to find him.

I got out of the Ford and asked its owner how much I owed him.

"But don't you want me to wait for you?" queried the surprised fellow.

"I'll be going back in a friend's car," said I, hoping that I was a true prophet; and I paid him.

I stepped down the line of cars to the Buick. A glance inside showed nothing unusual; everything in place, even to the key in the ignition lock. That, if nothing else, I told myself, gave proof of Jeff's restraint; for never willingly would that careful Irishman have left the car without locking it and pocketing the key. I took the precaution to do that and turned to retrace my steps to the entrance of the hotel. And there, from between the revolving doors, emerged coincidence in the person of Miss Kitty McCarthy, in a short fur jacket and a jaunty little toque. She was passing me with a casual glance.

"Hello, Kitty," I accosted her, putting myself in her way.

She looked up defensively for a moment, then showed her prominent teeth in a smile of recognition.

"Oh, it's you, is it?" she returned and studied my face while her smile broadened. "Well, you sure turned me down like a dirty deuce Saturday night."

I took her arm. "Here," I said, "let's go where we can get a quiet drink. I want to talk to you."

"All right," she agreed, after a momentary hesitation. "Are you game to go down and let Tony serve us?"

"Certainly," I told her.

She shook her head, serious all at once.

"No, no, big boy. That's no place for you."

"Why not?"

"Ever hear the story about the lamb in the packing house?"

The way she said it gave the words a sinister meaning.

"I'm hardly worth shearing—and would make tough eating," I laughed.

Just then a party of young folks, some half-dozen of them, and all feeling the effects of their liquor, roistered out of the revolving doors and barged into us.

"Come on, let's get out of this," said Kitty, laying her hand on my arm. "I don't want a drink, anyhow. We'll go down to the Greek's and get a bite to eat."

We turned the corner of the hotel, down the side street to the section of the town alongside the railroad tracks. The houses, small frame structures, were brightly lit and uproarious with phonographs and self-playing pianos. We turned another corner and found ourselves before a showily painted diner, quite a pretentious affair.

"Here we are," said Kitty. "This guy puts out the best hamburger you ever ate, and his coffee is something grand."

I opened the door and we stepped inside. With its nickel and monel metal fittings the place was clean and shining. The warmth, the odors of fried onions, coffee, and hot grease, a certain orderly and compact coziness, all seemed mighty pleasant to Kitty and me, coming into it that way from the chill of the night. I realized that I was hungry.

There were two young couples on high stools before the counter, behind which was a fat and middle-aged swarthy fellow in a white bibbed apron. These, and two girls seated at one of the side tables, were the occupants of the establishment. All looked inquiringly at us, and the fat proprietor and the two girls smiled and nodded at Kitty.

"Howdy, kids," she greeted the girls; and to the man: "Commy savar, Gigi; let us have two hamburgers and a couple of mugs of Java, back in the booth."

When we were seated in the semi-privacy of the tiny cubicle, the narrow table between us, she lit a cigarette and leaned back against the wall, eyeing me expectantly.

22

Here in the brightly lit diner I could see that the vividly made-up face which confronted me was strangely altered. There were lines about the weakly pretty mouth and a querulous wrinkle between the carefully penciled brows. I looked more closely and told myself if that wasn't a skillfully camouflaged black eye I missed my guess. Naturally I gave no sign of my observation. The girl puffed her cigarette and continued to stare at me.

"So you think I turned you down Saturday night, eh?" I grinned at her.

"What would you call it? You said you'd come—and then never showed. Wasn't that a turn-down?"

She leaned forward to knock the ash from her cigarette to the tray upon the table. I laid my hand on hers.

"Listen," I told her. "You were playing stool pigeon for Colleti. I was the fall guy. Then the play went sour. That's the straight dope, isn't it?"

She pulled her hand from under mine and resumed her former position, leaning back against the leather-cushioned wall, smoking her cigarette with slow puffs and regarding me doubtfully. Then, before she could voice the denial I expected, we were interrupted by the arrival of our order.

For a time neither of us spoke. When we had finished I took out my pipe and waited to hear what the girl had to say for herself. She lit a cigarette and puffed awhile in silence. Then, her elbows on the table, she propped her chin in her hands and fixed her eyes on mine.

"I wonder if I'd be cuckoo to play ball with you. I wish to God I knew," she muttered, half to herself.

"You promised to tell me who killed Snowden and Mrs. Randel," I reminded her.

She shook her head.

"That was a stall—just to get you to start down here."

"And Colleti ribbed you up to that, didn't he?"

She sat up sharply, a wild look coming into her eyes.

"What are you trying to do—get me killed?" she demanded, breathing hard.

"Poppycock!" I laughed. "Nobody's going to kill you."

"Gus would—in a minute—if he knew I was ready to double-cross him."

"Are you ready to double-cross him?"

She gave me a dark look as she crushed out the end of her cigarette.

"Do you see this?" she said, laying the tip of a finger to the discolored eye. "That's the thanks I get for doing his dirty work for the last three years. Whatever else he's done, he never hit me before."

Her voice breaking in a sob, she fell silent, her eyes moodily downcast. I let her alone, knowing I should hear all the more by keeping quiet. Presently she went on:

"I've been his girl for three years. I didn't mind him playing around with other women, as long as it was a matter of business—not even that Randel dame. At first he said he was just using her to promote a piece of change. Well, that listened all right. Later on we both had to be nice to her because she had stole something from Gus—something that could be sprung as evidence to send him to the chair. Once he got that back, he'd give her the gate, he always said. Then she gets croaked, and Gus pretty near goes nuts. I got sore over him singing his torch song day and night—and he gave me this."

Once more she paused, sobbing. After a short silence I said:

"You aren't telling me any news. I know Colleti killed Muriel Randel, and I know he killed her to get something he wanted from her. What puzzles me is how he came to kill Snowden. How did that happen?"

While I was speaking, the girl exhibited signs of a surprise too genuine to be doubted. As I finished she leaned across the table, wide-eyed and open-mouthed.

"What are you talking about!" she demanded fiercely. "Gus kill those people? You're crazy!"

"Certainly, he killed them," I said. "And then he tried to kill me afterward, because he feared I'd convict him of the crime."

Kitty grasped my wrist, shaking it in vehement protest.

"Listen!" she insisted breathlessly. "You've got this all wrong! Gus wanted you out of the way for another reason altogether—and, on top of that, he was sore on you for knocking him out the day you and Muriel were down here."

I saw my advantage and pressed it.

"That won't do, my girl. Colleti was in Muriel Randel's room at three o'clock Saturday morning. He killed her with a knife he got up at Snowden's place the day before. After he had killed her, he stole what he was after. I can prove all that."

The girl stared at me for a space. I could read indecision in her eyes. At length she seemed to make up her mind.

"Listen, Mr. Holt," she said, a certain note of piteous entreaty in her voice. "If I tell who killed Muriel, and all the rest I know about the business, will you play fair with me?"

"Kitty," I told her, "if you are trying to shield Colleti, give up the idea."

"He don't need any shielding, because he didn't do it," she insisted once more. "But supposing that in showing you how he come to be tangled up in this proposition—not doing any killing, mind you—I have to tip off another piece of work. Would you keep the dope to yourself?"

"I'll promise to mind my own business, if that is what you mean. There are just two phases of this affair that interest me; I want the man who killed Muriel and Snowden—also, Kitty, I want my servant, Jeffries, free and unharmed. I suppose you know they have kidnaped him?"

She nodded. "That was to throw a scare into you, so you'd behave."

"Where is he?" I demanded.

"Promise you'll play fair, and I'll tell you that, too."

"All right," said I, glad of the chance.

"There's one thing you've got to get straight," Kitty began. "You've got Gus wrong. God knows, I'm no squawker; but I'm not going to see him get in Dutch over that Randel woman—not when I can get him off the spot by telling the truth. You can play that bet both ways from the middle—even if I am all washed up with him and taking it on the lam."

"You mean you're quitting Collet!?" I asked.

She nodded, her eyes fixed on vacancy.

"I'm quitting him—and I'm quitting this racket. I'm through."

"You're a wise girl," I told her.

"I've got a kid, up in Detroit," she said gently, her face softening. "And I've saved a little bankroll. I'm going back home and get a decent job and live straight."

"Good for you," I said, wishing she would get on with her disclosures, but afraid to rush her.

She was thoughtful for a bit; then she lit a cigarette and leaned forward on the table.

"We'd better speak low," she said, with a quick glance over her shoulder. I bent toward her, and there we sat like two conspirators, our faces not a foot apart.

"This thing started six months ago," Kitty went on. "Everything was going good, and we were sitting pretty. Then one day Gus told me a couple of fellows blew in from Chicago and made a play to go partners with him. He turned them down. They started cutting in on our game—stealing our customers, and so on.

"We tried a little discipline on them, but they didn't scare worth a cent. Gus was all for the rough stuff. He'd have bumped them off himself, only I begged him to lay off. He did for a while. Then things got worse, and he begun to talk again about putting the doxology over the trouble makers.

"'Don't you do it,' I told him. 'If it's got to be done, get some outsider, like other people do.'

"About a week after that, one night Gus comes down from town with a stranger—a young fellow by the name of Cosmano. The minute I set eyes on him I knew what he was. 'Torpedo' was written all over him. I was scared, but what could I do? I kept my mouth shut.

"That was a Thursday night, I remember. Saturday morning, about six o'clock, Gus woke me up. He came into the flat, smiling all over.

"'There's been a bad accident,' he told me. 'Somebody gave the works to those two bums who've been making us trouble. They'll never do any more muscling in.'

"I asked him if he was mixed up in it—if there was any chance of us getting in trouble. He laughed and said some of the best people from out in the East End could swear he'd been running the roulette wheel over at the hotel all night.

"But that wasn't the end of it, by a long ways. Gus was suspected, and the police had him up for questioning. He had a strong drag and a good alibi. They had to turn him loose. But they knew he'd had a hand in it. There wasn't a word against the real killer. I knew who that was, all right.

"Not long after that, Gus told me he'd lost his card case. In it was a letter from Cosmano—I guess you savvy how he was tied up in the proposition. The letter was an answer to one from Gus, setting a price on doing the job. Gus was holding it just in case Nick—that's Cosmano—got gay with him later on. A damn foolish thing to do! Well, besides the letter, there were a couple of canceled checks, cashed by Nick, amounting to what they'd agreed on. Pretty bad evidence—you'll admit that. Gus was mighty hot and bothered about it, but time went on, and we never heard anything of it till about three months ago.

"Gus came to me one night, all steamed up.

"'You know that dope I thought I'd lost. I was wrong,' he says.

"'Well, that's a relief, anyway,' I told him.

"He gave a nasty laugh.

"'Yeah!' he says. 'It'll be a hell of a relief to you to know it was stole from me, and that it's being used to shake me down.'

"I could feel my knees getting weak under me.

"'Who stole it? And who's shaking you down?' I asked him.

"He looked kind of cheap at that. Then he told me it was Muriel Randel. Of course I wanted to know how she could have got her hands on it. He didn't know, he said, but I had my own idea. Anyhow, she had the goods on Gus. That afternoon he'd tried to collect from the Randels for liquor he'd sold them. Muriel had refused to pay. Told Gus to try and get it. Then she sprung the news that she had Cosmano's letter and the two canceled checks. Gus tried to laugh it off. Said he'd take the letter and checks and call it square.

"'Now I'll tell one,' says Muriel; and to make a short story of it, not only does she refuse to let loose of the papers but she touches Gus for five hundred bucks. Well, what could he do but cough up? It was either do that or kill her; and if he did that, where would the papers be?

"I told him: 'Your playing around with that girl has got us in a nice jam. Now all we can do is to act as if we liked it, and watch our chance to get the stuff back.'

"That's what we did. You saw how things were the day you and Muriel came down here. By that time I guess she'd made him like it. She kept kidding him along, promising to give the papers back to him—and other promises, besides; I've a damn good idea of that!

"Friday night—the night of the Randel dinner, you know—we were over at the hotel. Gus had a phone call from Snowden to bring him up some liquor. I didn't see anything more of Gus till he woke me up early the next morning—about four o'clock it was. He came in raging and raving and tearing his hair. When I asked him what it was all about, he told me Muriel had been murdered. At first I was glad; then I was scared.

"'Did you have anything to do with it?' I asked him.

"He carried on like a crazy man at that. At last I got this story out of him. And one thing you can bank on: it's true—every word of it. If you really want to find the man that killed Muriel and Snowden, don't doubt it. Don't go kidding yourself it was Gus.

"He had delivered the bottle of booze to Snowden and was coming away. Muriel came out and started to chin to him. He said he had never seen her act just like that before. She kidded him along, and finally ended up by telling him he could come back to her at three o'clock. Gus went on uptown and was back at the Randel joint in time to keep the date.

"He left his car up by the road and took his flashlight and went down to the house. Everything was quiet. Of course he knew where Muriel's room was and how to get to it. Maybe he'd been there before—how do I know?

"Well, anyhow, he climbed up and got in the window. Naturally, the room was dark. He couldn't see a thing. He daren't speak loud. When he whispered her name and didn't get an answer he thought Muriel was asleep. Stepping easy, he went over to the bed. There was just enough light for him to make out that the covers were pulled up over the pillow. He thought Muriel had covered up her head—acting smart, that way. He spoke to her again. There was nothing doing. Then he snapped on the flash and saw what had happened. The sheet was all bloody. There was the handle of a knife showing above it. And what scared him as much as anything else was that he knew the knife. It was a swell kind of dagger that he'd often seen up at Snowden's. He'd taken a great fancy to it, and just that day Snowden had given it to him, when he'd stopped there with an order of liquor. He'd put it in his pocket, and when he thought of it again, when he got back home, it was gone. So you can bet the sight of it there scared him stiff. He told me:

"'Kid, when I saw that chive sticking up out of that bloody sheet, I could feel them putting the straps on me—and me in the chair. Then, before I could get onto myself, I heard someone in the room. I couldn't tell if they were just come in or, maybe, had been there all the time.'

"I guess when he heard that, it didn't take him long to get back to the window. He daren't get out—just huddled there, up tight to the wall, behind the curtains. Whoever it was, was over by the bed. Everything was still for a minute. Then the handle of the door turned and someone else came in. The next thing Gus knew, the lights were on and two people were chewing the rag at each other in whispers. Gus looked through the crack of the curtains, and, mister, I'll give you three guesses who he saw."

Kitty came to a dramatic pause. The China-blue eyes, usually lackadaisical in the vacuity of the baby face, opened wide in the crisis of disclosure. We studied each other for a moment in silence. I shook my head.

"One was the very man who had given the knife to Gus—Campbell Snowden himself," declared the girl. "And who do you suppose the other was?"

Again she paused, considering me with the air of a sibyl.

"Lea Donnay," I said to myself, though decidedly less confident this time.

Once more I wagged my head negatively.

"Well," said Kitty, with great satisfaction, "it was that other old buzzard, Marshall!"

"Marshall!" I echoed.

"The surest thing you know! Gus said the two of them were standing there by the side of the bed, whispering—gabbing away at each other and making motions, like a couple of old tomcats. He couldn't hear a word they were saying. It was just for a minute, anyhow. Then Snowden pushed the other old guy over to the door. The lights went out, and Gus heard the door open and shut. He said he was scared worse than he had ever been, but he wasn't going to leave without those checks and the letter. He knew Muriel carried them hid in her brassiere. It didn't take him a minute to find it and get the papers. Then, you bet, he wasn't long in getting out of there. He got back to his car all right and beat it down here to me."

The girl came to a sudden stop. For the first time since beginning her story she dropped her eyes from mine and leaned back, relaxing after the stress of her recital.

"Well, that's all there is to it," she concluded, lighting another of her inevitable cigarettes, her manner one of relieved finality.

"Not quite," I demurred. "You haven't explained about your telephone call to me."

"Oh, that!" she deprecated airily. "Gus was afraid maybe that Randel dame had showed you what she was holding out on him. He said guys like you often took photographs of stuff like that, and the pictures could be used for evidence as well as the real thing. That's what had him worried. Of course he was sore on you anyway. But, really, I don't think he was going to do you any damage. All he wanted was to get you to leave town."

"Perhaps," I laughed. "Anyway, we'll let it go at that. Now I want to know what they have done with my man. Where is he?"

"You needn't get hot and bothered about him," Kitty assured me. "He's O. K. They've got him over in Cosmano's room at the hotel."

"For what purpose?"

Kitty looked embarrassed.

"Why, you see, Gus was going to send you word tomorrow that if you'd leave town quick, you'd get your man back in good condition."

"What if I refused?" I persisted.

She raised her shoulders in a disapproving shrug.

"Oh, well! Of course, we hoped you wouldn't do that."

"Just so," said I. "Now, where is this room of Cosmano's?"

"It's on the eighth floor; back at the end of the hall —841 is the number. Why? Are you going over there?"

"Yes," I said, looking at my watch. "It's twelve-thirty; I'd better go at once. Too bad to disturb Mr. Cosmano if he has gone to bed."

He would be watching over Jeff, the girl assured me, adding:

"If you're going over there, the sooner you start the better. Right now you'll find Cosmano alone. Gus'll be up on the top floor, taking care of the suckers."

"Right," said I, getting to my feet.

Kitty rose also. I helped her on with her jacket. Outside the diner she came to a stop and extended her hand.

"I'll be leaving you here," she said; and added, as I returned the pressure of her fingers: "Good-bye—and good luck. You're not a bad guy at that."

I asked if I shouldn't see her safely to her flat,

"No," she replied. "It's right near here; besides, maybe, it's better we're not seen together."

So I remember the last sight I had of her, standing there at the steps of the garish diner. I hope she carried out her good resolutions; that she got back to the kid in Detroit, and that all is well with her.

Back on Main Street I found the sudden quiet that comes to country towns at midnight. The sidewalks were bare of the early crowd, and but few cars remained parked along the curb. I grinned to see the old Buick, demurely respectable, still occupying its position. In the lobby of the Cambridge Arms things were equally quiet as I entered and made my way to the elevator, and when I got out at the eighth floor the long hall lay deserted before me. The layout of the place was exactly similar to the approach to Colleti's rooms on the floor above. I had no difficulty in locating room 841. I was at the extreme end of the hall, and, as I stood facing the door, immediately to my left was a partly open window. Through it came faintly the sound of revelry from above. Then I was conscious of a movement beyond the door. Someone coughed, sneezed, and loudly cleared his throat, and I recognized Colleti's pleasant baritone:

"What's wrong, punk? Beginning to weaken?"

There was the sound of a low laugh; and again Colleti's voice:

"Maybe tomorrow we'll send your ears to your boss—just to teach him to mind his own business. I wonder how the smart Mr. Holt would like that."

I quietly tried the lock. It was unfastened. I stepped inside and pushed to the door behind me,

"He wouldn't like it at all, Colleti," I assured him.

23

The flash of my first glance photographed upon my memory every detail of the scene. I can still see Colleti sprawled in a big wicker chair by the side of a brass bed upon which Jeff was spread-eagled, handcuffed and leg-ironed to the four corners, a strip of adhesive tape across his mouth. The picture shows the third occupant of the room in the person of a slim, sleek-headed fellow, scarcely more than a boy, very natty in blue serge, who, hands in pockets, stood at the bedside and stared at me with malevolent black eyes. I knew him at once, though he lacked the modish blue overcoat and the tan-colored soft hat in which I had last seen him.

"Hello, Cosmano," I greeted him. "How's Larry?"

Neither of them said a word—just glared at me, too confounded to move. Fortunately for me they were both on the same side of the bed and nicely in line. I stood watching them, my hands holding my coat lapels—a pose they both well understood.

"Well, boys," I went on pleasantly, "where are your manners? Say 'Good-evening,' can't you?"

From the bed came the sound of protesting springs and a grunt from Jeff as he tried to sit up, only to fall back under the restraint of the handcuffs.

"Just a minute, Jeff," I told him, never taking my eyes off the precious pair before me. "What's wrong?" I asked, "afraid to go for me? It's two to one."

They neither moved nor spoke. I kept my hands on my lapels and said:

"Well, you don't seem to want to shoot it out. You won't even talk. It looks as though we're deadlocked. Just turn my man loose, and we'll say 'Good-night' and be on our way."

There came a growl from Cosmano.

"You'll never make it, buddy."

I turned on him with sudden anger.

"Listen, you!" I told him. "Take off those irons, quick! Make one false move and I'll put a bullet through your greasy head and shoot the buttons off your coat while you're falling!"

He seemed to know that I meant it. Eyeing me doubtfully the while, he deliberately produced a key and unlocked the shackles; then, holding his hands at the level of his shoulders, he retreated beyond Colleti's chair, getting as far away from Jeff as possible.

That long Irishman left the bed like a bear coming out of a cave. Naturally my attention was centered upon the others, but I heard his growled profanity once his mouth was free of the adhesive tape. I think, if left to himself, he would have instantly attacked Colleti and his henchman, in which case he certainly would have gotten himself killed. However, at a word from me he came to heel.

"Get that jewelry ready for your friends," I told him. "We'll see how it becomes them."

"Come on, you two," I said to them. "Onto the bed with you. Lie face down and stick your hands behind you."

"You put those things on me!" threatened Colleti, "and I'll kill you, if I go to the chair for it!"

"Do as I tell you, or you'll not live that long," I assured him; and he knew he was listening to true words.

So that was the way we left them, handcuffed, arm in arm, face downward on the bed, each with a pillowslip over his head. Yes, we had played in luck. The interruption that I had feared might come at any minute hadn't materialized. We casually took the elevator and, unmolested, descended to the street. It all seemed ridiculously easy. There was the old Buick waiting for us. We got it headed for home without loss of time. Jeff drove.

"Step on it," I told him, and that for a while was the extent of our conversation. I knew how he felt, and, not wanting to add to his humiliation, I forbore questioning him.

At length, when we had left the town well behind us and were doing the old car's best of forty miles an hour up the highway, Jeff spoke. Inconsistently, I thought, he began by reprimanding me:

"And I never fancied that it would be yourself passing by a chance like that—you having the murdering hound at your mercy, as you might say, and leaving without getting the truth from him."

"Hold on!" I retorted. "The next thing you'll be telling me you were sorry to have me interrupt your party. I suppose you were doing a little sleuthing on your own account"; and, so losing patience, I asked him how he came to get into such a mess.

He was quick to defend himself.

On his homeward trip that afternoon, on a lonely stretch of road, he had been overtaken by "a fine big car" which crowded him to a stop. One of its occupants, gun in hand, had met Jeff when he alighted to "give them a bit of an argument."

"Sure I was up against it," declared poor Jeff ruefully. "'Back at the wheel with you,' says the lad, jabbing the gun into me, and both of us getting into the car. If I did as I was told, I would not be hurt, he says; otherwise, he would shoot my head off. Oh, you can laugh, sir; but what was I to do?"

The remainder of the story was about what I should l have expected. They had driven down to the Cambridge Arms, and under threat of death Jeff had gone unresisting to the place where I had found him. Colleti, I was told, hadn't put in an appearance till shortly before my I arrival.

"Well, Jeff, you needn't feel bad about it," I told him. "Really, your experience has been a blessing in disguise.

What I have learned tonight while looking for you will go a long way toward solving our problem"; and with that I was about to recount my interview with Kitty. However, Jeff was not to hear the story at that moment.

For some time our course had followed a succession of long curves which marked the base of the hills on the easterly side of the highway. Now we were making a fast run down a long gentle declivity. The mirror flashed the light from a car far in our rear. There should have been nothing particularly alarming in this, but when I looked I back and discovered that we were being overhauled with a rapidity which showed our pursuers traveling at twice our speed—I suppose we were doing forty-five miles an hour—I knew we were in for trouble.

"By George!" I said. "I believe they are after us."

"Sure enough," Jeff commented; and I think it spoke well for his nerve that our pace remained steady. Later, when I mentioned it, he disclaimed any credit. "The old bus could go no faster," he said. "And sure I did not think yourself would be stopping to wait for them."

That, however, was what I instantly decided to do. I had no mind to continue a flight which would end in our being the target for sub-machine guns. By good luck I remembered the piece of road which at the moment we were covering. It formed one side of a long dip in our path, the opposite slope being the stretch of highway which we had been traversing on Saturday night when held up by Colleti's mob.

"Slow down," I said. "A side road cuts in hereabouts. We'll take it."

Jeff grasped my intention at once. There was a screech of brakes as he checked our progress.

"There it will be," he announced, as a dark opening among the trees at our left showed the correctness of my topography.

In this bypath we came to a stop. I cut off the lights and we got out of the car. Now, among the trees and undergrowth, it was pitch dark. The starlit highway, a stone's throw distant, appeared light by comparison. Beyond it I could see an open stretch of country, and farther still—far away, on the other side of the river—a few scattered lights.

The car that followed us had been traveling at a speed which would bring it upon us in short order. That it had not already appeared was pretty good proof that it carried Colleti and Cosmano. Jeff, crouched beside me where I stood in the shelter of a tree, expressed the same thought.

"They would be noticing our lights as we turned. Going slow they will be."

"They will think twice before they come in here after us," I replied; and when we had stood there in the chill of the night mists a bit longer and nothing happened, I began to consider our danger a thing of the past.

"I believe they have given it up and turned back," I told Jeff.

With my words there came the sound of a rapidly approaching car. The opening to the highway sprang into prominence, illuminated by the glare from powerful headlights. A car roared by, its cut-out full open, its passage accompanied by the staccato rattle of machine-gun fire, the sound merging in the clamor of the car's exhaust. For an instant around us was the rip of bullets. Then darkness again, and the diminishing whine of the already distant car.

"Did they get you?" I asked, backing away from the tree against which I had glued myself.

Jeff answered from the ground.

"Glory to God, they did not then! Just 'whish!'—and did they go by!"

He got to his feet, and I heard him brushing away at his clothes.

"That," said I, "comes of underrating the intelligence of your adversary—always poor strategy."

"Are you thinking they scouted ahead, like—finding where we would be and all?"

"They didn't shoot for the fun of it. However"—and I smiled to myself, thinking how their technique had justified what I had told Colleti—"they stuck to their car when it came to delivering the goods. They lacked guts to come in here looking for trouble."

"Are you thinking they will be back to see if they did us in?"

"They must pass here to get back home," I said; and an idea suggested itself. "A good time to teach Colleti a lesson," I went on. "As long as he thinks we are always on the receiving end, he will be a menace."

"And what would you be doing?"

"I'm going to throw a scare into them," said I, starting for the highway.

"What will I be doing, then?" Jeff called after me.

Unarmed, he could do nothing. There was no sense in exposing him to danger.

"Lie low; and be ready to back out when I yell," I directed and left him grumbling.

Out on the highway, as far as I could see in either direction, there was no sign of life. Of course, that didn't mean a thing. With that fast car, Colleti could pop out of the distance like a jack-in-the-box. He would pass in a flash. Probably another fusillade would be directed into the opening of the side road.

With this thought in mind I retreated a hundred yards in the direction of Cambridge and looked for a place to conceal myself at the roadside. At this point the highway was bordered on either hand for the distance of a mile or so by a row of poplars, spaced by some fifty yards. None of these, however, was of a diameter to afford me protection as a bulwark, and I was glad to discover an ideal spot at a point where a shallow drainage culvert passed beneath the roadway. Here, in the shelter of the bank, I stretched myself and awaited developments.

Time passed and nothing happened. The ground under me was damp and cold. Soon I was pretty well chilled through. I began to censure myself as a jumper at conclusions. After all, there was little upon which to base the belief that Colleti and his cronies would again pass this way. However, I had a strong hunch they would, and, if so, there was a double reason for my waiting for them. First—I'll admit it—I felt the itch of resentment, the desire to dose these hoodlums with some of their own medicine. Our future safety might depend on it, I told myself. On the other hand, I had no wish to start back home and run into them on the road. So I continued to lie there, thinking of my warm bed, and clenched my jaws to still my chattering teeth.

At length, away off somewhere, a clock struck two. As though it were a signal, close upon the last stroke, my patience was rewarded. Far up the highway, in the direction of Glen Athol, there was a sudden gleam of light, the headlights of an approaching car. Never for a second doubting that it was the one I expected, I slipped my .45 from its holster and settled myself deeper in the covert of the bank.

As I watched the increasing glare draw nearer, the thought of Muriel came to me; I thought of what Kitty had told me. It had rung true. Nevertheless I was far from convinced that Colleti's part in the happenings of Friday night had been satisfactorily explained. Everything pointed to him as the slayer of Snowden and the girl. And here he came, delivered into my hand by his own deviltry. The temptation was strong to go further than a mere gesture calculated to intimidate him. I seemed to hear Muriel's husky voice: "Give him hell for me, old-timer."

I shook my head. No, I decided, I was not cast in the part of avenger—beyond proving his guilt and handing him over to the police. For the time, a shot or two across the bows of the enemy as he passed, a token of our attitude if forced to harsher methods—that, thought I, was the thing to do.

Now the glare of the headlights was close. The car was coming at high speed, though not at the racing pace it had traveled up the road. Quiet, too, it was; the cutout closed, merely the hum of the tires and the purr of the splendid engine to announce its presence. Suddenly, however—it was fairly on top of me, passing the opening of the side road—it spat darting flashes from its side, the tattoo of the sub-machine gun rolling over my head; and without conscious volition I had risen to my knees and was shooting into it as it swept by.

At the time I couldn't have told how often I pulled the trigger. Afterwards I found three cartridges in my gun and knew that I had sent five bullets at the flying car as it skimmed by in its headlong rush. Of course, the result was greatly due to chance, for it was like shooting at a swallow on the wing. Probably it was my last shot that did the business. I remember delivering it, turning on my knees, as the car flew past me.

What followed was over too quickly for me to know exactly what had happened. There was the jump of the gun in my hand; the sharp screech of tires ripping across the surface of the roadway; a crash, the jingle of broken glass; then silence, and two pencils of light directed straight upward from beside one of the poplars, a hundred yards down the road.

For a time I remained kneeling behind the sloping bank, prepared to repel boarders, and wishing for another clip of cartridges. I waited in vain. There wasn't a sound. If the occupants of the car had escaped the crash, they were keeping quiet, machine guns ready, no doubt. I didn't investigate. Under the circumstances I wasn't interested to the extent of risking another run-in with them.

Back at the side road, I found Jeff and the Buick—he having anticipated orders. At a word from me he backed out on the highway. I took another look down the road. Far away there was the light of a car headed toward us. No doubt at that moment the driver had his eye on that upflung radiance from Colleti's headlights and was wondering about it. I got into the Buick, beside Jeff.

"Home, Jeff," I told him.

24

"One thing is sure," said I, helping myself to a second portion of bacon and eggs—"supposing he is able to talk, they will get no chit-chat out of Colleti. If it should become known that we are connected with the fracas last night, it won't be through him."

Jeff, having finished eating—he lacked his usual appetite that morning—merely grunted as he slowly filled his pipe, his eyes fixed on a patch of thin October sunshine on the wall of the dining room. It was long past our regular breakfast hour, we having overslept—as a result of not getting to bed till three o'clock that morning. The story of my interview with Kitty had been told, and we had discussed the encounter with Colleti—Jeff full of conjectures and eager to go down to the village to learn the outcome of the crash.

"We'll know soon enough," I had told him, determined to avoid publicity if it were possible.

Jeff lit his pipe deliberately and emitted a few thoughtful puffs.

"A good job it will be if he has cheated the hangman, the murdering scut! Sure it is not believing the girl's story you are at all?"

"Well," I replied doubtfully, "it sounded true, the way she told it. She believes it—I'll go bail on that."

Jeff shrugged. "I am thinking she was pulling the wool over your eyes with her fairy tales."

"A great deal depends on Agnew's report," I replied—"whether he finds fingerprints on the statuette, and, if so, whether we can identify them."

That thought sent me to the telephone to call Piermont. A minute later I was talking to Agnew. Yes, he told me, the statuette had shown fingerprints, clear and distinct. He had made some enlarged photographs.

"By the way," he laughed, "I have heard from Mueller. No mistake this time. He says the hair is from the head of an elderly man. I think he is prepared to supply further details—character of party, et cetera. Might be interesting, eh?"

No doubt, I agreed, and told him I would send for the enlargements. So along towards noon, I being engaged at my work, Jeff set out for Piermont.

It wasn't long after that when I was disturbed by a knocking at the back door. Vexed at the interruption, I threw down my pen and went out to the kitchen. I found the intruder was none other than Mrs. Randel's pretty housemaid, Amelia. And very pretty she was, in her short-skirted black dress and frilled white apron, standing there looking at me through the screen door, an expression of embarrassment on her young face and the wind taking liberties with her bobbed brown hair. My ill humor vanished.

"Why, hello, Amelia," I saluted her and waited to hear what had brought her.

"I saw your man go off in the car," she said, serious, and, I thought, half scared. "I want to see you alone."

I pushed open the screen door.

"Come inside," said I, "and tell me about it."

She slipped past me into the kitchen. I turned to encounter her look of questioning uncertainty.

"Is it so, what Simpson says?" she asked, eyeing me inquiringly. "That you're a kind of detective and trying to find out who killed those two?"

Obviously it was hopeless to explain my status to Amelia.

"Well, let it go at that," I told her.

The pretty face took on an expression at once pleased and spiteful.

"Then there's something you ought to hear, something about that stuck-up thing over there. Why, Mr. Holt, she'd give you a pain! The way she goes around with her nose in the air, never paying no more attention to you than if you was the dirt under her feet!"

"And who is this haughty creature?" I asked; though I could pretty well fit the description.

Amelia bridled and sniffed disapprovingly.

"Why, that Svenson woman, to be sure."

"You don't like her?" I suggested.

"Like her! She thinks nobody's wise to her. But she's kidding herself."

"I thought she was a friend of yours," said I, adding fuel to the flames. "Wasn't she making a dress for you, the night of the dinner?"

She might call it a dress, Amelia declared; as for herself—

"Why, I wish you could see it on me, Mr. Holt!"

"Probably she is jealous of you—doesn't want you to look too nice," I suggested.

She rose to the bait.

"Jealous! She was up in my room Sunday afternoon, and when I put on that dress and told her it made me look like a frump, she said you couldn't make a silk purse out of a sow's ear!"

"Clearly a case of jealousy," I insisted. "I'll wager she wishes she were as pretty as you, Amelia," I added, laying it on.

"That's what I told her," triumphantly declared the girl. "But she just smirked at me and sailed out of the room like a duchess. And, mind you, it was that very night I saw her burying the things!"

"What things?" I cut in.

Amelia turned her back, wiggled a bit and, facing me again, held up for my inspection two objects—a squat two-ounce bottle of blue glass and an empty silver-trimmed sheath of green sharkskin.

"These things," she said, handing them to me.

The empty sheath was so obviously the scabbard of the dagger which had been used to kill Muriel that for the time I gave it little attention. The squat blue bottle was devoid of label. When I had removed the glass stopper and had shaken the contents out into my hand, I found eleven gelatin capsules, of perhaps five grains each. None the wiser, I poured them back into the bottle and replaced the stopper.

"Of course, you know," I told Amelia, "I shall have to keep these."

"Sure," she nodded. "That's what I brought them over for."

"You saw Olga Svenson bury these, you say?" I asked, pocketing the sheath and the bottle.

"Yes, I did; Sunday night. It was this way: It was raining when I went to bed, and I left the window closed. The room got so warm I woke up later on. I got up to see if it had stopped raining. It had, but it was still awfully black.

"I was leaning out the window for a breath of fresh air, when a funny thing happened. Up on the road, right on a line with me, somebody stopped their car and turned it round to go the other way. The headlights shined right in my eyes. I looked down quick, and on the ground below my window I saw something else. There's a narrow flower bed runs along there, close to the house. Olga was standing beside it. She had on a black coat, but I could see her plain—the light from the car shining on her red hair.

"She was bending over, sort of poking at the dirt. The car turned round quick and went off. I couldn't see Olga then. There wasn't a sound. I went to bed after that, but next morning, early, I found where the dirt had been turned over. When I poked at it with a stick I found a napkin with those things wrapped in it.

"I didn't tell anybody. Just hid them in my trunk. Then Simpson said how you were a detective, looking for the one who did the murders. I got to thinking I ought to let you know. I've been waiting to tell you, but I didn't get a chance till this morning."

She paused and smiled up at me as much as to say: "Just see what a good girl am I!"

"You had better be careful, Amelia," I cautioned. "You are sure it was Olga who buried the things?"

Her smile became tolerant.

"Oh, yes; certain. Why, I could see her just as plain! I'd never mistake her red head."

I thought this over for a minute or two,

"Well, you were a good girl to bring your find to me. Now here's something else: You were with Olga, up in Mrs. Randel's room, for quite a while on Friday night, weren't you? If I remember, you went up with Simpson when he took the Ovaltine to Mr. Marshall's room. That was a quarter to twelve. Right?"

She nodded, and I went on: "Now I want you to think carefully and tell me exactly what happened—every little thing, mind—while you and Olga were together."

Amelia puckered her pretty forehead in a thoughtful wrinkle.

"It was this way, Mr. Holt: Svenson had been sewing on my dress. It was lying on the davenport. I had a tray for her—cake and tea; but she didn't want anything and began talking about the dress.

"'We'll try it on,' she said, and she went over to the davenport to get it."

"Was the door still open?" I interrupted.

"Yes," she nodded, "it was. I went to shut it when I was going to try on the dress—Mrs. Randel and Mrs. Harry passed, going down the corridor, just as I was going to close it. Svenson said: 'Nobody's going to see you. Don't shut the door. I like to hear the music.' They were playing the big Victrola downstairs. So I left it open."

"You say Mrs. Randel and Muriel passed by the door together. They were going to Mrs. Harry's room, I suppose?"

"Yes, they were; and it was only a few minutes later—and me there in my slip—when Mrs. Randel and Simpson went past again, going downstairs. Svenson just laughed and said, 'Simpson won't bite you. He's only a tabbycat'; but I was mad then and I did close the door."

"How long after that were you in the room?" I asked.

She wasn't sure; quite a little while.

"I put on my old dress again, and Svenson worked at the new one; and later on we went out to the head of the stairway, watching the folks down in the hall. Pretty soon they all started to come up to bed and I left. I guess it was after one o'clock."

Amelia had given the account without hesitation. I pondered over it during a short silence, staring at the big house beyond the hedge, visible through the kitchen window. A remarkably straight story, I decided. And yet . . .

I turned to the girl.

"Listen, Amelia; you are positively certain you've told me everything? You haven't omitted any little detail?"

No, she declared with a shake of her head, that was all.

"And Svenson was in the room with you all the time? Think well now."

She flushed at my persistence.

"Only the few minutes she was in the bathroom."

"By George!" I exclaimed. "When was that?"

"Just before we went out to the head of the stairs."

"How long was she in the bathroom?"

"Long enough for me to eat the cake I had brought her—maybe five minutes."

"And the door of the bathroom was closed—and locked?"

"It was closed; I don't know if it was locked or not."

"And then she came out, and the two of you went to the head of the stairway?"

Amelia nodded.

"Did she look any different from usual—or act differently? Think well, Amelia."

"No, Mr. Holt; she was like she always is—cool and high-hat."

"Well, Amelia," said I, "you've been a great help to me, and I thank you very much. Now I want you to help some more—just promise that you won't speak of this to anyone else."

She colored with pleasure.

"Oh, I won't tell a soul, Mr. Holt!" she assured me; and I believed her.

Certainly she had given me food for thought, and after she had gone and I had returned to the living room, I closed the desk on my manuscript and sat down with my pipe before the fire to think the thing out.

Jeff's return put an end to my cogitation. I heard him drive up to the back door. Immediately he came in and handed me a large envelope and the box containing the statuette.

"These will be the pictures the doctor man made," he said and waited, curious, I could see, to have a look at them.

However, they were more or less of a disappointment to both of us. I don't know what I had expected, but a look at the twists and whorls depicted in the photographs left me more mystified than ever.

"I don't seem to recognize Mr. Marshall—do you?" I commented.

Jeff merely grinned.

"Of course," I went on, "you might run over and ask him for a sample of his fingerprints to compare with these."

My man's grin broadened.

"And what fingers shall I ask him to print off for us?"

"For choice," said I, "you might make it the thumb and fingers of his right hand."

Jeff laughed outright.

"Sure, sir, on my way down it was some thinking I have been doing; and a pleasant surprise I have for you." He left the room to return in a minute bearing a tray upon which rested a bottle and several glasses. I took a second look and recognized the bottle of Haig & Haig we had had in the evening Marshall had called.

"Well, you lazy Irishman!" I exclaimed. "You never washed those glasses!"

"I did not, then," Jeff admitted. "We being so worked up that night. I just put the tray on the shelf in the pantry, where it has been ever since—it being Scotch, and we preferring the rye."

"And one of those glasses is the one old Marshall used?"

"As ever was, it is, sir," Jeff affirmed delightedly. "And now," he added, "you can do some checking, as you might say."

"Agnew shall have the lot tonight—along with the enlargements and something else I have for him," I said; and thereupon I told Amelia's story and exhibited the little blue bottle and the sheath of the dagger.

It was three o'clock before we sat down to a late lunch. We had finished eating, when the telephone bell rang. I took the call.

It was Jane's voice I recognized with a start of pleasure: "Frank, I am out here at my aunt's. I've been sick. I am still sick, in fact. Sick and worried. I want awfully to see you. Do you think you could come out?"

"Certainly."

"This evening—about eight?"

"Delighted to. How long will it take me to drive out?"

"Oh, about an hour—in that old car"; and she gave me the necessary directions.

"I'll be there," I promised; and she said good-bye.

I went out to the kitchen, where Jeff was cleaning a chicken, bought that morning for our evening meal.

"That was Miss Maxwell," I told him. "She wants to see us. Tonight we go to the East End. We'll start early and stop at Piermont to see Agnew."

The evening papers from the city were delivered late in the afternoon. I scanned them eagerly for news of Colleti. The incident had excited brief notice—merely a few lines reporting the affair as an accident due to a tire blowing out. (The result of that last shot, I told myself.) Colleti, Cosmano, and a third man—name unknown—had been occupants of the car, which had been demolished by collision with a tree. Cosmano was dead. Colleti and the unknown, both seriously injured, were in the Valley Hospital. On the whole, a very satisfactory report. I congratulated myself.

We dined early, the *pièce de résistance* being Jeff's chicken. I say *"pièce de résistance"* advisedly. It was tougher than leather.

"And it was killed this morning," Jeff protested.

"That accounts for its toughness," I told him. "We're eating it too soon—or too late, if you like. Immediately after it had been killed it would have been tender enough, probably. Keeping it six or eight hours this way, the muscles tighten and make it tough. Later on there would be a loosening of the fiber and it would become tender. I have often noticed that when eating game I've shot."

This was news to Jeff. He was much interested.

"You would be wondering sometimes at the funny things in nature," he affirmed sagely. "And, after death, would a person get stiff and limber up again like that?"

"Certainly," I told him. "That is what they call *rigor mortis,*" and at the word I sat up sharply, staring drop-jawed at my man.

Jeff ceased his gnawing at a drumstick to regard me inquiringly.

"And is the word scaring you?"

"The world's champion numskull!" I muttered, pushing away my plate, my appetite gone.

And though he pressed me to know what was the matter, I refused to enlighten him.

"Wait till I've talked to Agnew," was all I would say.

25

"Ordinarily," said Agnew, "I am, I suppose, the least inquisitive of mortals. However, I admit it, I am curious to know what has set you upon this inquiry concerning cadaveric rigidity."

Seated beside him at his big flat-topped desk, I met his rather disconcerting stare.

"All in good time, my dear Doctor," I grinned; and added seriously: "For the present, just answer my questions, like a good fellow; add to my obligation—you have been most obliging and helpful."

"Nonsense!" he scoffed. "It has been all the other way. A nice load you removed from my shoulders when you convinced the police that my escaped patient wasn't a murderer. I'll get the fingerprints for you—and analyze this capsule; glad to."

I thanked him. "Now about this *rigor mortis?"* I suggested.

"Well, what do you want to know?" he asked. "Not that I am an authority on the subject. You already are aware that it is the stiffness of the body after death."

I nodded. "How soon after death?"

He shook his head. "Can't lay down an iron-clad rule—it varies, according to the muscular and fatty tissues of the individual; six or seven hours, sometimes longer, for complete rigidity. The more muscular, the sooner; the more fat, the later."

"A strange condition," I commented. "What causes it, by the way?"

He refused to commit himself. "Probably coagulation of albumin in the muscle. You know that the condition changes later, don't you? Yes; after twenty-four to forty-eight hours it disappears."

"Suppose," I interrupted, "the body bled copiously—would the rigidity occur more quickly?"

Agnew gave me a sharp look.

"What are you getting at? Thinking of the Randel girl, eh? No; hemorrhage would not effect *rigor mortis*—except in this way, possibly: undoubtedly cold hastens the condition, just as heat retards it."

"Let us consider the case of Snowden and Muriel Randel," I said. "Snowden's body, when I found it, showed no indication whatever of the rigidity of death. I lifted the arm; it was perfectly supple. The fingers, I chanced to note, were flexible. On the contrary, the body of the girl was stark and unyielding; the fingers of both hands rigidly clawed. You tell me that cold hastens *rigor mortis* and heat retards it. Also, the more muscular, the sooner; the fatter, the later. Right?"

The doctor gave me a slow nod; and I went on:

"Muriel Randel was, as you know, thin and muscular; the body had been pretty well drained of the warm blood, and exposed—practically uncovered—to the cold air from the open window. Snowden, fat as a pig, was bundled up in a warm room. Now what I want to know is this: taking those conditions into consideration, would it be probable that both had been dead approximately the same length of time?"

Agnew smiled and shook his head.

"No, sir," he declared positively. "If your description of the state of Mrs. Randel's body is correct, you may rest assured that she had been dead five or six hours, maybe longer."

"And Snowden? Not so long?" I asked.

"Positively not. I should say, judging from what you tell me, two or three hours; perhaps less."

We looked at each other, the same thought in the mind of each. Agnew's strange eyes showed a hint of ironic amusement.

I said: "It's damn odd that McClennen didn't bring out all this at the inquiry."

The big man's expression didn't change a jot.

"Of course he would immediately notice these conditions," I declared. "Why—even myself—I can't imagine how I was so stupid!"

Agnew held up his hand.

"Suppose we don't go into that. By the way, did you know that Piermont is a state institution? Yes; you might say mine is a political job."

I suppressed a smile at his demure air.

"I recently heard that our friend McClennen cuts quite a figure in politics," I commented.

Agnew nodded. I had been correctly informed, he averred.

"Well, Doctor," I assured him, "a word to the wise is sufficient"; and I got to my feet and held out my hand. "Good-bye and thanks, I am anxious to learn the result of your comparison of the fingerprints and the analysis of that capsule."

If I would call him in the morning he would let me know, he promised, shaking hands cordially. So I left him.

Our destination proved to be a modest two-story house of gray stone in the Park district. In response to my ring, the door opened and I was confronted by a two-hundred-pound elderly negress, black as the ace of spades. I told her my name. She displayed parallel lines of ivory in a wide smile. Yes, Miss Jane was expecting me and would I please come right on up. I rather looked for the aunt to appear, but there was no sign of anyone save the black maid, and I followed her to a room on the second floor. Entering, my first glance showed Jane in bed—a much subdued Jane, pretty despite the flu.

"Oh, I *am* glad to see you!" she greeted me; the smile I had grown to know so well lighted the attractive face.

"You're hoarse," I said, looking down at her. "What are you trying to do—be sick?"

"I'm a lot better now," she smiled; then, suddenly grave: "Except in my mind."

"What's the matter with your mind?" said I, trying to appear innocent.

Jane didn't answer at once. She hitched herself over in the bed, making room for me, and I sat down.

"It's a wonder you wouldn't have called me sooner," I reproached her.

Her face became inscrutable, and she closed her eyes. After a short silence she looked up at me.

"It's all right," I told her. "Your young man is no longer a prisoner."

"I know," she nodded. "I have talked to Ann every day."

I protested: "You were able to phone Mrs. Randel every day and never gave me a call."

"Now don't pretend that you care," she smiled mockingly. "I'll wager you haven't given me a thought." She came to a sudden stop. Instantly she was serious. I wasn't, she assured me, to suppose that she didn't thoroughly appreciate what I had done; quite the contrary.

"As a matter of fact, Frank," she admitted, "I was ashamed to call you. Then I was so worried I decided to see you and confess everything. I hope you'll believe every word I am going to tell you. It will be terrible if you don't."

I tried to make my smile reassuring.

"Don't let yourself be unhappy about that—and don't, I beg of you, be afraid to confide in me."

She drew a deep breath. "Here goes then: You wouldn't believe that I am a liar and a thief, would you?"

I laid a finger on her lips.

"Quit libeling yourself and tell me everything just as it happened."

"Well, to begin with, Friday afternoon I went to Piermont to see Harry. I had had no word of him for weeks, and I was terribly worried. Oh, you'll think I'm horrible—worrying about the husband of another woman!"

"Sometimes we can't help those things," I told her.

"No, but really," she went on, "it was pity as much as anything else. Remember, we had grown up together. We had been very close to each other always. I was his only friend—it seemed to me. Muriel, the little two-timer, treating him as she did! And Ann never seemed to care for him as a mother should. With her it was always Tom, Tom, Tom, till it would make you sick!"

"Some mothers are like that," I commented. "The complex of maternal affection for the first-born."

"Well, anyhow," Jane went on, "I thought I should let him know there was someone who hadn't forgotten him. It was pitiful, how glad he was to see me. At first he seemed just as he used to be. I suppose it was my fault—I mean the change that came over him. I told him of the house party. Naturally he wanted to know who was to be there. I skipped Campbell's name in my list of guests.

"'Is Snowden one of the crowd?' he asked; and when I had to admit that he was, Harry began to rave. He called Campbell everything you could think of. Then he got on the subject of the pearls."

Again she came to a stop and gave me a questioning look.

"Oh, you don't know about them, do you?"

I shook my head.

"They were a string that Campbell had given Muriel before they were divorced. Of course she had kept them. That made Harry furious. Often they fought about that like cat and dog. He was always at Muriel to return them to Campbell. That was the reason I didn't tell you of my visit to Piermont. I was afraid you would get to know all this, and believe that Harry had killed Campbell because he was jealous of him and his money."

"Half-confidences are never good," I interrupted. "I hope you will remember that in telling the rest of your story."

"I will," she promised contritely; and went on: "When Harry learned that Campbell was to be one of the party, he frightened me, the way he talked. He vowed he would escape from Piermont and—as he expressed it: 'Cram those pearls down the old wretch's throat.' And: 'To think that my wife should be wearing that badge of infamy!' Over and over, he kept repeating those words." At last, to pacify him, I said, 'Harry, if you will promise to be good, I'll see that Muriel never wears those pearls again.' He believed me—you see, he always did trust me. Finally it was agreed that I should go to Muriel's room that night, when she was asleep, and take the pearls. Later on we would send them to Campbell anonymously. He is—was, rather—as penurious as an old miser—except when it came to making a display. He would keep the pearls—they were worth a lot of money—without saying a word to anyone."

"A fine scheme!" I growled, much relieved to hear this daft recital.

"It would have worked perfectly," Jane insisted, "if this other horrible thing hadn't occurred. I waited to go to

Muriel's room till I thought everybody was in bed. I didn't have a bit of trouble—just slipped in to her vanity, where I knew I'd find the pearls, and there they were, and I took them and went back to my room."

"Did you see Muriel in the bed?" I asked, thinking of the condition of things in that quarter at the moment.

"No; I just tiptoed to the vanity, never raising my eyes. You see, I had a little flashlight—one of those like a pencil. It made a tiny spot of light on the floor—and on the vanity, when I came to look for the pearls."

"And now there is no longer a Mr. Snowden to whom to return them, you find yourself embarrassed by their possession. That's your trouble, eh?"

"Oh, I am sick with the worry of them," she cried.

"Where are they?" I gravely inquired.

"Hidden in my bookcase, down at the apartment."

"And you want me to shoulder the responsibility, eh?"

"Oh, if you only would!" she exclaimed.

"Well, if it will make you happy, consider it done. I'll look after the pearls and see that the insurance people hear about it. And perhaps they won't be pleased!"

She was duly grateful and said a lot of nice things, none of which I took too seriously, however. Then I decided to do a good job while I was at it.

"You will be glad to know that before long any possible suspicion of Harry's complicity in the tragedy will be removed. It looks as though he were out of his troubles—homicidal, matrimonial, et cetera."

Considering the importance of my news, she didn't display the expected emotional reaction.

"Oh, I am so glad," she said gravely and was silent for a little; then: "Does that mean the police are soon to arrest the guilty one?"

"Something like that," I replied.

"Do you know who it is?" she asked in an awe-stricken whisper.

I decided to ignore what I had said of half-confidences.

"Look here," said I. "You can help, if you will. Tell me all you know of Mrs. Randel's maid, Olga Svenson."

She looked surprised, but answered without hesitation:

"I know she is a superior sort of lady's maid that Ann brought home from a visit to a sanitarium some years ago. She is absolutely devoted to Ann—a kind of obsession with her, I think. From little things Ann has let slip, I believe Olga was in serious trouble when they first came together, and Ann got her out of it."

"Why," I asked, "would she harbor a resentment against Muriel, a feeling sufficiently strong to be a motive for murder?"

Jane looked at me in wide-eyed horror.

"Olga kill Muriel! Is it she who is suspected?"

"Can you answer my question?" I somewhat tartly demanded.

She shook her head. "I can think of nothing—except, perhaps, she disapproved of Muriel for her actions with Tom. She saw it worried Ann. Anything that made Ann unhappy would be hateful to Olga."

For a long time neither of us spoke. Remembering some of Muriel's hints, I thought I had found the missing pieces of the puzzle.

"That would be it," I muttered to myself.

Jane was quick to take me up.

"Do you believe she did it?" she demanded incredulously.

"It all fits together," I told her. "I thought she had a perfect alibi—being with Amelia all the evening. I have found the weak spot in her story. She had ample opportunity to kill Muriel"; and I proceeded to recount what Amelia had told me.

"So, you see," I finished, "she had merely to pass from the bathroom through the adjoining chamber, cover the short distance down the corridor, enter Muriel's room, draw the sheet over the head of the sleeping girl to avoid the danger of bloodstains, strike the one quick, sure blow, and return to Amelia. All thoroughly within the bounds of probability. We know she had the dagger. Now we have the motive. The deduction is obvious. As a matter of fact, if we are to believe the evidence at our command, she is the only one who could have done it."

Suddenly Jane sat upright in the bed, oblivious of charming disclosures. She gripped my hand like a vise.

"You are wrong!" she cried. "It is a terrible, a horrible mistake! She couldn't have done it!"

Her absolute conviction staggered me.

"A mistake?" said I. "No; I don't think so."

"She couldn't have done it," she repeated and added slowly: "All through the evening the door between my room and the bathroom was locked—bolted, on my side!"

"Just a minute!" I stopped her. "At the police inquiry the Svenson woman stated that you went into Mrs. Randel's room with her and her mistress, and that you immediately went to your own room, passing through the connecting bathroom. I am almost sure you told Olsen the same thing."

Releasing my hand, Jane sank back in the bed and drew up the coverlet.

"I don't know what Olga may have said. I am very sure of what I told your policeman," she contended. "He asked me what I had done after I had left Mrs. Randel. I told him I had gone at once to my room. I didn't mention the bathroom."

"Perhaps not; but Olga did," I insisted.

"Very likely she did," Jane admitted. "I can easily see how she made that mistake. You see it was this way: I didn't want Olga coming into my room, trying my things on, perhaps—a fashion some girls have, you know—so before I went downstairs to dinner I locked the door between my room and the bathroom. To be exact, I bolted it—there was one of those turn-bolt arrangements. When I said good-night to Ann and Olga—in Ann's room, you remember—I *did* go into the bathroom, thinking to pass to my room. You see, I had forgotten bolting the door. When I found it locked I had to go back through Ann's room and out into the hall to enter my room by the other door. Then I unbolted the door to the bathroom and went in for a word with Ann. When I left, of course, I went back through the bathroom. That is probably what Olga was thinking of when she talked to your policeman."

I puzzled over this for a while.

"And you could swear that your door was locked all the evening?" I persisted.

"Oh, Frank!" jane exclaimed irritably. "I could swear it on a stack of Bibles as high as the house!"

"Well, that's that!" I told her, feeling that the ground had been well cut from under my feet. "But never mind," I added. "Your young man won't suffer as a result of the slip-up. His skirts are clean whatever happens. Also, you can trust me in the matter of the pearls."

And, though Jane assured me I had been "wonderful," I left her shortly after that, feeling—if I must confess it—pretty cheap.

26

My interview with Jane had left me uncertain and perplexed. Next morning, as I shaved to the accompaniment of pattering raindrops on the bathroom window, I was still reproaching myself for jumping to conclusions. I even began to doubt that Marshall was the old rascal we had pictured him. After all, perhaps Agnew wouldn't find that his fingerprints checked with those on the statuette.

"You ought to know better—at your time of life, having seen so many good bets go wrong," I told my lather-covered visage, reflected in the mirror.

Back in the bedroom, I stood before the dresser tying my tie. There came the sound of a car outside, and I went to the window in time to see the Buick go round the house toward the back door.

"Now what is that long Irishman up to this morning?" I asked myself.

Before leaving the window I took a look at the big house beyond the hedge. Viewed through sheets of rain blown in diagonal lines by the strong west wind, it appeared lonely and deserted. This was Friday morning, I remembered. Just one week ago today what a different sort of place it had been, alive with bustle and high spirits in prospect of a gay week-end. For the moment, oppressed by melancholy, I turned away.

Jeff grinned cheerfully at me when I went out to the kitchen to say good-morning. He had, he informed me, made an early trip to the station to get all the city papers in hope of learning some news of Colleti.

"I'll be thankful when we have forgotten that name," I told him.

"And I am telling you we are not done with him yet," Jeff prophesied, wagging his head. "Mind you this, sir: alive or dead, he will be heard from again before this business is over."

"Well, let us eat, anyway," I suggested; and I helped him carry our breakfast into the dining room.

We had finished our meal, and I was lighting my pipe when Jeff produced a letter from his pocket and handed it to me.

"Waiting in the box at the post office this morning it was, and me forgetting it entirely," he apologized.

A glance showed a Boston postmark and the typed address in the script lettering of my young niece's portable. I slipped a finger under the flap of the envelope and drew out the single sheet of heavy vellum, folded in two. Opening it, my eye was attracted to a line of red lettering which stood out from the black-typed words. I was familiar with this odd affectation of my young niece, who uses a two-colored ribbon on her machine and switches to the red line when she wishes to add emphasis to her correspondence. On this occasion, however, the quaint mannerism caused me no amusement, for the words which seemed to spring out at me held a sinister import that gave me an odd feeling of impending destiny: *"will have her knife in me!"* I read it again; and I laid down, the letter and thoughtfully lit my pipe. I didn't like the expression. There had been overmuch of knives lately, I told myself, picking up the letter. However, the effusion was casual enough.

"Beloved Avuncular Relative:

"The dress is divinely beautiful, and you are a darling old skeezicks! Of course I shall wear your lovely gift the night of the great event—and won't all the other girls turn green with envy! Every single one of them will have her knife in me! But your little pal can take care of herself. A true daughter of the dear old state of Massachusetts, my motto shall be the same as hers:

"'Ense petit placidam sub libertate quietem!'

"Now, 'fess up! You have forgotten both the motto and necessary Latin to translate it when you see it in the original, haven't you? So I shall be nice, darling, and tell you that it means:

"'We'll have peace, even if we must fight for it!'

"That's not quite it, but you wouldn't know the difference!

"Anyway, thanks for the gorgeous dress; and I'll write and tell you how it all turns out on the big night.

"Yours,

"Fannie"

Casual? Yes. But, somehow, its reading left me strangely perturbed. I laid the innocent cause of my disquiet upon the table, and pipe in mouth and hands thrust in my pockets I tipped back my chair and sat with eyes fixed on the words which, doubly pregnant with meaning in their significant coloring, seemed to carry a hidden message for me.

Jeff sat at the other side of the table, busy scanning the columns of the morning papers. He continued his search for news of Colleti. His silence told me that he looked in vain. Again I read Fannie's letter from the beginning. I noted what the minx had to say about my forgotten Latin. I grinned to myself. She was right, I admitted. Certainly she was correct in her assumption that I didn't know the motto of my native state. I doubted that I had ever known it. As to the Latin—well, let's see; and my attention centered upon the words of the motto.

"'*Placidam sub libertate quietem,*'" I read, muttering. I believed I could manage that. "'Peace and quiet under liberty,' or something like it. '*Ense petit* . . .'"

Puzzled, I raised my eyes from the type words, looking for inspiration.

The windows of the dining room rattled in the rising storm. From where I sat I could see the bare, wind-tossed branches of the sycamores which bordered the hedge, and beyond them, over the wide lawn, the big house looming mistily through the rain. I thought of the disturbing influence which recently had been removed from that quarter. They were free of her now—the entire lot of them. "Peace and quiet under liberty," thought I.

My glance returned to the letter. The red line stood out clearly: "will have her knife in me!" I shook my head.

"A propos, by God!" I muttered, struck by the gruesome parallel.

Once more my attention centered upon the first two words of the Latin tag. "*Ense petit* . . ." It had me stumped.

"And devil a word can I find about him at all," Jeff suddenly declared and threw down the paper.

The thread of my thoughts broken, I reached for the letter and pocketed it.

"I'm going to call Agnew," I said, getting to my feet

Two minutes later I was listening to the big man's voice.

"Plenty of fingerprints this morning," he informed me. "I expect I've got yours, and your man's, too; so both of you had better watch your step. One thing sure—I have the mates of the ones I found on your little image. Yes, sir! Beauties!"

"I looked for that," I returned, in nowise surprised.

So that settled the old sharpshooter, I told myself.

"How about the capsule?" I asked.

"Hyoscine; a nerve depressant and mydriatic alkaloid," I was told; and there followed a technical account of the formula of this particular preparation, all of which was so much Greek to me.

"Hold on," I at length interrupted. "What I want to know is how the damn stuff works—what it is used for."

"It is used to produce sleep," replied Agnew; and he went on: "You see, hyoscine is usually given hypodermically—especially in cases of mania or delirium; it's fine for the D.T.'s, by the way. And you've heard of twilight sleep, haven't you. Well, it's produced by hyoscine given together with morphine. But that wouldn't interest you"; and he came to a pause, chuckling to himself.

"No," I agreed, "it wouldn't. What I want to know is: if the average adult should swallow one of those capsules, how soon would it begin to work on him, how would he look, and what would be the general effect?"

That, in a great measure, would depend upon the individual, I was told; and Agnew continued:

"This preparation of yours is rather an unusual one. I should say that, after taking one, the average adult—as you put it—first would become active and excited, though he might complain of dizziness. Shortly, however, in fifteen or twenty minutes perhaps, he would feel tired and drowsy. He would become less active, less talkative, and would soon fall asleep. When he awoke he might not remember having seen certain objects or having had pain. There being less action of the sensory area of the brain, fewer sensory impressions would be received; consciousness would therefore be lessened and sleep would be produced."

He was becoming technical again.

"Just a minute," I once more interrupted. "What would the party look like?"

There was silence for a moment; then;

"Now I wonder what the hell you've got up your sleeve! Look like? Well, the pupils of his eyes would be dilated; and you might notice that his speech had become difficult and indistinct. His pulse and his breathing would be slow—though, as far as looks are concerned, you probably wouldn't be able to determine that." He paused for a moment and added: "Have I told you what you wanted to know?"

Had he, indeed!

There was a short silence; then Agnew's voice again: "Hello, Holt! Are you there?"

"Right here," I assured him.

"I asked if all this is any good. Does it tell you what you wanted to know?"

"Yes; I have learned much," I replied, "And here is something else I want to ask you: do you know what *'ense petit'* means?"

This time he was the surprised one.

"Do I know—*which?"* he inquired, after a pause.

"'Ense petit,'" I told him. "Latin, you know. Can you translate it?"

"My God!" he groaned. "You *do* ask the most fascinating questions! What was it again?—spell it."

I did so and was told to hold the line.

After a lengthy wait there came Agnew's voice again. "I must say, Holt, this is damn peculiar. What are you trying to do—preserve a record of the Randel affair in the dead languages?"

"What has the Randel affair got to do with it?" I asked.

"Well," returned Agnew, "I chance to have a Latin dictionary handy, and I should say that a broad translation of your phrase would be: 'an attack with a dagger'; *'ensis'* being poetic Latin for 'a sword, or dagger'; and *'petitio'* signifying 'an attack.' To me that savors strongly of the matter under your consideration."

"It does sound suspicious, doesn't it?" I admitted; and, disregarding his protests, I said good-bye.

Then I did what I might have done in the first place: looked for the motto of the state of Massachusetts in the judge's encyclopedia. Both Agnew's translation and my own had indeed been broad enough. But if ours had been liberal versions, nevertheless, they were equaled in their significance by the nicety of strict interpretation, for the words I read were these:

"With the sword she seeks quiet peace under liberty."

"A strange coincidence!" I marveled, considering this recondite presentment in connection with Agnew's report in the matter of the capsules; and thoughtfully I replaced the book upon the shelf. Then, having arrived at a sudden determination, I secured from the desk drawer the several articles collected in the course of my investigation—the little blue bottle, the statuette, and the sheath of the dagger. With these in hand I returned to the dining room, where I placed my exhibits upon the table and covered them with a napkin. Out in the kitchen I found my man washing the breakfast dishes.

"Listen," I told him. "Something is due to break, and here is where you do your bit. Go next door and get hold of that butler, Simpson. Fetch him over here."

Jeff looked surprised. "And supposing the laddie-buck objects?"

I wasn't sticking at trifles.

"Fetch him, nevertheless. Furthermore, see to it he talks to no one before he comes."

Jeff slipped into his raincoat. Through the window I watched him cross the lawn, his head bowed to the driving rain, to disappear at the rear of the big house. In a surprisingly short time he reappeared, accompanied by a stocky figure swathed in a yellow oilskin. I recognized Simpson, his short legs doing their best to match Jeff's long stride.

"Yes, sir, Mr. Holt; good-morning, sir," the little Englishman greeted me, coming into the dining room, where I sat with my pipe. He had left his oilskin in the kitchen and appeared impeccably attired in his sleeved vest and striped trousers. His face wore a look at once apprehensive and expectant.

I motioned toward a chair. "Sit down," I told him gruffly.

He took the chair, looking more scared than ever.

"Simpson," I proceeded, "I regret to tell you that you are in an exceedingly difficult position."

I paused to allow this to sink in, the little Englishman staring at me in horrified amazement.

"Difficult position!" he gasped. "Oh, don't say that, sir!"

"Difficult position, indeed," I repeated, with a wag of my head. "I have every reason to believe that you withheld important evidence in your interview with the police."

Simpson started from his chair, his hand uplifted.

"As God is my judge, sir, I told the truth!" he protested.

"Yes," said I, with a sly nod, "but not all the truth, Simpson!"

In pop-eyed dismay he continued to stare at me.

"If I omitted telling anything, it was because I was not asked, sir," he stammered at length.

I had to agree with him there. The questioning had been superficial. I suddenly assumed an air of benign tolerance.

"Very true, my man; I have considered that point. However"—with a quick return of magisterial ferocity—"I want the entire truth now—unless you want me to turn you over to the police as an accessory to murder."

The wretched man fairly writhed in his chair.

"You may depend on it, sir. I shall tell you all I know."

"That may prove to be your salvation," I admitted doubtfully. "And remember this"—I wagged an impressive finger at him—"I already know a great deal. I shall ask you questions the answers to which I have unearthed in my investigations. If I catch you tripping, it will be too bad for you."

Once more he protested his willingness to reply truthfully, and considering him sufficiently disciplined for interrogation, I went on:

"First of all, I am aware that you knew Harry Randel was an inmate of Piermont, though it was generally believed that he was absent on a protracted business trip. Now I want you to recall what happened the night he was taken away—the night when he, his wife, and his brother had the scene which led to his removal. Was Mrs. Randel, senior, present on that occasion?"

The answer was prompt:

"She was indeed, sir; and very miserable the poor dear lady was as a result."

I asked how she had manifested her feelings. The recollection caused Simpson to shake his head mournfully.

"Indeed, sir, she fainted when they took Mr. Harry out to the ambulance; and recovering her senses, she bitterly reproached both Mr. Tom and young Mrs. Randel for their behavior. She was particularly bitter in her remarks to Mrs. Harry. I couldn't avoid overhearing that. You see, fortunately, all the other servants were absent that evening—there was only Olga and myself, and conditions were such that it was necessary for both of us to be in the room at the time."

"You tell me that Mrs. Randel seemed most to resent the part played by her daughter-in-law. Can you recall what she said?"

Poor Simpson fought hard against a lifetime training in suppression. Finally, however, fear conquered loyalty.

"My mistress was distracted—unaccountable for her words. She did, I remember, revile Mrs. Harry for being—as she expressed it—'an unnatural wanton'; adding: 'Not content with ruining Harry, body and soul, and shaming us by your conduct with my brother, you spread your net for Tom.' And when Mr. Marshall protested, and Mrs. Harry merely laughed and made some light remark, my mistress cried bitterly and said God would not allow such things to be. I wish I could have forgotten it. It was most distressing, sir."

The man's feeling was so evidently genuine I pitied him.

"All right, Simpson," said I. "Now how were things later on—any further mention of the occurrence?"

The little chap made an effort at self-control.

"Not a word, sir; and quite remarkable, too, if I may say so. Next day—and thereafter—everything was pleasant as a May morning. I told Olga later: 'After all, we of the lower classes have the deeper feelings. Fancy being able to forget so easily!' But Olga merely laughed and said I should not judge others by myself."

I grinned, picturing the exchange. Olga—and the "lower classes"!

"Now, Simpson, before we leave this unpleasant phase of the subject, I must ask you if you ever observed anything unusual in the relation between young Mrs. Randel and Mr. Marshall."

The query brought a look of doubt to the honest face.

"A puzzling question, sir; and—if I might make so bold—one I have often asked myself. I have fancied that Mr. Marshall—well, entertained a sentiment toward Mrs. Harry—if you understand what I mean, sir; and that she took advantage of the situation, so to speak, to get money from the old gentleman. She did get money from him—I know that. Once I overheard him complaining to her of her extravagance. He was, if I may say so, bitter."

I uncovered the sheath, the statuette, and the little blue bottle. If I had expected that the sight of them would produce any effect upon Simpson I was doomed to disappointment. He looked at them with interest, nothing more.

"Ever see any of these before?" I asked.

He shook his head. The eyes he turned on me were honest.

"Never, sir," he denied flatly; and I believed him.

I covered the exhibits and resumed my inquiry.

"You always got your liquor from Colleti, didn't you?"

At the mention of the bootlegger, Simpson showed surprise; also—perhaps it was imagination—I thought he looked relieved at the shift in the topic of conversation.

"Always, sir," he replied. "And very good liquor it was," he added appreciatively.

"On the day of the dinner party Colleti delivered an order of wine over at your house," I reminded him. "He delivered it about noon. Now you go on from there; tell me every detail. Remember what depends on your sticking to the exact truth."

My grim manner made the butler sit up sharply.

"Yes, sir; quite so. I recall the incident perfectly. It was this way, sir: On Friday morning Mrs. Randel and I talked of the menu for the dinner. She suggested champagne with the entree, and I told her our supply of champagne was practically exhausted. I recall her words: 'Fortunate you mentioned that, Simpson. I must call Mr. Colleti at once.' Immediately she went to the telephone, and I heard her place the order. She returned to me and said: 'I caught him just in time. He was about to leave with some liquor to be delivered at Mr. Snowden's.' Then we resumed our discussion of the menu.

"About twelve o'clock Colleti drove up to the back door. Mrs. Randel and I left the dining room and went to meet him. We carried the wine into the basement, and I left Colleti and Mrs. Randel there while I went to give Amelia some orders about the silver. When I returned to the cellar, Colleti had unpacked the wine and was arranging it in the bin. Mrs. Randel stood at the side, watching him, the two of them conversing."

"Stop right there!" I interrupted. "Had Colleti removed his overcoat?"

The butler gave me a startled glance.

"Why, yes, sir; and his under coat also. They were hanging from a hook on the wall. He finished with the wine almost at once and then resumed the garments. I recall that, distinctly. Then I accompanied him out to his car. We talked for a little before he drove away."

"Anybody else present during all this?" I asked.

Simpson gave a decided shake of the head.

"No, sir; no one, sir. I am positive of that."

"Where was Olga—and young Mrs. Randel—all this time?"

"I can tell you that, too, sir," Simpson eagerly averred. "Olga was upstairs, making some alterations in the arrangement of Miss Donnay's room. Mr. Tom, Mrs. Harry, and Miss Donnay had driven up to the city."

I gave him a searching glance.

"You are certain that no person but yourself and Mrs. Randel was in Colleti's company—not even Amelia, nor the cook, nor the chauffeur?"

"Absolutely certain, sir. No one saw Colleti but Mrs. Randel and me."

So that was that, I told myself.

"Now," said I, "we will pass to the time you and Amelia went upstairs together about midnight Go from there—and skip no detail."

Simpson showed no concern.

"There was nothing to that, sir; I gave a full account if you remember, at the police inquiry."

"Just repeat it," I told him.

"Very good, sir. As I said, Amelia and I went up together—she taking a tea tray to Mrs. Randel's room for Olga, I having a tray on which were a glass of Ovaltine and several of the Swedish crackers Mr. Marshall is in the habit of taking at bedtime. Of course, with the refreshments and the drinking downstairs he wouldn't be likely to take them, but that was the custom, and I adhered to it.

"As I stated at the inquiry, I left the tray on the bedside table in Mr. Marshall's room and started to return below stairs.

"As I came down from the mezzanine I saw my mistress standing at the door of Mrs. Harry's room—I think she was just coming out, as a matter of fact. At any rate, she looked up and saw me. She smiled at me and, turning, spoke to Mrs. Harry."

"What did she say?" I demanded, though I remembered what he had told at the inquiry.

Without hesitation Simpson answered: "She said, 'Here is Simpson, come to take me back to my guests.'"

"Was there any reply? Think carefully."

"Yes, there was, sir. For I recall Mrs. Randel's rejoinder. She laughed at what Mrs. Harry had said, and: 'Oh, absolutely,' she remarked. Then she said: 'Sweet dreams, dear' and closed the door. I had come down by that time. I accompanied my mistress up the corridor and we descended the stairs together. You remember, sir; you were standing there, waiting to say good-night."

"Did you actually hear Mrs. Harry's voice in the short conversation you report? Think well."

Simpson became frowningly thoughtful.

"No, sir," at length he replied slowly. "When I come to think of it, I don't believe I did." He paused, considering the point. "No, sir," he declared, with a shake of the head. "I am sure I did not."

"And yet the stairway from the mezzanine is practically opposite to the door of the room Mrs. Harry occupied. Think a minute. You must have heard her reply."

But Simpson wasn't to be shaken. He was honestly telling his story and sticking to it.

"No, sir. The more I think of it, the more certain I am. I heard no reply to the remarks addressed by my mistress to Mrs. Harry."

I got to my feet.

"All right, Simpson; that will be all. You can go now; and I don't think you need worry."

The butler gave me a look at once grateful and appealing.

"I hope it will all come out right in the end, sir. As for my unfortunate part, I only did what I thought was my duty."

"I believe that, thoroughly," I told him, with a hearty clap on his fat shoulder; and Jeff and I shepherded him out to the back porch. He wrapped his yellow waterproof about him and, with his formal little bow, stepped out in the rain.

Looking after him as he traversed the path, my glance lifted to the big house beyond the hedge. There was a familiar coupé drawn up at the back door. Standing motionless at its side, observing us with inquisitive intentness, was Dr. McClennen.

27

At once the big man turned and went into the house.

"I'd give a dollar to know what's in your mind, old boy," I thought, watching him disappear.

Suddenly it occurred to me that much which had seemed strange in McClennen's attitude throughout the affair was made clear in the light of my recently acquired knowledge. Following this line of thought, I was convinced that Simpson would immediately pass through a rigorous third degree concerning his visit with me. McClennen would learn that I had the statuette, the sheath of the dagger, the little blue bottle. He would hear an account of my interrogation, and, by the significance of the questions, he would know that, at least, I was perilously near the truth. Already I had dissipated the smoke screen laid down by him in foisting Harry Randel upon the police as a logical suspect. Was that the only failure for which he had to thank me? At the thought I shrugged dubiously. Since I had learned of McClennen's connection with the Cambridge Arms I little doubted—Kitty's assurance notwithstanding—that a deeper influence than Colleti's rancorous fear had been responsible for our attempted abduction and the subsequent kidnaping of Jeff. If, indeed, McClennen were behind all this, under the shadow of a new and greater danger of exposure—for so it would appear to him—to what devices might he resort?

These thoughts passed rapidly through my mind as we stood watching the yellow-clad figure of Simpson bob along the path through the gusts of rain to vanish at the rear of the Randel house.

Jeff closed the door and turned expectant eyes upon me. He was, I saw, puzzled by my procedure with Simpson and eager to know what the interview foreshadowed. I was in no mood to satisfy his curiosity. Indeed, having at last learned the truth, I was more than willing to forget the distressing affair. Certainly, I told myself, I should take no further action in the matter. However, there remained one last duty for me to perform.

I had Jeff get the car, and, through a miniature cloudburst, we drove down to the village. We were a quiet pair; I deep in conjecture as to the final outcome of the tragic business, Jeff curious but, seeing me silently thoughtful, too considerate to ask questions. Arriving at Jane's shop, I found that I was expected. The little helper greeted me with a smile.

"After your book, are you?" was her pert salutation.

"Evidently you have talked to Miss Maxwell this morning," I countered.

"Go right on up and make yourself at home," she nodded and handed me the key.

Once more I stood before the bookcase in the tiny living room; and when I had removed the volume of Shakespeare I retrieved the valuable little bundle from behind the *Decameron*. Also I took a book at random; and so downstairs to return the key to Miss Pert.

Presently we were back home, Jeff to resume his interrupted dishwashing, and I to my writing, trying, unsuccessfully for a time, to forget the shocking revelation of the morning. At length, however, I did succeed in losing myself in the recollections of far-distant scenes, and when Jeff called me to lunch I ignored the summons. Absorbed in my pleasant task, I continued to write, and it was late afternoon when I finally laid down my pen. For a while, during my work, I had been aware of Jeff's presence in the room. He had come in quietly, considerate as always, had taken a book from the case, and for some time had continued its perusal; then tiptoed out as silently as he had entered. As the judge's books would make heavy reading for Jeff, this oddity of interest occurred to me as I got to my feet, stretching muscles stiffened by long sitting. Suddenly alive to the fact that I was hungry, and also could do with a drink, I went out to the kitchen. There was a pleasant smell of frying. Jeff was hashing potatoes in a skillet—to the whistled melody of "Come Back to Erin," sweet as the song of a meadow lark.

"What's for dinner, Irishman?" I asked him.

He stopped his whistling to grin at me.

"Hashed-brown potatoes there are, and fried chicken—a fine and tender young rooster, this one; and him not dying of *rigor mortis* at all; and you will be liking the waffles that will be along with him."

"Jeff," said I, calmly, "you are a treasure! I think a little Overholt is clearly indicated—pronto!"

Notwithstanding my afternoon of industry and Jeff's good dinner, as the evening advanced I found myself more and more inclined to brooding melancholy, the horror of my discovery lying heavy on my mind, I had, I decided, come to hate this place where I had expected to find quiet and studious seclusion.

We sat by the living-room fire, I with my pipe and a volume of Macaulay's essays, the whisky and a siphon at my elbow, Jeff, at the other side of the hearth, deep in the evening papers. For two hours neither of us said a word. Not since our return to the house at noon had there been an allusion to the subject uppermost in the mind of each.

At length, the clock striking ten, Jeff laid down his paper.

"I think it is hitting the hay I am," he yawned, stretching his long arms; and he rose to knock out his pipe on the andiron.

I looked up from my book and caught his eye, knowing well what was in his mind as he stood smiling down at me, fiddling with the pipe in his hands. A last smoke and a bit of a gab, with an accompanying nightcap, was a custom dear to both of us. Nothing loath, I laid aside Macaulay.

"Sit you down," I said, reaching for the bottle. "Sit you down and load your pipe."

With a pleased grin he reseated himself and took the glass I had filled for him.

"Sure it is a hole you have made in that quart," he commented, replacing the emptied glass upon the tray and eyeing the lowered level within the bottle. "Drunk, you will be getting."

"Nothing like it," I indignantly denied. "There are times when I find a little good whisky an aid to thought; likewise—since it can work either way—it helps me forget, when to remember is to became the prey of melancholy." Then, serious once more and arrived at a sudden decision: "Jeff, I'm sick of this place. Let's move on. What do you say?"

In the act of setting a match to the bowl of his pipe Jeff paused, his hand poised, his quickly raised glance directed upon me. Then he lowered his eyes and lit his pipe in deliberate puffs.

"Sick of the place, is it?" He tossed the match into the fire and sank back in his chair to observe me thoughtfully, conning my abrupt proposal.

"Yes; sick of the place," I repeated. "I can't look forward with any pleasure to a winter spent here. The result of first impressions, no doubt—we getting off on the wrong foot, so to speak."

Jeff continued to stare dubiously. "Would you be leaving Colleti to get away with the murdering and all? Sure, sir, if I may make so bold, is it yourself would be doing the like of that?"

The mention of Colleti's name was to me like a red flag to a bull.

"Damn Colleti!" I stormed petulantly. "He had nothing to do with it. Get that now! Colleti had nothing to do with it!"

My man looked both surprised and hurt.

"Have it your own way, sir," he returned gently.

"Here's the point, Jeff," I went on, with less heat, somewhat ashamed of my outburst. "We have done what we agreed to do—given Miss Maxwell her young man. As far as you and I are concerned, the case is finished. We'll forget it."

Reassured by my return to normality, Jeff's good nature asserted itself.

"Why, then, fine it will be suiting me to be moving—and me born with the itching foot."

"Good!" I exclaimed and rose to go up to bed. "We'll pull out of here tomorrow."

It spoke well for Jeff's discipline that he asked no question as to our destination. However, I had the place in mind. Later, as I lay waiting for sleep to overtake me, in fancy I saw again a long stretch of white beach upon which the surf frothed, the wide rollers beyond sweeping in, wild horses tossing their manes in the salt breeze. I fell asleep undecided whether I would see Jane before we left.

And next morning as I stood before the bathroom mirror, drawing the razor down my lathered cheeks, I propounded the same question to the middle-aged face in the glass. Now, with the clarity of perception which comes with the first hour of the new day, I arrived at a definite and wise conclusion.

It had turned colder in the night. The morning was dismally overcast, and I went downstairs in no very happy frame of mind. A good log fire was blazing on the hearth in the dining room, and Jeff, coming in from the kitchen, gave me a cheery "Good-morning" as I took my place at the table. He was, I saw, all agog at the prospect of new scenes.

"I left out a note for the milk man telling him it is leaving we are," he said, placing the cereal and a jug of cream before me.

"And there's your chance to stop the papers," I told him, a glance through the window showing me the newsboy, mounted on his bicycle, coming down the lane.

Jeff was absent for some time. I was starting on the bacon and eggs when he reentered, his eyes, big with astonishment, fixed upon the open paper in his hands. At once I knew from the look of him that something had happened.

"Now what's wrong?" I asked.

Being much interested in what he read, he didn't answer immediately. Then he raised his eyes to regard me with a look that held a certain triumph.

"There now! And what was I all the time telling you!" he exulted and handed the paper to me, his finger indicating a headline. I read: "Killer Admits Guilt; Confession of Underworld Character Clears Mystery of Recent Murders."

I looked up to find Jeff, goggle-eyed with excitement, grinning at me. Without comment I sat back in my chair to read what followed the headlines:

> "A police investigation which for the past week has been conducted to apprehend the person

> or persons responsible for the killing of Mrs. Harry Randel and Campbell Snowden, both socially prominent in the Glen Athol valley, was unexpectedly terminated early today by the confession of Augustus Colleti, a notorious underworld character who for the past two years has frequented the locality.
>
> "Colleti, an inmate of the Valley Hospital as the result of an automobile accident, admits that early on the morning of Saturday, October 24, he entered the Randel home for the purpose of robbery, his object being a valuable pearl necklace, the property of Mrs. Harry Randel.
>
> "According to the man's confession, Mrs. Randel was killed to prevent her sounding an alarm when the unfortunate woman was wakened by the intruder.
>
> "Mr. Snowden, a house guest, disturbed by Colleti's movements, surprised the murderer when he went to investigate. Seeking to escape the attack directed upon him, Mr. Snowden sought refuge in an adjoining room, where he was followed by Colleti and silenced by blows of a blackjack, the killer then making a successful getaway.
>
> "It was stated at the hospital today that, owing to Colleti's condition, no further details of the affair were available at present."

I laid down the paper and resumed my interrupted breakfast.

"And was I not right, now?" Jeff crowed, sitting down opposite to me.

I ignored the challenge.

"Did I tell you," said I, helping myself to another egg, "that where we are going we shall get some excellent wild-fowl shooting? I hope you have kept my Parker in good condition."

"Wild-fowl shooting, is it!" hooted Jeff. "Would yourself be thinking of that, with news the like of this coming?"

"They are mostly black ducks," I went on, unheeding him. "Some few mallards, and an occasional canvasback."

My man persisted, careless of my hint.

"Sure it was that chicken we had the other day that got you fooled—him with the *rigor mortis,* as you call it," he chuckled knowingly. "*Rigor mortis!* Yesterday afternoon it was—and you at your writing, and the two of us in the room beyond—I was reading about it in one of the big encyclopedia books in the case. A tricky thing it is, by all accounts—and you being so sure how long the two of them over there had been dead when found. Why, sir, the big book will tell you a person could be having this *rigor mortis* in a minute, as you might say."

"Hard on the person," I laughed. "Tough—literally."

"Oh, you may laugh, sir; but so it says; and me minding the exact words, which are these: 'After electrical shock *rigor mortis* occurs instantaneously.' Tricky, I would be calling it."

I was tempted to remind Jeff that the unfortunate couple had departed this life by other than an electric route, but forbore, well satisfied to have him persuaded as he was. Also, I was minded to have done with the subject for good and all.

"Last night we agreed to forget the case; and that goes, Jeff, in spite of this 'news'—as you call it," I declared, getting to my feet. "And now," I added, "I am going to call the Pennsylvania station."

The operator at the Glen Athol exchange had difficulty in getting my call through to the city. It was some fifteen or twenty minutes before I had secured reservation for a drawing room on the Sea Gull Express, the crack night train for the shore. I would, I was told, be required to call for the tickets before three o'clock, which meant an extra trip to the city for either Jeff or me. During this colloquy I had heard a car drive up and stop at the front of the house; there had been a ring at the bell, and Jeff had admitted a caller whose deep bass betrayed McClennen as our early visitor. Now, as I hung up and turned from the instrument, Jeff was at my elbow.

"The doctor man is wanting to see you," he whispered.

I nodded and started for the living room.

28

"Have you seen this?" was McClennen's greeting.

He extended the morning paper, his finger on the Colleti scare head, his keen eyes surveying me intently over the top of his spectacles.

"Why, yes," said I. "My man just called my attention to it. Interesting; very."

"Humph; yes; interesting indeed," he growled. "O'Brien thinks so, at any rate. He telephoned me this morning. Asked me to see you. It seems Colleti's confession develops a phase of the routine end of the affair which makes it desirable that we have a conference. Come along; we'll go up together."

Recollection of the tickets popped into my head.

"Well," said I, "that fits in very nicely. Thanks; yes," and I excused myself to give Jeff directions as to our baggage.

And so it was, some five minutes later, at about 9:30 on the morning of that blustery last day of October, I found myself a passenger with McClennen in his Cadillac, little suspecting that I was setting out upon my most hazardous experience of that memorable week.

Proceeding cityward along the highway, we had covered perhaps half the distance to Piermont. Suddenly my companion checked the speed of the car. On our right, viewed across some half-mile of meadowland, was the broad and yellow Ohio; on our left the road was bordered by a high palisade of cliffs, broken at this point by a narrow canyon-like valley into which disappeared a macadam-surfaced byroad.

"Ever been up here?" McClennen asked, and not waiting for my reply he shifted his gears and gave the big car the gas, swinging its bonnet between the overhanging sides of the gully.

"We make a right turn, a bit farther on, taking the hilltop road," McClennen explained as we entered the ravine to follow a track which, though of good surface and seemingly well traveled, was scarcely wide enough for two cars to pass abreast. "You like variety; getting off the beaten track will appeal to you," he added.

"And our appointment with O'Brien?" I suggested.

"Oh, plenty of time for that," he laughed and swung the Cadillac round an abrupt curve to meet a rapidly increasing gradient.

For the next mile or so we continued to climb a road which had been blasted from the rocky side of the hill; then to come out on a long stretch of plateau across which lay the narrow ribbon of macadam, paralleling the river and the highway far below. Up here, out of the mists which hung over the lowlands, the air was brighter; a faint sunshine showed in occasional breaks in the rack of gray clouds, and a sturdy wind from the north whistled in the open crack of the window at McClennen's side. Climbing the stiff grade, the car had smoked a trifle, and, thinking we should be the better for some fresh air, I made an attempt to lower the window beside me. It resisted my efforts. I glanced at McClennen. If he had noted my action he gave no sign. Now, upon the level road which lay deserted before us, he accelerated our pace and sat motionless, his gaze directed ahead, a look of cynical amusement on his swarthy face. In the gray light the Mephistophelian profile appeared more satanic than ever. Reacting to my glance, he turned to me.

"There is a spot beyond here a little way that may interest you," he said, with gravity which might have been real or assumed; and, I remaining silent, he went on: "'The Lovers' Leap.' Hasn't Jane acquainted you with its sinister history? It's her best story."

No, I told him, I had never heard of the place.

"An oversight," McClennen declared. "It is the scene dear to the morbid imagination of the local thrill lover. Quite romantic. We'll stop and have a look at it."

Five minutes later my companion brought the car to a momentary halt. Here the road curved to the left, away from the edge of the plateau, which, after continuing its direction for several hundred yards, also swung north, following a bend of the valley. Across the elbow thus formed ran an ill-defined path, winding through high dead grass and scattered bushes to disappear in a fringe of scrub oak. Over the uneven surface of this trail we now proceeded at a pace in keeping with the rough going, passing through the outlying coppice, at length to find ourselves fairly on the edge of the cliff, with a fine view of the valley and the river and the hills beyond.

It was, I at once decided, a ticklish position. Immediately before us the ground sloped alarmingly, a checkerboard of brown turf and loose gray shale. We had made the quick stop demanded by the situation not a minute too soon. McClennen's right foot descended heavily upon the service brake, where it remained to hold the car on the incline. Surprised by his failure to apply the emergency brake, I instinctively reached for it and gave a pull at the handle. It came back loose and unresisting. I caught McClennen's quick sidewise glance.

"It's out of commission," he growled. "Don't worry—the foot brake will hold us all right"; and he shut off the engine and rested back in his corner to regard me with eyes which showed hard and bright behind the lenses of his spectacles.

However, when he addressed me it was in a voice which carried a tone of gentle sadness strangely at variance with both his aspect and the conception which I had formed of his apparent sardonic personality.

"And now, my dear Holt, the time has come to speak of many things!" he said, and he stirred uneasily, releasing by his movement the pressure on the foot pedal so that the car slid forward a few inches to be instantly checked once more.

Half ashamed of my caution, I shifted my position to send a secretly exploring hand rearward to the handle of the door. Finding it, I discovered also that it no longer performed its appointed function. Round and round under my groping fingers it turned, useless. Suddenly it occurred to me that I had allowed myself to be nicely taken in. Here I was, practically a prisoner, ambushed in the scrub oak which screened us from the road, in a lonely spot well adapted to an act of violence, with a strong probability of willing hands to perform the deed.

I resumed my former position, with a half-formed idea of sticking my gun in the doctor's ribs and holding him hostage for my safe delivery, when he spoke.

"A sad business," he said, and all the irony had left the deep voice, leaving it strangely pensive. "However, time enough for that later. First let me fulfill my duty as cicerone. I was to show you the locally famous—'notorious' is the better word—the notorious 'Lovers' Leap.' Well, here we are. What do you think of it?"

"Assignation or assassination—equally well suited to either," I retorted, edging away from him so I might easily reach the pistol under my left arm. At once it was plain he understood my action. He smiled at me and shook his head. The car moved forward a couple of feet and stopped with a quick jerk. I began to realize there was something behind all this that I wasn't getting at all.

"I don't think much of the local taste for scenery," I added, merely to say something.

McClennen shrugged.

> "'*The very place puts toys of desperation,*
> *Without more motive, into every brain—*'"

he quoted grimly; then, with one of his ironic smiles and a nod toward the near-by brink of the precipice: "And if you'd cast an eye over the edge yonder, you would see an abandoned gravel pit, a matter of a hundred feet or so below you, and possibly an acre in extent, full of spring water—a good forty feet of it. From its depths they dredged the car containing the two misguided young persons from whose tragic end this spot derives its title. They went over the cliffs one moonlight night, about five years ago, with the notion that by so doing they would square a sordid triangle. A mistaken idea, of course, but a damned conclusive action."

He had kept his eyes fixed upon my face during this recital; now, coming to a pause, he shifted his gaze to stare straight ahead. As he slightly altered his position, again the car slid smoothly forward a few inches, seemed to hesitate, and became stationary.

I didn't like it. I didn't like it at all. And yet, for the life of me, I didn't know what to do.

"Better watch that foot," I said, trying to make my voice unconcerned. "If you're not careful, you know, you'll have us looping the loop."

McClennen turned on me quickly; his eyes were bright behind his glasses, and his teeth showed in a wide, mirthless grin.

"Not unless you are asking for it, Mr. Holt. As a matter of fact, it is up to you."

"Up to me?" I said, taken quite unawares.

"Up to you," he repeated fiercely. "I hold the lives of both of us in the hollow of my hand"—his big body shook in sudden ironic laughter. "'In the hollow of my foot' would be more nearly anatomically accurate. Let me once release this brake, and we'll be off at the deep end before you can stop us,"

I camouflaged my uneasiness with a laugh which I flattered myself sounded as genuine as his own reckless jocundity.

"Fancy that now!" I exclaimed. "I in the role of *deus ex machina!* Literally so!"

"The time for pretense between us has past," he said. With the words he turned on me savagely. For the moment our eyes held. I nodded, and he went on: "Of course you are perfectly aware that Colleti's confession is fiction. By the way, it may interest you to know that Colleti died at five o'clock this morning. Colleti, Cosmano, Larry—you, yourself, have some ability as a murderer, Mr. Holt!"

That was nonsense; I had merely defended myself. "Self-preservation is nature's first law," I reminded him.

He was quick to take advantage of the expression.

"You believe that, do you?" he demanded. "That, to preserve one's life, it is ethical to take the life of another?"

"It is a right recognized by the laws of every land, at least," I contended.

He shrugged. "There are rights which supersede man-made laws. And we may find dearer things in existence than mere life—honor, good name, the happiness and welfare of those dear to us; you agree with me, do you not?"

"No doubt," I acquiesced somewhat dryly, seeing where his logic was leading me.

"Why, then," said he, "by your admission you justify my sending both of us over the brink yonder; for I am fighting for the honor and happiness of one who is dearer than life to me."

"And that is why you have tricked me here with your trumped-up story of an appointment with O'Brien, is it?" I demanded.

"No," he replied and glanced at the watch on his wrist. "It is eleven o'clock. An hour from now O'Brien will be looking for us to walk in on him. As a matter of fact, he wants to be sure that you are satisfied with the way things have turned out. He's politic, is O'Brien. Through you he would like to curry favor with your powerful friends at Washington."

"So you took advantage of the occasion to bring me here to threaten me with sudden death unless I promise to keep my mouth shut," I added.

"I am ready to sacrifice you, and myself with you, to that end. If by the use of the word 'threaten' you mean I am not sincere in the determination that you shall keep your mouth shut, dismiss the thought."

"But why sacrifice yourself?" I asked. "Why deviate from the machine-gun, kidnaping policy already employed? Why not use one of your mob of hoodlums to eliminate me?"

"I had considered that," was the calm answer. "It probably would have worked next time; your luck couldn't hold always, you know. But, to be honest with you, such underhand methods do not appeal to me. I show my sincerity of purpose by accompanying you on your journey from this vale of tears."

"You are not trusting too much to Colleti's confession," I commented.

He shook his head. "I never for a moment thought it would deceive you—not after I questioned Simpson and talked to Olga."

With that we fell silent, each occupied by his own thoughts. Suddenly I wanted to smoke. I got out my pipe; McClennen, watching me fill it, took a cigar from his pocket, and we lit up together, sociable as you please. Since then I have thought that perhaps that simple act had much to do with the result of the affair. At any rate, after we had smoked for a time, I looked at my watch and said:

"It is 11:30; isn't your foot getting tired?"

McClennen chuckled; then he said earnestly: "Listen, Holt; I believe you to be a gentleman and a good sportsman. I should like to call you my friend. I want you to know that, however this may turn out."

"Oho!" I exclaimed. "And a minute ago I was 'the god in the car'!"

"You are! You are!" he protested. "Man, consider! A promise from you will preserve the honor and security of one of the best of women, who considers her mad deed an act justified by God; it will reunite two lovers who never should have been separated, and it will maintain the newly wedded happiness of two others joined only yesterday; it will bring relief to a tortured old man. You notice I say nothing of my own life and yours, both of which it certainly will save."

"I had no idea I was so important," I told him; and I added: "You said, a bit ago, that the time for pretense between us was past. Suppose you tell me the circumstances of this unhappy business, just as you know them."

He thought for a little. "Fair enough," at length he agreed. "I might state it this way: A moment ago I told you that it lay in your power to reunite two people. I had in mind a boy and a girl, two young lovers, parted as the result of a good woman's mistaken enthusiasm. The boy was the younger and—in all fairness I must say it—by no means the favorite of the woman's two sons, upon the elder of whom she lavished a devoted affection which bordered upon fanaticism. That all her love was for her first-born, however, didn't mean that she lacked ambitious plans for her younger son.

"The woman, as I have said, was a good woman—one of the best; but, I must admit the fact, she loved social distinction. Family pride, the honor of the name, these things bulked large in her mind. That she lacked the wisdom to appraise correctly what stood for her ideals was the weak spot in an otherwise admirable character.

"The girl was the daughter of a man who had ended his life—a bankrupt and a suicide. Born rich, now she was dependent upon herself for a livelihood. It was no part of the mother's plan that these two should marry, and she set herself against the match.

"The boy was weak and easily led. It was not long till the mother had succeeded in breaking up her son's love affair. However, embittered and disillusioned, he was caught on the rebound by a young divorcee with a goodly slice of alimony from her former husband, a dissolute old rip if ever there lived one.

"Now this new inamorata was endowed with undeniable charm—of the sophisticated variety, it is true, but charm, nevertheless. She had personality, too; plenty of it; and the ability to wind her way into your heart—not masculine hearts alone, but also into those of her own sex, sisters—let us say, more normal than herself.

"In the beginning the girl seemed madly devoted to the boy. I suppose his very innocence and lack of sophistication proved tempting bait for her. The mother saw only Madame Messalina's desirable side—the charm, the distinction, the not inconsiderable fortune. To the best of her ability she furthered the match, only to realize, when it was too late, the pair married and living in the same house with her, that, indeed, 'the devil hath the power to assume a pleasing shape.' Now, with the opportunity of close association, she had glimpses into the secret places of her daughter-in-law's character which showed her, all too plainly, that she had unwittingly consigned her son to ruin."

McClennen paused and relighted his cold cigar. As yet he hadn't told me anything that I didn't know, but I was in no mind to interrupt his statement of particulars. I remained silent, waiting for him to continue, while for a time he smoked thoughtfully.

"Do you know, Holt," he resumed, "sometimes, in my profession, one gets the notion that, after all, there may be a scintilla of truth in the ancient superstition of vampirism? There was much about this girl that, when I consider her abnormal tendencies, puzzles me—accustomed though I am to encounter the bizarre angles of human conduct. At any rate, soon after she had been welcomed into the home of the unfortunate lady of whom I am speaking, the mistress of the house experienced the horror of one who, all unaware of the diabolic nature of the incomer, admits the vampire, and by so doing must henceforth grant hospitality to the demon. That is the belief of vampirism, you know.

"Be that as it may, whether the case was psychological or physiological—a proposition in demonology or a demonstration of the ductless glands, or mere cussedness, perhaps—the girl was a menace which threatened ruin. Did I tell you that the situation had its financial angle? It had. The girl spent money like a drunken sailor; and, having made ducks and drakes of the settlement from her former husband and bled white the resources of the present incumbent, she turned to other and less reputable means of supply. Blackmail wasn't too strong a game for her, and there was a fourth member of the family circle, the elderly brother of the mistress of the house, upon whose senile infatuations this charming young woman failed not to profit.

"I ask you to picture to your imagination the torments of the unfortunate lady, hag-ridden by this knowledge, a prey to self-reproach that she herself should have been responsible for the condition. Too proud to show her suffering to the world, terrified by the thought of the scandal which would follow the exposure of the family skeleton, she hid her repugnance under the guise of affection for this Frankenstein's monster. One person alone shared her secret—a woman deeply under obligation to her and devoted to her service. And that, my dear Holt, was where the poor lady erred on the side of discretion, for there was a man—he had loved her with a hopeless passion since he and the lady had been boy and girl together—to whose power and will she might have safely trusted."

McClennen paused. He was, I could see, much affected by his own story. For a time he smoked meditatively; then shot the butt of his burned-out cigar through the crack of the window and turned to me.

"However," he resumed, its accustomed note of cynicism returned to his voice, "the unfortunate lady chose to ignore the instrument ready to her hand. And then there loomed upon her horizon a cloud which threatened a new and greater catastrophe.

"The favorite son, home for a visit, for the first time met his brother's wife. Against his will he was drawn into an association which presaged a sordid crisis. Scenes occurred which wrung the mother's heart. She had visions to contemplate which appalled her. In imagination she saw her idolized son the betrayer of his brother's honor; she conjured up the picture of her darling, ruined physically and morally by this sinister conjunction; and when she discovered that, yielding to the girl's importunities, the boy had agreed to disappear in her company, the distracted mother determined to act as the instrument of the Power she had invoked. She had, I think, come to believe that she herself—responsible, in a measure, for the girl's presence in the house—had been appointed by the Omnipotent as the authority to frustrate the shameful design. We may well believe that, distracted by fear and worry, she was not accountable for what followed. You may credit this when I tell you that—without a plan, though she knew the time for the proposed elopement was at hand—she waited for the sign which she was convinced would be granted to her."

The big man ceased speaking. His eyes, which had been directing a somber gaze across the depths of the valley, turned and rested challengingly upon mine.

"And sign there was—to her, at least, it seemed so," he added solemnly.

I nodded, looking into the keen grey eyes behind the spectacles.

"The sight of Snowden's dagger in the pocket of Colleti's overcoat, as it hung from the hook in the wine cellar," said I, knowing that I was right in my surmise.

He bowed gravely. "You are right; it was the sight of the dagger that decided her. That very night, in a cup of the coffee Snowden had brewed, she administered a drug to the girl, accompanying her soon after to her room, where the penalty of distorted nature was paid."

"Ten minutes," I commented. "The time was short."

McClennen's eyes grew hard.

"It was abundant," he remarked darkly.

"And the presence of the butler in the corridor; and the conversational exchange he overheard when the unfortunate lady made her exit?" I queried, though I knew the answer.

He shook his head.

"Merely to impress upon the man the belief that her departure was a casual one. A bit of quick thinking."

"And the demise of the ex-husband?" I suggested tentatively.

"Snowden? The old goat!" He threw aside all pretense at ambiguity. "He and the other ancient satyr! Two superannuated black rams contending for the white ewe! Snowden interrupted the other in his attempted gallantry, and, the condition of the mistress of the room having been discovered by the first interloper, mutual accusations flew thick and fast. Then, terrified by the presence in the bed, the pair adjourned to the big room at the end of the corridor where the wrangling continued. At length Snowden threatened to alarm the house. The other, panic-stricken, picked up the statuette. Of course he never intended to kill the old roue. In the scrimmage that followed, probably one of his wild swings accidently landed. However, he escaped to his room. There he was overcome with nausea—you've heard that part of the story. What you don't know is that when I went to him next morning he made a clean breast of the whole business. Naturally I shielded him."

"I don't see why I should follow your example. The old sharpshooter nearly did for me"; and I told of the experience.

McClennen chuckled at the account. "Poor old brother Reuben, ineffective as always! Well, don't cherish animosity. At best—or worst—he is not long for this world."

"His heart, I suppose?"

"Simply rotten. How it keeps going is a mystery. Don't allow your decision in this matter to be influenced by any ethical nonsense concerning your failure to hand the old boy over to justice. He is already sentenced by a higher tribunal. From, motives of kindness I have kept him in ignorance of his impending fate."

Somewhat dryly I congratulated him upon the ability he had displayed in the role of dissembler throughout the affair.

"You see, I have some influence with the police department," he admitted modestly. "That stood me in good stead; though if I had had Chief Medical Examiner Burnham to contend with, in place of the little assistant, Burgher, it might have turned out differently. As it was, I had him under my thumb from the first."

I was not a little ashamed of the stupidity which I had exhibited in that encounter, and I changed the subject.

"Did you know that Colleti was behind the window curtains in the death chamber during the meeting of the elderly swains?" I asked.

He gave me a quick look of surprise.

"Did you?"

"Oh, yes," I told him. "I knew it. By the way, how did you secure that confession?"

"Merely a case of *quid pro quo,*" he returned. "You see, Colleti had a wife and a youngster out in Chicago. When he knew he was dying, the thought of their future got to bothering him. Having nothing to lose by it, he was willing to exchange the confession for my assurance that I would look after the woman and her child. Simple, wasn't it?"

I asked to whom he referred in speaking of "newly wedded happiness." I had the idea that it might be himself and Mrs. Randel. However, I was wrong.

"Not what you're thinking. I'm sending Mrs. Randel to a sanitarium. Perhaps, after what she's been through, she'll have to stay there. No, this is 'a reversal of the usual order,'" he said, smiling grimly. "In this instance it is a case of off with the new love and on with the old. Tom Randel married the Donnay girl last night. I left them at the house this morning when I came over to your place.

Now that the police restriction is lifted, they will go back to France on their honeymoon."

"And young Harry," said I. "What are his prospects?"

"Very good, indeed. He is conscious this morning—thoroughly in his right mind; better, in fact, than he was before we sent him to Piermont. The bullet wound in itself doesn't amount to much, and the injury to his head—the result of his fall—is less serious than I had feared. He'll do all right now."

Well, after all, he hadn't told me much that I didn't know. There didn't seem a great deal more to be said. We were silent for a bit; then I asked:

"How is the foot holding out?"

He grunted. "It's getting tired. If you're going to make that promise, I would be grateful if you'd do it in a hurry."

"A promise made under such conditions as these would hardly be binding, would it? Easy to change one's mind when out of the lion's mouth, you know."

I did myself an injustice, he assured me; he would accept my promise.

"That being the case," I told him angrily, "I think you're making damn fools out of both of us. No need to go through all this melodramatic nonsense. When I hit upon the truth of this business I made up my mind to keep my own counsel. You are supposed to be taking me up to the city to get my railroad tickets to clear out of here tonight. You'll forgive me if I say I don't like the locality."

"Sorry to lose you," McClennen declared gruffly; and we both laughed, each of us, I think, relieved to have the strain over.

Without further word we backed up the hazardous grade and returned to the road.

"Wait a minute, Doctor," I said. "Let's clean the slate for good and all before we leave here"; and I reached into my pocket and brought out the little tissue-paper bundle containing the pearls.

"Merely as an evidence of good faith," I grinned and handed it to him.

He gave me a sharp look and took the packet, opening it without comment. Seeing the contents, he looked up at me, a twinkle in his gray eyes.

"What a hell of a kick you must be getting out of this!" he growled and stuck out his big hand. I took it.

"'The rest is silence,'" I returned.

Print-on-demand titles available at
CoachwhipBooks.com

Ebook titles available at
Coachwhip.com

BRUTAL
Question
by
OLIVER WELD BAYER
author of
"AN EYE FOR AN EYE"

Crime
is of the
Essence
Joe Csida

DEATH
BEATS
THE
BAND
IDA SHURMAN

MURDER AT
DRAKE'S ANCHORAGE
E. LEE WADDELL

MURDER ENDS
THE SONG
ALFRED MEYERS

MURDER
A LA
MODE
ELEANORE
KELLY
SELLARS
CLASSIC RED BADGE PRIZE MYSTERY

MURDER IN
MALAYA
FATAL SHADOWS
DEATH OVER
HER SHOULDER
DOROTHY
COLE
MEADE

MURDER
IN A WALLED TOWN
KATHERINE WOODS

MAUDE PARKER
MURDER IN
JACKSON HOLE

ODDS-ON MURDER
DANCE
JACK DOLPH

THE FIRES AT FITCH'S FOLLY
KENNETH WHIPPLE

FULL CRASH DIVE
ALLAN R. BOSWORTH

NARROW
GAUGE TO
MURDER
CAROLYN THOMAS

NOW I LAY ME
DOWN TO DIE
ELIZABETH TEBBETTS-TAYLOR

DEATH
OVER
NEWARK
ALEXANDER WILLIAMS

THE JINX
THEATRE
MURDER
ALEXANDER WILLIAMS

DRESSED
TO KILL
Emma Lou Jetta

MURDER
ON THE
FACE OF IT
Emma Lou Jetta

VIRGINIA RATH
DEATH AT
DAYTON'S FOLLY

MURDER ON
THE DAY OF
JUDGMENT
VIRGINIA RATH

HIDE AND GO SEEK
with, GOING TO ST. IVES
HOTEL
COLVER HARRIS

THE HOUSE THAT JACK BUILT
with, MURDER IN AMBER
COLVER HARRIS

THE CAT
SCREAMS
A HUGH RENNERT MYSTERY
TODD DOWNING

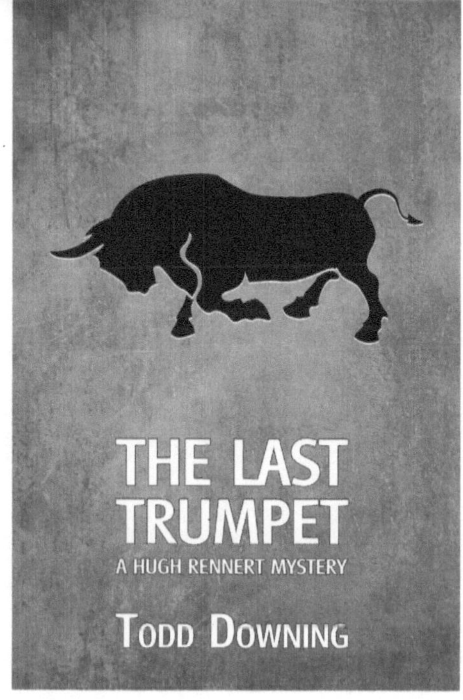
THE LAST
TRUMPET
A HUGH RENNERT MYSTERY
TODD DOWNING

www.ingramcontent.com/pod-product-compliance
Lightning Source LLC
LaVergne TN
LVHW091026080826
845145LV00002B/372

* 9 7 8 1 6 1 6 4 6 5 0 8 7 *